BEYOND THE BANKS

RANDY ANDERSON

For Norah, Grayson, Eden and Emma
The Lord will never fail you!

Chapters

Chapter 1

The Scarred Warrior

All of the colors and sounds were true as life.

Acts stood looking down at his own face as only in a dream one can; his attention suddenly turned to the Red Sea. He could see the walls of water on each side of the wide path the Children of Israel had walked to escape the Egyptian Army. The walls were churning, moving as though being held back for an intended purpose. As if climbing back into his own body, Acts watched as the walls of water suddenly began to fall in from the top down, crushing the army of Egypt beneath the weight of the water. The whole scene was spinning and with a sudden stop, Acts found himself standing on dry ground. He was in front of Moses who stood on the rock overlooking the path that was now being swallowed by the water. The falling of the water was so powerful that it shook Acts to his very core. He watched as the Snake of Mist moved over the water and now had many other creatures doing its bidding. Each creature held the souls of two soldiers in each of their talons. The Snake of Mist turned its head to look Acts in the eyes, but this time he didn't feel the fear he had felt before. Acts flashed back to the first time he had met this creature.

Many scenes moved through his mind, each a new memory every time he opened and closed his eyes. The pictures in his mind started with the night the mist passed over the land of Egypt taking with it the firstborn of the land. It was in seeing the lamb's blood, which the Israelites had applied to their doorposts, which prompted the creature to 'Pass Over' their homes. Next, he saw and heard his father yell at him to get away from the door as Acts peered out to see this creature for the first time. This memory was followed by the picture of Acts and his sister holding each other as they listened to the cries of Egyptians in the distance who were losing members of their families.

As quick as a thought, Acts was back standing in front of the rock with the creature looking at him. Tilting its head, it looked deep into his eyes and then it looked above the head of Acts to focus on something behind him. As it did it recoiled and shrieked in fear. Acts did not turn completely around but felt a hand on his right shoulder. As he glanced over to look, he found the same scar from a hole that had pierced through the hand of this mighty Warrior. This was the same Warrior as before in earlier times, in other visions. Acts understood it was Him; The Warrior... He was once again, coming to his rescue. Acts jerked his head back to see the Snake of Mist moving toward the rock where Acts was standing. Their eyes caught in unblinking gaze: studying each other. No fear on the part of either. Acts looked as deep as he could into the eyes of the creature for understanding. To his surprise, he felt deep hate and loathing from the Snake Mist. It despised man and the Warrior. It also had a great desire to be worshiped by man and seen as a god. He didn't understand how he knew this, but he was sure of what he felt.

Changing its gaze to the Warrior behind Acts. The creature screamed violently, rose above the ground several feet, and then pushed hard into the dirt, taking with it all of the other hideous creatures that were under its command and every single soul of the Egyptian army. Acts could see the face of each Egyptian that was being taken and the fear that was etched on their faces caused a chill in Acts that felt 'unholy'. Not one soldier had escaped. Acts looked up across the sea and saw the king of Egypt, Pharaoh as if he were only a few feet away.

Pharaoh's face held a look of complete devastation in the amazement of total defeat. As Pharoh looked up from the opposite side of the sea, he could see Acts staring at him. He gave Acts a blank expression and then his eyes looked above Acts casting his gaze upon the Warrior. Acts could hear Pharaoh speak to the Warrior, "If only I had not hardened my heart to the people. If only I had worshiped You... as my Lord." As Pharaoh spoke the expression on his face, the tone of his voice, and the choice of his words, was the saddest thing Acts had ever witnessed, but it was too late. Acts began to turn his head to look at the Warrior that had caused the creature such terror and the heart of Pharaoh to break.

A bright light filled his eyes so that he could not see the Warrior's face as everything then quickly faded into brilliance.

~

A new face started to come into focus in the place of the Warrior, Acts realized it was his sister Klee. She was kneeling beside him asking, "Acts, can you hear me? Can you see me?"

He blinked a few times and nodded his head to his sister, letting her know he could hear her. As he looked around to regain his bearings, he could see Salmon walking toward him with Moses and Joshua. As they came near, Acts asked, "It happened again, didn't it?"

Salmon answered, "Yeah, but Klee and I caught you before you hit the ground." He paused a moment, "You did miss Moses' and Miriam's song though." Salmon smiled at his friend and commented, "I think I might be getting used to you doing this!"

Acts cut him a half frown and then asked Klee, "Did it last very long?"

"Your jerking around didn't last long, but when you didn't wake up, I sent Salmon to find Moses and Joshua," Klee answered.

"I missed Moses and Miriam's song, huh?" Acts asked.

Salmon smiled and said, "Yea! They sang a song about the Lord delivering us and crossing the sea. It was awesome!"

Acts looked at his best friend again with a bothered smirk. Acts then looked up into the eyes of Moses. He saw the man of Great Compassion staring deep into his soul. No one spoke for a moment and then Moses said in his stutter-like talk, "Acts, I th…think it's time you and I did have that talk."

He smiled at Acts as Joshua and Salmon helped him to his feet casting a look of thanks to each.

Klee put her hand on his cheek and said, "Don't worry about anything little brother. Moses will be able to help you understand."

Acts followed Moses over to the rock, to the very place he had stood for all of the Children of Israel to see him as they made their way up the steep grade out of the Red Sea. It was from this rock he had closed his hands to bring the walls of water down on the Egyptians. The waters, now lapping against the rock, had a calming sound. It wasn't until after the waters fell that the people understood - the nation's army which had held them in bondage for over 400 years was dead: no more looking over their shoulders and no more chase.

Moses looked into the eyes of the young man and began to teach him, "Acts… the Lord is allowing you to s…see things even as He shows me… not exactly the same way, but in like manner. There are things I see in and through His Spirit; except… I don't usually fall."

He smiled at the young warrior and then motioned for him to sit down. Sitting there on the ground with their backs against the rock they both paused a moment to just listen to the water speak softly to them. Moses handed Acts a skin of water and said, "Just get a small s...sip. It is part of the last of our water supply."

Acts took a sip and savored every drop as it went down his throat. Moses began, "The Lord shows you... and me, things that are of natural and s...supernatural realms.

We see things that have happened, are happening, and things that will happen. It's not the f...fake magic the sorcerers performed in Egypt. It is of the very Spirit of God. He leads us through our very inner self... our spirit."

Acts sat looking into the face of this humble man, ready to listen and receive what he had to say, just as dry ground thirsts for water.

"Why He chooses to reveal Himself to us this way, I don't know. And the f... fact that you see things so clearly is a mystery to me as well." Moses smiled at Acts and asked, "Do you also s...see everything in color?"

Acts thought for a moment, "Yes. Yes, I do see all distinct colors. As clear as I see the colored linens we have from Egypt." He paused a moment and added, "Sometimes it starts in only black and white though."

Moses smiled as he thought for a moment about what he was trying to explain to this young man who had been introduced to the Lord for only a short time. The exodus, in leaving Egypt had kept everyone so busy that Acts had not had time to learn more about this New Great God. Or the fact that He is the Only True God.

Moses began, "The people who are chosen to receive from the Lord... they do so in different ways, as the Lord sees f...fit. He knows each person better than they know themselves. He knows the absolute best way to speak to them... to you. I don't know all of the ways or pretend to understand them, b...but I trust our God." Moses paused and smiled with a chuckle, "But you... are the only one who falls to the ground."

Acts smiled sheepishly back at his teacher.

Moses told his young student, "Know this; each time the Lord speaks to you in this way, He will not allow you to be harmed."

Acts had never thought about the fact that it was the Lord speaking to him. This helped him relax a bit concerning the visions. Moses looked at him and asked, "I can see that your reaction to this ability has changed just a little. Tell me how you are feeling."

Acts thought for a moment and combed back his long brown hair with his fingers. "You remember how the Snake of Mist put terror into my heart at first? Moses answered, "Yes, Yes I do remember."

Acts looked into Moses' eyes, "Well... this time I had no fear at all. When the Warrior with the scarred hands and feet appeared beside me, it was at that point my fear was taken away?"

The Snake looked right at me, and I just looked back. All of a sudden it screamed in terror because of the Warrior standing behind me. He commanded such a presence that it caused the creature to fear Him, without the Warrior having to say a word."

Moses straightened up to look into the young man's eyes. "And now you have no fear of it at all?"

"Well, I don't know about the next time, but this time I just knew I was being protected from the start and all that I witnessed of the Egyptians was final." Acts paused a moment to search for the right words. "It feels like… the Lord is closing the past up in a way I won't have to look over my shoulder again." Acts then thought of something for the first time; "Even within my own family."

Moses smiled at Acts, "You have learned so much; beginning from the night in Egypt when you first came face to face with the S… Snake of Mist. Which, by the way, is also called, 'The Death Angel'… and it is not like our God. In fact, it is no god at all. It is a created being and limited in what it can do, but still powerful compared to human standards. Although, I think I like your name for it better." Moses smiled, "We are going to be walking into new challenges and even greater times of t…testing. The Lord is going to use you to maintain courage in those around you; even Joshua." Acts looked back into Moses' eyes with amazement and question.

Moses continued, "Yes, even Joshua will need encouragement, but you m…must use wisdom and insight in your approach and in your words. You must be subtle in talking to the people around you. Don't worry about it though… You will know what to say when the time comes."

Moses got to his feet and Acts mirrored him. He placed his hands, on Acts' shoulders, "You and I are on a journey that will take the rest of our lives to complete. And at the journey's end..." He looked up across the sea and then back to the eyes of Acts, "We will meet the Warrior of the Lord who bears these scars… face to face."

The countenance of Acts suddenly lit up as he smiled. The thought had never crossed his mind, nor entered his heart and in that teaching, a new hope was birthed in his spirit. It was a hope that would need to be protected and cultivated so that it could grow. It was a hope that caused his faith to stand firm just by hearing the words Moses had given him. Acts repeated the words, "At the journey's end we will meet the Warrior of the Lord who bears these scars… face to face!"

Moses looked over the mass of humanity called 'The Children of Israel' and said, "A time of t…testing is upon us." He paused to study the people. "Acts… the next hours will be very trying because the Lord is going to show each of us what is in our hearts. Do these people have the *heart* to follow Him, or will they be a people who t… turn back to the only way of worship they have known for hundreds of years? Will they turn back to the idols of Egypt?"

As Moses finished his sentence, he looked up to see Nahshon, Salmon's father, walking toward them. Moses looked at Acts one more time and whispered, "We will talk more at a later time."

Acts smiled and answered, "Yes Sir." Moses gave him a fatherly hug and Acts turned to walk to his sister and soon-to-be brother-in-law, Joshua. As he looked at them, he whispered a prayer of thanks to the Lord for giving them this new family and pondered... Now that they were safe from the Egyptians and even their own father, the wedding between his sister and Joshua could be planned, giving them all something to look forward to.

As he walked up to Klee she asked, "Are you alright?" Acts smiled and said, Everything is just fine.

Chapter 2

The Family

Nahshon, the leader of the tribe of Judah, walked up to Moses and gave him a hug and they both sat down. "The song you sang with Miriam was exhilarating! Did it just come to you as you sang?"

Moses looked back and answered, "Do you think I already knew w…what was going to happen!?" The two men laughed as they took in the sight of the people still praising and dancing before the Lord with gratitude. Looking at all of the people, Nahshon stated, "I must say, Moses, I am completely intoxicated with the freedom and deliverance the Lord has brought us into." He paused a moment and then looked at Moses, "So what now? In what direction do we travel to reach the land promised to Abraham, Isaac, and Jacob; and to us?"

Nahshon had a completely childlike attitude. It was refreshing as Moses thought to himself; "this is what he is… a child in the Lord." Nahshon, like the people, had much to learn about God, and their relationship with Him needed to be more defined.

After four hundred years of captivity, the people standing before him had only heard bits and pieces of their history. They only 'knew' the names of Abraham and Isaac. It was Jacob they knew most about. It was Jacob whose name was changed to Israel.

Jacob had been the father of Joseph. Joseph had been the 'savior' of Egypt as well as other regions when the Great Famine hit the entire country. It was Joseph who stood as second in command to all of Egypt, alongside the 'Good Pharaoh' who had welcomed Joseph's family. But when Jacob and Joseph died the honorable deeds were forgotten and the next Pharaoh put the people of Israel into bondage because their numbers had grown so large. He used them for their labor and their skills. Moses himself didn't know all of the history concerning Abraham and Isaac. He, just like the people, was learning where they came from, what is safe, what is dangerous, and how to trust with obedience. Even though the people were learning that Yahweh is the only true God, they still did not *know* Him. Moses thought to himself, "Did Nahshon expect the Lord to give him a land already inhabited by people, without any obstacles and walls already established, without developing a relationship with this wonderful

God? A land they knew nothing about. What did mere slaves know of battle?"

Moses looked at him as a mere child in faith. They had only been through the waters a few hours. The Children of Israel had started down into the heart of the sea as twelve tribes, fleeing Egyptian slavery. And then, they emerge on the other side as a victorious people delivered by a mysterious God who claimed them as His people. They went into the heart of the sea in fear and were raised out of the water a single nation birthed by God. Moses did not judge Nahshon or set up a standard too high for him to understand. Moses chuckled to himself, "I'm only a toddler in this new faith myself."

He looked over at Nahshon and said, "We have m…much to learn about our faith in the Lord. We must learn how to combat the things in life that want to pull us away from knowing and trusting our Lord, God." He paused and repeated the statement in a whisper, *"We have much to learn about our faith."* He patted Nahshon on the shoulder and said, "Let's join the people in celebration because tomorrow we must be r…ready to move out. If you will see to your tribe, it will be one less thing for me to be concerned with?" "By all means," Nahshon said, as he turned to begin the task. He glanced back at Moses and said, "I know I have much to learn."

~

Moses smiled as Nahshon walked off and whispered to the Lord, "And our first test after being delivered is going to be a big one, isn't it Lord?"

The Lord chuckled at Moses, **"Do you see that small child over there?"** The Lord pointed him out to Moses. **"He is learning to walk; he trips, falls, and gets back up. See how close his father is. That baby may trip and fall but that father will not allow his son to fall on something that could injure him. I AM closer than that father is to his child concerning the people of this company. They are my people, and they are learning how to trust and obey Me. Don't worry my friend… I will provide."**

Moses smiled, "I know that you will… but this people...?" The Lord spoke to His friend in a calm assuring tone, **"I know, Moses, just do as I command you. This is what I ask of you."**

~

About that time Joshua came walking up with Aaron, Moses' brother to find out the orders. The three of them sat down on the rock and Moses began giving instructions:

"We are going to travel south into the d…desert of Shur. I don't know exactly where, but that doesn't matter right now. The Lord is going to test the people and show them certain things about His character, His care, and *our* faith. They are just now only learning about the Lord… just as you are Joshua." Joshua smiled, "Yes, I know."

Looking to Aaron he continued, "You and I w…will be in the front just as we have been. The Lord will show us where to stop with the pillar of cloud. I want the people to understand that we are following the Lord God's instruction just as they have been given to me." He looked at Aaron and asked, "Will you tell our tribe of Levites to spread themselves throughout the front four tribes?" Aaron nodded in understanding.

Moses turned to Joshua, "I want the tribes in three groups: four tribes in each group with the exception of the Levite tribe. The tribes of the first group are Reuben, Simeon, Judah, and Issachar. Make sure Elizur, Shelumiel, Nahshon, and Nethanel," *speaking of the tribal leaders in the order he had mentioned.* "Make sure they know to stay in the m…middle of their tribes so that they can be accessed by anyone in their tribes. Nahshon knows what to do with Judah. I want Salmon in this first group close to me in case I need him for something special."

"I know his mother will like that," Joshua added.

Moses continued, "Next will be Zebulun, Ephraim, Manasseh, and Benjamin. I want Acts to be in this second group with 'You're...'" *looking into the eyes of Joshua his young captain,* "soon to be bride and his sister, Klee.

Joshua put a grin on his face from ear to ear. Moses smiled and said, "I think that Acts' sister is ready to have him by her side, especially because of the trouble she faced on the way here. I would like Klee and Acts to travel with your family Joshua, for they are soon to be part of your family."

About that time Telok came walking up to the group of men and Moses said, "Good timing Son."

Telok smiled and asked, "What'd I miss?"

Moses caught him up on the groups of tribes and then continued with the plan, "The last f…four tribes will be "Dan, Asher, Gad, and Naphtali. Once again Naphtali will bring up the rear guard. I want you Joshua and Telok between Asher and Gad." Joshua tried not to show disappointment as Moses acknowledged, "I understand your time with Klee will have to wait, but this is what I need for you to do." He studied his young captain's eyes and knew he would do what he asked with all of his heart.

Telok knew his friend had some disappointment, but he could also see how well Joshua managed it.

"Ahiezer can s…send runners to you from his tribe of Dan if he needs you. And Ahira was pretty put off concerning the trouble you had on the way to the Red Sea and also in coming through the Sea, with members of his tribe. He has put strong capable men he trusts from all of the clans of the tribe of Naphtali on alert to look for any sign of trouble. Pagiel has done the same with the men of Asher, but I still want you and Telok in position."

As Moses looked into each man's eyes, he questioned in his heart how much to reveal to them. He thought a moment and decided not to tell them. It was the Lord's test, not his. He would have told Moses to tell them if He wanted them to know.

"We n…need to get started. Make sure Acts and Salmon are ready and in position. We will start moving in the morning. We will keep the signals with the ram's horns the same, starting and stopping. The flags and tribal standards will be used to keep the people moving in a straight line. Make sure each tribe has enough runners to have effective communication and men with horns to give the signals to each tribe, clan, and family. Moses smiled and said, "Be strong and courageous; and let's see what the Lord will do."

~

It took most of six hours for the men to give the instructions to the runners after they arrived and were sent to pass the orders on to the next set of runners. Both Acts and Salmon kinda wanted to travel together, but they understood the role they had been given. Klee was the one who would be most disappointed. She would have to wait until the whole company stopped again to see Joshua.

After Joshua shared the instructions with Klee, She smiled at him and said, "This will only give me more time to spend with your mother and dad in planning the wedding." With a small kiss and a hug, the two parted.

Telok looked over at his best friend, "You are truly blessed, my brother."

"I know!" said Joshua. "It amazes me every day." Joshua thought a moment and added, "I think you need to tell Naoon what's going on. She needs to know where you are... I mean where we are." Telok cut him a sly grin and Joshua raised his eyebrows in a moment of enlightenment. "Hey! Why don't you see if Naoon would like to move up with your dad and my family? It would be a wonderful time for Klee and her to get acquainted."

"That… is a good thought." Telok stopped to really think the idea over and he said, "In fact, I will do just that." Both of them began looking around to estimate the distance from where Naoon was to the tribe of Ephraim. It wasn't far around the edge of the Red Sea and Telok knew he could have her there in plenty of time to get her settled so that she could rest before the company moved out. He looked back at Joshua as he headed out and said, "I'll meet you in the tribe of Benjamin at the tent of Abidan."

"I will be there after I have met with Gamaliel in the tribe of Manasseh" Joshua replied.

~

Naoon was still very taken with Telok and his relationship with her people, who were now *his* people. She thought his Egyptian dark skin and his light green eyes were extremely handsome. She watched him begin to walk up to the cart from his run. He smiled at her and looked down at the baby. She was playing with a soft pillow Naoon had made for her. He looked to the young man who had come to her aide, summoned by Telok while they were crossing the Red Sea. Guni was still standing with her to see to any of her needs. He had been given the privilege of getting Naoon and the baby up the final portion of the steep grade out of the Sea. He stayed with her while Telok went back down to assist others to the top of the long grade where Moses stood on the rock.

After a short greeting, Telok shared with Naoon and Guni, "Moses has given instructions and we, being Joshua and myself, are to travel between the tribes of Asher and Gad. The tribes are to travel in three groups with four tribes in each group." Placing his gaze on Guni, he explained, "Acts will be in the tribe of Ephraim. Salmon will be with the tribe of Judah. Salmon will be with the first group of four tribes and Acts will be in the second group. Telok looked at Naoon, "His sister and Joshua's family will be with the tribe of Ephraim in the second group. Joshua and I will be in this last group." He watched as the smile on Naoon's face dropped a bit. He looked at Guni and said, "I will be moving Naoon and the baby up with my dad, to the same tribe with Joshua's family." He looked at her and finished, "If that is alright with you?"

Naoon smiled, "That would be very nice."

Telok looked at Guni and said, "I would like for you to walk with your family and spend time with them until we have stopped as a company. I will get word to you as to what I will need for you to do as I receive word from Joshua and Moses. This is a time your family will need you for we are going into a time of testing. This is all that Moses said about it. So, we will walk in this test together learning each day as we walk, trusting in our Lord. Stay strong and courageous and wait until I send for you." He paused and added, "I don't know just when that will be, but I will not forget you."

Guni was relieved that he was not going to be dismissed. "I will enjoy my time with my family, and I will stay strong. I will be ready to hear from you." He looked at Naoon and smiled. She reached out to take Guni by the hand and said, "Thank you so much for your bravery. I look forward to seeing you again. And so, does 'baby.' His smile was as wide as it could go, and he turned to set out to find his family.

Naoon smiled and said, "That was very considerate of you to speak to him that way. I just know that his heart is about to burst from the excitement of working with you. He did mention it, you know?"

Telok looked back puzzled.

Naoon said, "He knows who you are and of the trouble you had with a man named, Korah?" She said in question. "He knows that you are a trained warrior within the special guard of Pharaoh, himself. He knows that you are now very dedicated to Joshua and Moses. He also knows you are a man of honor."

"I had no idea that he knew those things," Telok said surprised. "I just grabbed him because he looked available. I guess I will have to give this young man a closer look," he said thoughtfully. He looked into Naoon's deep brown eyes and got lost for just a moment and then he realized he was staring and cleared his throat, "I hope you don't mind me speaking for you before asking if you want to move up to where my father is?"

"I didn't mind and in fact, I found it comforting knowing that you have not only been thinking about us but also planning what you think best in our situation." She was careful with her words so that she wouldn't make him feel uncomfortable or give away too many of the thoughts and feelings she had been experiencing in getting to know her 'guardian.'

As he turned to begin moving the cart he gave a good rub to the ox and spoke softly to her, "Are you ready to move this mother and child up to a new family?" The oxen moved her head into him, and he took that as a 'yes.' Making sure she was ready to move, he prodded the oxen only a little and she began to pull the cart with ease. As they moved Telok would glance back to see how they were doing.

Naoon grinned and said, "She is sleeping…. with a smile on her face."

He turned back to lead and spoke a silent word of thanks in his heart.

~

It didn't take long for Telok to lead the cart to where his dad was and when his dad turned around to see him coming, he smiled and said, "I was wondering when I would see you!" He walked up to his son and gave him a grand hug and then holding him at arms-length he said, "I have missed you! You running back down into the Sea worried me for just about this long." Holding his thumb and index finger out about an inch apart; showing that his worry was small. Kemuel stepped to Telok's side and gazed at the beauty of Naoon and then he noticed the baby.

Telok turned to look at Naoon as spoke to his dad, "This is Naoon and her baby girl. I would like, if it is all right with you, for them to travel with you and the clan."

Kemuel smiled without hesitation and said, "Mind!? It would be an honor!"

Telok told his father, "We met while crossing the Red Sea and have become good friends in only hours."

Kemuel looked at Telok and then to Naoon and replied, "I too have made lifelong friends in only moments. It will be good to make another one… or two," glancing down at the baby as he walked up to the cart for a closer look. "I think Naoon and Klee should meet as well. It seems to me Klee and Acts are both new to the clan and they can all get through their 'newness' together."

Telok smiled at his dad and said, "Thank you, father."

"You're welcome, son."

"Then if I could, I have duties to attend. Joshua and I are to move with the company between the tribes of Asher and Gad." Telok told his dad of how the tribes were to be arranged and where Salmon would be and that Acts was to travel with Klee in Nun's family which, just happened to be the same clan as Kemuel.

Well, you better get to it then. Naoon and the baby will be just fine. I'll make sure her oxen are fed with mine and then I'll make sure we're ready to go in the morning. We will be walking right next to Nun and his wife so everyone will get to know each other."

With a hug from his dad, Telok turned to Naoon as Kemuel moved around the cart checking it over.

"I know that you will be safe here and that if you need anything…"

She put her hand on his lips and said, "All I need to do is ask?" She released her finger from his lips and waited.

Telok took in a deep breath and answered, "Yes. All you need to do is ask." He smiled and touched the baby's cheek and turned to move toward Joshua's position, but not before turning once more to look into her beautiful brown eyes.

Kemuel looked back at Naoon as she watched Telok run off. He smiled to himself and walked back to take a closer look at the baby. "She is beautiful."

"Thank you!" Naoon replied sweetly.

"With everyone getting things ready to move out in the morning and trying to grab a few hours' sleep, I think we will wait until we are on the march for you to meet all of the family," Kemuel told her. "I suppose you've met Joshua?"

"Only once; and that was very brief" she answered.

"Well, Joshua is the servant of Moses; you might say 'his right-hand man'. Telok serves with Joshua as his 'right-hand man'." He paused to make sure she understood and continued, "Joshua is engaged to a young lady by the name of Klee. Her little brother, Acts serves Joshua, as his other 'right-hand man' and then, there's Salmon." Kemuel paused to think and said, "He is kind of Joshua's 'left-hand man'." He chuckled as he said it. "Acts and Klee are both traveling with Joshua's mom and dad who are only a cart or two away from ours. Once we are on the move and everyone is settled in with the pace, I'll make sure you meet them because I know they are all going to want to meet you."

"Why would they want to meet me?" Naoon asked.

"Well, they…. they are good people and if you're going to be traveling with the clan, you're going to need to know who's in it. Klee and Acts are new to the family because they don't really have anyone else" Kemuel explained.

"Did their family die in Egypt?"

"No… their family didn't exactly die. Their father and brothers didn't want them, and Klee and Acts didn't need to be around that, so… when Joshua and Klee got engaged, Nun and his family took them in."

"Well, that was very nice of them" Naoon spoke with a bit of surprise.

"Yea. Joshua is a blessed man, and I know he is going to be a blessing to Klee. Even before we left Egypt, Joshua had thought of Acts as his little brother. They're gonna make a fine family!" Kemuel said as he turned to finish some last-minute packing.

Naoon looked around her at the people of the tribe of Ephraim and wondered in her heart if she too, could find a family here. Her heart was filled with hope, but she kept it to herself.

Chapter Three
The Crash

It was a bit further than Telok had estimated to the tribe of Benjamin and as he walked the last half mile to catch his breath, he could see Joshua standing with Abidan the tribal leader. A smile on their faces welcomed him and Joshua held out a skin of water that was half full. Telok took the skin and with much care only took two sips and handed it back to Joshua.

"It was a little further than I anticipated."

"I found that to be the case too!" Joshua agreed. "Well, how'd it go?"

"She is with my dad, and they will be walking only a couple of carts away from your mom and dad," Telok responded.

"This is concerning a young woman, is it?" Abidan asked inquisitively.

"A young woman and her baby girl we helped as we passed through the Sea" Telok replied.

"Yes, Joshua was giving me a little of the history. It sounds... most promising" Abidan said with a smile. "I will let you two get on with your duties." as he turned to take care of his family.

Telok looked at Joshua with a straight face and said, "Giving out some 'history'?"

"Yea, While... we were waiting, we just got to talking and it kind of came out." Joshua shrugged and grinned with a raised brow, then quickly changed the subject. "Well... we better get to it. I have called for all of the runners of the last four tribes, and they should be getting here within the next few minutes. While we wait, let's see if we can find any more water."

"My water skin is drained," Telok replied letting his friend off the hook. They both looked for several minutes before finding one of the last water carts. The water was three inches from the bottom. They had to tip the cart all the way on its back gate to get the water out, but they were able to fill their skins, and they would use it sparingly. There was also enough remaining in the cart to fill a few more skins.

They looked up and could see seven runners coming toward them. As they walked up Joshua looked at each one and then to their skins of water. He asked, "Do all of you have at least a little water?" Each one said, 'yes. "Good! Now, is there any water left in your tribes?" Each boy looked to the other and they all shook their heads left to right. Joshua shook his head with concern, "I was hoping that there was still a little bit of water in some of the carts." He paused a moment and told the young men, "Use your water wisely." As each young man gave a nod of understanding he continued, "Here are Moses instructions. We will begin moving the front four tribes just after sun-up and then, after an hour we will begin moving the second group of four. After another hour, we will get the last four tribes moving. I want you to only tell the tribal leaders that we won't be stopping. The people will find that out for themselves." He cut a small smile to the boys and that helped them to relax. "It will be a tough walk and that is why I want you to use your water sparingly. If I should need you, I want you to be able to come as quickly as you can. Try to make sure the other runners in your tribes have at least a little water, also." Each boy was completely taken with the opportunity to serve Joshua and Telok. After the instructions, Joshua looked to Telok and asked, "Did I miss anything?"

Telok replied, "No My Captain."

Joshua turned to the runners and said, "Be strong and courageous and hand the word down as I have given it to you."

The boys all said in unison, "Yes, My Captain."

This took Joshua off guard, and he chuckled as they ran off to perform the duty given to them, Telok looked at Joshua and commented, "They will make fine warriors." Joshua smiled and agreed, "Yes, they will."

~

It took a little more than 12 hours to get the people ready to move out with runners taking the word in all directions. Joshua and Telok were able to get a few hours of sleep before being up in time to see the pillar of fire give way to the pillar of cloud. The sun had just started to make its appearance for the day. They knew that the front group of tribes would be moving out any time with the pillars changing. Then it would be an hour before the second group would begin. All the tribes began lifting up the different banners of which the people rallied around. Each tribe had its own banner and color of flags for their runners. With the sound of the ram's horns, it was only minutes, and the first four tribes began to move. The entire group gave a huge shout, and the march began. This was the start of the trial or test, and the sound of their voices could be heard around the shoreline of the Sea. All of the other tribes knew that it wouldn't be long before they were moving as well. Moses set a slow pace. They were not in a hurry, after all it was not the destination that was the focus. It would be the actual journey. The things that had taken place, the destruction of the Egyptian army and their deliverance was so fresh on their hearts and minds they were ready to follow wherever Moses led. By mid-morning all of the company was moving and as they moved away from the Red Sea, the bodies of the soldiers began washing on shore. The emotions of the people ran from total fear of this new God to praise and thankfulness. It was from the moment of the first ram's horn that Moses began to count the three-day journey.

Salmon walked with his family telling them all about his experiences coming through the Red Sea. From Acts sticking his hand into the wall of water to touch a smooth fish and the giant sea creature they saw.

"It had a neck that was at least four horses long and its tail was even longer. It had a mouth that could swallow a whole cow. It had two large flippers toward the front of its large body and a whole mouth full of teeth. The eyes were like a cat, with the black spot, slit up and down." He laughed as he looked at his family with all of them wide-eyed and their mouths open. "I know! I wouldn't have believed it if Acts had just told me about it, but we all saw it and so did a lot of the people around us. Telok said, he had heard some of the sailors tell of a creature such as this and they called it 'Leviathan,' the 'gliding serpent'."

He told them about the people stopping to rest and he and Acts having to 'ask' them to keep moving. He told them how Joshua showed up and they suddenly understood that Acts was not playing around.

Nahshon and his wife looked at their son and suddenly realized that he was a young man and now held a certain position, in the very ranks of Moses. They smiled with pride for him and just let him keep right on talking. His mother whispered to Nahshon, "I have never heard him talk so much."

~

Moses and Aaron walked silently for a while and then began to discuss what was now taking place.

"I only had a couple of people say something to me about the water supply" started Aaron.

"Yes, Nahshon and Joshua both said something to me," Moses answered back. Quiet was the moment and Aaron said, "Moses, I know that I don't know our Lord nearly as well as you, but I am learning by being at your side. I know He is a God who can provide anything we need... even dividing waters for us to escape." He thought for a moment. "I guess what I might be trying to ask or say is... How far is this God going to go with us? I don't want Him to get tired or frustrated by us, causing Him to leave us."

Moses smiled at his brother and said, "Do you grow tired and dulled by your sons?" Aaron looked back at him and Moses continued, "Our God cares for us just as we care for our children and our grandchildren. His love goes far beyond what we can think or ask or hope. It is His personality we will be learning. It is His w...ways we will be experiencing and in all of this, His love is a love that n... never will leave us or forsake us as long as we follow Him..."

Aaron thought a moment... 'As long as we serve and worship Him: What happens when we don't? What happens when we trip up and fall? I know I can't be perfect in everything He commands.'

Moses paused for a moment, "Remember the Pass Over Lamb? Remember how the Death Angel was kept from touching our people?" Moses laughed a little, "Acts calls it the Snake of Mist."

Aaron laughed with him. Moses looked out over the wilderness, and said, "I think if our God was willing to allow death to pass over us and provide escape from bondage and the destruction of our enemy... I think He is willing to take us the full distance. Even to our final day when we die and go to Him. He will not abandon us. Our God m...made a promise; He promised that we are His people and that He would be our God. This I do know my brother... our God is a consuming fire and is very fierce in what He says and the promises He makes. It is impossible for God to lie. He will not leave us!"

And then Moses proposed a question to his brother. "What if your younger sons Eleazar and Ithamar decided to become Egyptian while we were still captive... What do you think you would have done?"

It was a question Aaron had never even thought of. His first two sons, Nadab and Abihu, were always rebellious toward him and lived on the edge of his authority as their father. He wouldn't have put it passed them, but Eleazar and Ithamar were very obedient and had great respect for him as their father. So, for Aaron to think of losing them to the Egyptians would have meant losing part of himself. "I would still love them. I would still stand to fight for them." Aaron's eyes began to open as he compared that to the love Moses was explaining. A love that was so much more than what he could comprehend... a love that was too wonderful to grasp.

As they walked and talked more of what they had learned and would be learning they relaxed in communion with each other and with the Lord. Within just a couple of hours, every tribe was moving east into the desert of Shur. With emotions still high there were no questions or reservations about following Moses and Aaron into the desert. The Pillar of Cloud now ran the full length of the company providing shade from the front to the rear guard. The Pillar of Fire would give light to the company at night to move about and it also led the people at night if they were to continue moving.

~

As Acts walked looking at the pillar of cloud he thought, "I sure hope Salmon's seeing this." At about the same time, Salmon thought the same for Acts.

The first day of travel was going well. Acts was walking with his sister and began to think aloud. "Moses said, to be careful and use insight when encouraging someone." He thought for a moment, "To be subtle in the words I choose to encourage Joshua and those around me."

"I'm sorry, what?" Klee asked.

"Oh, I was just running back over some of the things Moses said to me. He can get pretty deep very fast and it's always a lot to take in on the spot. I have to think about it for a while before it starts to become clearer." He told his sister.

"So... What about it?" She asked.

"He told me to be subtle and to use insight in the words I choose to encourage people. I think Moses is telling me to look at a situation and think of what I am trying to tell someone so, my words are encouraging and not misunderstood."

"Wow!" Klee said. "He really is getting you to think." She smiled, "I believe Moses is trying to get you to see you are special to him and that he has trust in you. I think he believes you have good instincts... your heart is good." She put her hand on his shoulder and said, "That is something I do know... your heart is good!"

He smiled back at her and asked, "But what is being subtle? I always thought if someone was being subtle, they were trying to get to you: to profit from you."

"That's kind a right!" Came a response from behind them. It was Joshua's dad, Nun. "Acts... it is being clever, but it is also being skilled in getting someone to think the way you think. Kinda like me working for a day's wage. I did the work, but when I come home in the evening it is Joshua's mom who is subtle and gets me to think about where it should be spent. It doesn't always mean someone is trying to profit, being subtle can be a very good thing especially when you're encouraging someone. If they are thinking in a dark light, maybe you'll be the one to help them change their focus and see the good light instead. And it's not easy to do."

Acts thought for a moment and said, "So, if someone is thinking in a wrong way, I can use insight in choosing my words to help someone alter their thinking, by being subtle?"

"Kind of wordy, but yeah; I think that's about it," Nun answered.

~

It wasn't but a few more steps when all of them heard a loud crack of wood splintering. It was a cart being pulled by two large oxen just to the left of them: the cart between Kemuel and Nun. As the right wheel broke, it began to tip, and the axle began grinding down hard. The man pulling the cart was Nun's brother-in-law. Nun and Acts ran to keep the cart from rolling over. The weight was tremendous and soon others were running to help.

Klee stepped in front of the oxen to stop them. As she held up her hands, she spoke to them and said calmly, "Whoa." And the oxen slowed to a stop. "Good girls," she told the pair of animals. She stepped out from in front of the oxen to see what was happening with the cart.

Kemuel and other men were running to help, but they couldn't make it in time as the cart began to roll. Naoon jerked her head to see what the sound was, but she was riding too low and couldn't see them on the other side of the large cart as it tipped away from her.

It seemed to be in slow motion to everyone. As Acts and Nun began stepping back away from the cart there was an unseen handle, long and of very hard wood. Acts was able to clear the cart itself. As Acts turned to run the handle struck him on the back of the head. It was the same spot on his head where Abiram had struck him and then Korah had followed with an even stronger blow during the altercation they had with Acts before crossing the Red Sea.

Korah had been embarrassed when Acts beat him in a fight that took place in front of the men who followed him. It had enraged Korah to the point that he took Klee hostage to draw Acts out for a rematch: A rematch that involved not only Korah but several of his men. They were going to teach this kid how real men of 'planning' handled problems like him. In the fight, Acts had been hit in the back of the head and suddenly the events of that fight flashed back through Klee's memory as she watched the handle strike Acts.

Chapter 4
Total Recall

As Acts fell to the ground, the cart crashed spilling its contents all around. Nun and Acts were covered with the items in the cart. There were colored linens from Egypt, pots, tools, and even some of the gold idols the people had come to worship in the land of slavery. All had been packed away. As he fell, past actions were taken, and emotions began to come into focus in his mind. His mind began to replay the confrontation with Korah and his men. All of the actions in his dream see-sawed between slow and fast. Every person who was present in the altercation was perfectly clear in his thoughts.

~

Acts first saw Klee. She was frightened and being treated roughly. A rope was around her wrists, as the men laughed and spouted boasts of what they would teach the 'boy'. The dream, vivid with colors, seemed so real that his body flinched and jerked in response to what he was seeing. The dream showed Acts in a position as if he were moving in a circle around the event and able to sense the emotions of everyone involved.

He could see that they appeared drunk and enraged with hate and vengeance. As if they had been drinking strong wine, but in reality, they hadn't been drinking at all. He could see Klee as she struggled with the pain of the rope and the fear she felt, knowing the trap they had planned for her brother. The situation now moved quickly, and he saw himself walking up to Korah and the group of men. They began to fan out to seal off his way of escape, but he could sense in himself he had no fear. Next, he heard Korah begin yelling, "You think you can talk to me like I am some child?" the sound of his voice echoed the sentence several times before fading away. Acts saw Klee being thrown to the ground and the sound of Korah's voice screaming again at Acts, "You will taste the beating of your life," The threat echoed as before.

Joshua's face began to come into focus like someone coming up out of water. He had the look of a warrior ready to kill, but his discipline and self-control kept him from killing Korah on the spot.

As Nun and Klee began pulling the articles from the cart off of Acts, they could see he was flinching, reacting to what he was seeing. Klee picked his head up tenderly placing it in her lap and applied pressure to the wound that was bleeding on the back of his head. Joshua's family was running to her aid. Naoon picked the baby up and as she walked around the spilled cart, she could see Acts on the ground and Klee holding him. She could hear Klee as she began yelling out instructions; "I need soft pieces of cloth and any water we can spare." As the family began arriving with the supplies, Klee rolled Acts' head to the side to look at the wound for the first time. She could see that his head was cut, but she couldn't tell how bad it was because of his hair and the dirt. Naoon stepped a little closer but stayed out of the way. She watched intently with emotions that empathized with Klee. Joshua's mom handed Klee some cloth soaked in water. Klee began to wipe his hair and the dirt away from the wound to see if a knife could have made the cut.

The scene in Acts' dream continued to flow in his mind. He could see himself falling hard to the ground on his back. With Acts' attention on his sister, Korah had caught him off guard. He tried to put his foot in the middle of Acts' face, but Acts told himself to roll. It was like he was coaching himself in the fight. Korah's foot slammed into the dirt sending a small cloud of dust out from around his sandal. The motion was so slow that the particles seemed to almost stop. The small dust cloud moved very slowly and then the actions sped up. Viewing the scene from the ground as if he were a bystander, he saw himself roll back against Korah's leg putting his right elbow to the back of Korah's knee, sending him to the ground. Now Acts could see Joshua pull Salmon back to keep him out of the fight for that moment.

Klee could feel her brother's body moving as if in a struggle. Nun asked, "Is he having a fit?" Klee just looked at Acts and replied, "No. He's... he's dreaming something. He's... fighting something in his dream."

In the dream, Acts now viewed the entire scene moving around in a full circle. He was between Korah and Abiram with Klee behind Korah. He watched as Abiram started for him. Acts felt himself pick up his foot kicking Abiram in the middle of his chest and fall to the ground. He now faced Korah and in a fluid movement, he rolled forward, headfirst, onto his shoulders, bringing the heel of his left foot over his body and putting it in the middle of Korah's abdomen. He saw Korah fall away. He looked to see Telok holding a man's arm and then slam his elbow into the man's jaw. The scene moved quicker as Salmon ran and wrapped his arms around another man. With the weight and force of his own body, the man fell hard with Salmon on top of him. As they fell the scene moved again to slow motion and Acts could see the force of the energy Salmon used etched on his face.

Acts watched Joshua as he was grabbing the hair on the back of a man's head. As Joshua began to pull on the man's hair the scene slowed; pulling with great strength he lifted the man off of his feet and then let go... Time seemed to almost stop as Acts watched the man float in the air before his body hit the ground. Even the muscles in Joshua's face seemed to move like ripples in water. It seemed such a long time as the man's feet flew up in front of him and Joshua let go. The man hit the ground high up on his shoulders, with all of the air in his lungs rushing out. Dust flew out from under the man and Acts could almost see each particle of dust stop in mid-air and then resume in natural movement.

Acts seemed to understand that he was watching the fight all over again, but he couldn't stop it or wake up. He felt that he had to see it through to the end and then... try to pull back to reality.

As the dream continued, he watched Joshua pull the hood off his head and reach to help Salmon up after he had body-slammed the man to the ground. Korah was up and moving again. Acts jerked his head back around to get eyes on Korah.

Klee could feel his body flinched as she held him.

Korah's fist was coming straight for his face. Acts grabbed Korah's wrist and then his elbow and threw him to the ground just in front of Klee. Her face filled with fear.

Suddenly Acts' head was forced forward with pain. Abiram had come from behind him and hit him in the back of the head with his fist. He felt himself dropping to the ground. He both felt the strike and watched it happen in an echoed rhythm, playing slowly over in his mind three times. Each time Acts could see more details, Abiram's facial expression of complete hate. Abiram's fist met Acts' head, and his hair moved from front to back. Looking at his own face, he could see the grimace he made with the hit.

"He's not waking up," Nun said with a very concerned voice. "Just… Just give him a minute. Sometimes it takes a little longer for him to come around." Klee said, with a fearful tone. She thought to herself, *"But this was not like the other times."*

Nun's family had gathered with more cool clothes from the very last of their water. Now there was no water left, but they were glad to use it for this purpose. To them, Acts and Klee were already family.

As the dream moved quickly again, Acts now watched Joshua strike a man in the throat and Salmon watching his captain, repeated his action. The man Salmon faced met with the same results, leaving both men gasping not only for air but also trying to swallow. Acts position now whirled around to watch Telok let go of two men. Both their bodies were in mid-flight after he had pulled them up by their hair, letting them land on their shoulders and the upper part of their backs. Time slowed again. He watched as Telok punched his fist hard into the top of the man's abdomen just under his breastbone. He could hear the force push all the air from the man. As the man bent forward Telok lifted his knee into the man's forehead, which brought the man back up into a standing position. Now Telok began to spin to his right and in the spin, he hit the man with his right elbow striking him in the jaw. It was with such force he lifted the man off the ground. The man did a cartwheel in the air before landing unconscious. Acts then saw himself slowly get up from the ground to face Abiram. Abiram's face full of surprise and mixed with fear could not stop this young warrior. Acts told himself to strike fast. He then responded in the dream as if he had heard himself. Acts hit Abiram under his chin with the palm of his hand. Abiram's head snapped back, and he fell to the ground unconscious. But even as Abiram fell, he could see Korah behind him. He was again moving toward him. He tried to tell himself to "watch out!" He saw himself drop to one knee and struggle to stand. Korah had moved into striking distance, and he watched Korah pull his fist back. With all the force Korah could muster, Acts watched as Korah hit him in the back of his head. He watched as blood appeared and began to soak his hair. He was falling toward his left side; feeling the strike and the air move around his body, he felt the ground stopping him. As he fell to his side he rolled to his back, and he heard something. It was Korah's voice. The word was coming to his ears in echoes but starting far away and then coming closer. The word was "YOU!"

Korah had now focused on Joshua's face in recognition. Joshua jumped over Acts to grab Korah and flip him over his shoulder. He watched Joshua's face grow in rage as he looked over to Acts' body and then to Klee. He watched as Joshua began to breathe deep and fast. He had never seen such an expression on his captain's face. It was the angriest he had ever seen anyone. As the rage built, Joshua began to move into action. The scene moved slowly. He hit the big man in the stomach bending him over in pain and then he saw Joshua raise his arm intending on putting his elbow into the man's spine at the bottom of his neck. It appeared he was going to end this man's life. Then he watched Joshua suddenly stop in movement before the blow. Now Acts focused not on Joshua's face, but on the man behind him; Telok had stopped Joshua's arm. As Joshua turned his head to see what stopped him Acts could see Telok speaking the words, but with no sound. Even so, Acts still could understand what Telok was saying. "They are finished, My Captain". Telok had ended the battle. Acts looked around at the men down; and then, he looked at Joshua, Salmon, Telok, and finally at his sister. He had watched the fight from beginning to end from several different angles. He still did not understand the hate and disgust these men had toward him, toward his sister and to Joshua. But what he really could not understand, were their actions while being rescued by the Only True God. How could they be so callous to not see the wonder happening around them? As the last question passed through Acts' mind, the dream began to whirl around like a dust cloud moving up into a funnel and out of sight.

~

Klee, holding her brother, suddenly felt him become deathly still. He had stopped breathing. She looked at her brother in complete fear for his life. Naoon watched in horror as she held her breath along with the rest of the family.

Klee said his name, "Acts!" She shook him and repeated it louder, "ACTS!!" She felt him take in a breath. She paused and said his name again, but in a calmer voice, and Acts opened his eyes. Everyone watching took a deep breath along with him.

Chapter 5
Two Realms Collide

Acts had been unconscious for more than an hour, longer than any time before. The gash to the back of his head would not stop bleeding and so Klee kept her hand pressed to the cut. As she looked up at Joshua's mother she could see the worry on her face. She checked his breathing and then felt his skin. He was breathing deep and slow, and his skin was cool. She asked for a blanket to keep him warm, and she put it over his legs. She didn't want to get him too warm, just enough to keep him from getting chilled. Joshua's mother had pulled out some thread and looked around to see if there was someone who could do the stitching because she was shaking too much. As her eyes caught Naoon's she felt in her heart that Naoon could do it. She didn't understand why because she didn't know who Naoon was, but just trusted her eyes. Naoon didn't even hesitate and handed the baby over to Joshua's mom. She took the needle and thread and watched as Klee turned Acts' head so she could see the cut. Naoon didn't say anything with her mouth, but the compassion she felt said everything in her eyes and Klee understood. She very tenderly pulled the hair out of the way as a drop of water hit her hand. She looked to see where it came from; it was Klee. Tears had well-up in her eyes and one escaped falling onto Naoon's hand.

Naoon stopped and put her hand on Klee's and said, "I will be as gentle as I can." Klee tried to smile, but it was a poor attempt. Naoon understood as she began to put the needle and thread to work. Having to stop several times to wipe the blood away she finished after putting twelve stitches to the cut. When she was done, she let out a sigh and looked at Klee. The look on Klee's face had relaxed as Naoon finished and in so doing stopped the bleeding. As she rolled Acts onto his back, she placed one of her hands on Naoon's and thanked her for being so kind. Naoon smiled, got to her feet, walked over to Joshua's mom, and took the baby. Everyone watched her. As she got the baby comfortable in her arms Klee asked softly, "Who are you?"

She smiled at Klee and answered, "My name is Naoon, and I am traveling with Kemuel, Telok's father." Naoon was beautiful in form and her face was captivating. Her dark brown eyes held such compassion that she didn't need words to convey her empathy. She smiled at Klee and said, "I will be just over there if you should need me for anything." She pointed to the cart of Kemuel and walked back.

Klee watched her and as she walked off, she called to her, "Naoon!" As Naoon turned to look at her, Klee said, "Thank you."

Naoon smiled, turning to see Kemuel watching the entire scene. She smiled at him and quietly said, "I think the baby is ready to eat."

Kemuel was standing just a few steps from Klee and began to explain who this beautiful young lady was. "My son and your soon-to-be husband came across Naoon as we were passing through the Sea. She needed some help and Joshua put Telok to the task of taking care of her. She has no other family other than that beautiful baby girl." Klee looked over in the direction of Kemuel's cart and asked, "What is the baby's name?" Kemuel thought for a moment and then shook his head and laughed, "I don't know!" Klee asked, "Does Telok have a special interest in her?" Kemuel nodded his head and replied, "You might say that. He brought her to me when he found out that he and Joshua were going to be stationed in another part of the company for this part of the journey." He paused a moment and added, "I like having the fellowship and that baby is the best little thing."

Klee smiled and as she looked down at Acts, he was looking up at her. "How do you feel brother?"

He was a little slow to respond, but he was able to answer her. "My head hurts and I feel really tired." He paused and then asked, "Did I hear you met Naoon?"

"Yes, I did. In fact, she is the one who stitched your head up." Klee smiled and added, "And she did a really good job."

"I only heard about her from Telok. He seems to really like her." His eyes closed slowly and then opened again. "I am glad you met." He got quiet and closed his eyes again. Klee could tell by his breathing that he was sleeping. She didn't worry as much at this point and held him tenderly.

~

As things started to calm down, their new family began planning how to care for Acts. A group of men had come with another cart and lifted Acts into it. The family talked among themselves, gathering the things that had spilled and planning a way to fix the wheel on the broken cart. She heard Joshua's dad, Nun, come up with the best plan.

"Let's just use this cart filled with these useless idols. We can leave the idols here and put all the clothes and tools in it. We don't need this cart anyway. These things are just waste in our lives. Which one of these idols can split the Red Sea?!" This brought a laugh to the rest of the family standing nearby.

Klee spoke to herself softly, "Which idol can split the Red Sea? Not a one."

As she looked down, she found Acts had woken. He looked into her eyes. He waited a moment and then said in a soft voice, "Not a one."

Klee smiled, "did you read my thoughts?" "Yea. Great minds think alike."

It was good to hear him spout out a little of his humor.

Even with the entire company of Israel on the move, the news of Acts accident spread quickly throughout the tribe of Ephraim. The tribe of Ephraim had 40,500 men of fighting age: not counting women and children. Before the journey began Moses had estimated there to be over 120,000 people in this tribe and it wasn't the largest. Only a very few had met Acts, but his actions in serving Joshua had become well known throughout the tribe. Acts wasn't a hero, but he'd come to have a place beside one.

~

The news of Acts getting hurt had reached Janue and Shade. They asked their father if they could go and check on him. He gave them permission and they quickly made their way to the cart that Acts was riding in. Shade stood back a few steps as Janue approached the wagon. She took a look and could see he was lying with his eyes closed. Klee walked up and was surprised to see the girls standing there.

"Janue! Shade! You don't know how good it is to see you." Klee said.

"We heard the news, that Acts had been hurt in an accident?" Janue told her.

"We had to come and see how he is doing!" Shade added.

Janue looked over into the cart and asked, "How bad is it, Klee?"

Klee smiled and told them, "One of the wagons had a wheel break and as the wagon rolled over, there was a long-handle garden tool and that is what hit the back of his head."

Janue asked quickly, "It wasn't the same place Abiram hit him, was it?"

Klee nodded her head and said, "Yes, it was. He's got 12 stitches holding his three-inch cut closed."

"Three inches?!!" Janue expressed.

Shade held up her hand, showing what three inches would be with her fingers. "That is a long cut!"

"It is the biggest he's ever had. Naoon is the one who sewed him up." Klee looked in the direction of Kemuel's cart. "She met Joshua and Telok as we crossed through the sea. Telok was put in charge of seeing her and her baby to safety. She is amazing. And she has the cutest baby girl. Without a word, Joshua's mom turned to Naoon and handed her the needle and thread. I turned his head so that she could see the cut and she put 12 good stitches in. In that one single moment, I knew I had a new sister."

Janue was listening, but she kept stealing glances over at Acts. As she looked at Acts once more, she found him looking at her. She was surprised and smiled at him. Klee saw the exchange and said, "Shade, I would like to take you over to meet Naoon." The slight encouragement told Shade that Janue and Acts needed a moment.

While they walked off Acts said, "You are a surprise!"

"Well, you can't get hurt without the entire tribe knowing." She countered.

Acts pulled himself up and leaned against some blankets so that he could see her better.

"How are you feeling?" she asked.

"My head hurts almost all of the time. It will ease off for a while but then it comes back with a vengeance."

"Have you been up yet?" She said, stepping closer to the wagon.

Acts replied, "I haven't yet. Klee has put the 'big sis' orders on me. I'm not supposed to get up until she says."

Janue laughed. She paused a moment and asked, "Did you see anything this time?"

Acts looked down at the blanket and then back to her eyes. He suggested she sit on the edge of the wagon as it moved. She hopped up on the tail of the wagon and got comfortable. As he was talking, he couldn't get over how beautiful she looked. "I saw the entire fight with Korah and Abiram again."

She got even more comfortable and said, "Tell me!"

~

Naoon was playing with the baby in the back of their wagon as Shade and Klee walked up.

"Naoon. There are two young women I would like for you to meet." As Naoon looked up she only saw Shade. Klee noticed and added, "Well, this young lady first. Her sister is talking with Acts. Naoon stepped up, put out her hand, and said, "I am Naoon."

Klee looked at Shade and then back to Naoon and said, "This is Shade. Her sister is Janue. I have known them all of their lives." Naoon looked into the kind eyes of Shade and said, "It is good to meet you." And then, she turned and said, "This is baby."

Shade loved babies and was very comfortable with them. "May I hold her?"

Naoon reached over and took the baby, "You sure can." Placing baby in her arms she began to coo and play with Shade's hands. Shade looked around and asked, "Where is her father?"

Naoon looked into the baby's eyes and answered, "He was killed a few months before she was born."

"Oh! I did not mean to bring up something bad." Shade said with emotion.

Naoon put her hand on Shades and replied, "It's alright. I have come to terms with all of it and now I am living a new life of freedom. I have much to be thankful for. The life in Egypt seems like another life to me."

Klee smiled and said, "That is a good way to put it. It does seem like a whole different life, and I don't think about it much anymore." She looked over at Janue and suggested, "Naoon, would you like to walk over and check your patient and how the conversation is going?" Naoon smiled and answered, "Yes, I would like that very much."

Shade never let go of baby as they walked over to Acts' wagon.

~

When Acts had finished telling Janue about the dream, she looked at him and said, "You are a very important part of all that is going on. I hope that this injury does not hinder you for long. I know you like taking care of what Joshua and Moses need done."

There was a moment of silence and suddenly they were aware of other people around them. They both looked to see Shade holding the baby as they walked up. Klee introduced Janue to Naoon. Naoon looked deep into Janue's eyes and said, "It is very nice to meet you." Her warm look and gentle handshake were very calming and inviting. Janue smiled and replied, "It is so nice to meet you, Naoon."

Naoon smiled at Acts, "And how are you feeling?" Acts perked up when he saw baby. "I'm feeling better."

Janue looked at Acts with a funny look and Acts corrected himself. "Well, my head still hurts, and I get dizzy at times." Klee looked at him, "And that is why you will stay in this wagon until I tell you or Naoon… says it's alright. You understand?"

"Yes, sis!" Was the reply.

The girls laughed and Janue said, "We need to get back to our family. Our father didn't want us gone for long."

"It was nice to meet both of you and I hope we can visit more," Naoon said with a smile.

Before Shade gave the baby back to her mom, Acts asked if he could hold her for a while. Naoon said, "Of course, you can."

Shade handed Acts the baby and all of the girls could see what effect the baby had on him. He was calm and his eyes bright. Klee and Naoon made a mental note of it. Goodbye hugs were given among the girls and Janue and Shade walked back to their family.

Klee and Naoon walked behind the wagon at the slow casual pace of the oxen. They were amazed at the way Acts responded to baby. Klee said to Naoon, "Now, that's interesting, isn't it?"

Naoon smiled and agreed, "It sure is."

Klee commented on the visit, "It sure was good to see the girls and it is always funny to watch Janue and Acts interact. They make me laugh."

~

As the company moved at a slow comfortable pace the mood was still high across the sea of humanity, but it only took a few hours for some of the people to notice that the water was gone. It wasn't that there was little water around those who were asking, there simply wasn't any. No one said anything though because they thought Moses knew where the water was and that he was leading them to the next oasis.

The evening was just about to begin with the sun fading in the west. The pillar of cloud began to lift away as the pillar of fire began swirling into a funnel and spread a blanket of light from Moses to the last man in the rear. It wasn't as bright as the day, but it was just enough so the people could keep moving. The fact that the ram's horn did not sound meant the company would not be stopping.

~

In the spiritual realm, a myriad of Angels surrounded the entire company, beautiful in form. All were much bigger than any human, even the tallest human. Moving around the company they looked in all directions for the enemy, but it wasn't just the human enemy they guarded against.

Satan and his minions were in tremendous turmoil not understanding why the One True God of the Universe was so interested in this homeless band of humanity. They were on every side, moving in and around the people trying to hear, trying to see the importance of these twelve tribes. They were listening as the people talked, trying to understand what the Holy One was doing with them. The threat of a demon coming face to face with an Angelic being in a confrontation was terrifying. To lose a fight with an Angel meant possibly being sent to the pit; a terrible place of holding until the very judgment of God. They did not understand what would come after the judgment; they only knew that they never wanted to be cast into the pit. No demon had ever returned from there and one swing of an Angelic blade or spear could put any one of them there for eternity. One-on-one there might be a good match between a certain angel and demon, but Satan was only focusing on Acts at the time.

Satan understood certain things concerning what was happening and he knew man. He had studied them since the 'Fall' in the garden; a time of great victory for him. He saw people as whimpering little children when they didn't get what they wanted. He knew just how weak the human body was. Case in point was the fact that these people were now walking in a desert with absolutely no water and Satan could see for himself there was no oasis within a two-day walk. He felt for certain that many of them would not survive long in such a hostile environment. "Even with The Holy One giving them shade by day and warmth by night," he thought sarcastically. "All I have to do is wait and let human nature work against itself. We shall see then, who wants to follow this human, Moses. They will turn on him; this I am sure of." Satan was paying close attention to those Moses had trust. But the young human known as Acts posed a problem.

Satan had sent one of his best demonic warriors ahead of the people to lay in wait for an opportunity to kill the boy. The demon had hidden just under the surface of the sand and as the cart rolled over him, he had sabotaged the wheel and caused the cart to almost land on Acts.

"We came so close my lord" the demon explained to Satan.

"But failed to finish the job" Satan sneered.

The fact that this minion had been able to work his evil right under the Angels' noses brought great pleasure to the demon sent by Satan. But his efforts did not impress his master. He had been able to penetrate his enemy's defenses and slip away but was unsuccessful in killing the boy. Satan remembered how *this* boy had been able to look him right in the eyes; the eyes of the Death, as he moved like a serpent throughout the land of Egypt, taking all of the firstborn. Even in such a close encounter, he could not touch the boy who was being protected by the blood of the lamb on the doorposts of the house. Because the boy had looked into him so intently, Satan knew the boy was special; that he could see things of the spiritual realm that others could not. This caused Satan to be weary of how the Holy One might use him. So, wait he would. He could wait until the opportunity presented itself again to take care of the boy and everyone in service to this leader of the people, Moses. Satan kept his place at the front where Moses was waiting to hear any new orders given to him by the Lord. He would wait close by to catch even the smallest whispers... if he could.

Chapter 6
Doubt Creeping In

Back in the realm of humanity, the walk was becoming more difficult. Now the children were beginning to cry. This made the parents edgy and the words they spoke were like that of snapping dogs toward each other. Still… no one said anything about the water.

They believed that Moses would find the water in the morning. And so, they marched, occupying their minds with the thought that tomorrow would bring what they needed. And even though the Lord had supplied for them in every way, even before leaving Egypt, they never turned their thoughts to the Lord God.

As a new day began, the first full day would be complete. And Moses knew there were two more days to walk in this 'Test of the Heart'.

Acts had been sleeping off and on since the accident and Klee was getting a bit worried. She could see how the air was beginning to dry his lips because unconsciously he was licking his lips to keep them moist while he slept. The news of him getting hurt had made it to Salmon in the front and to Joshua and Telok in the last four tribes with the message having been sent to the tribal leaders: Acts had been hurt, hit in the head in an accident involving a cart which had overturned, but was doing alright.' The particulars were sketchy, but this news would have to do for now. Even though they wanted to go to him, each of them felt in their hearts they needed to stay where Moses had put them. Even Moses wanted to go to Acts; wanted to be there for him and still, Moses knew that he must maintain his position in the front of the company.

As the dawn made its appearance in the east, the pillar of fire gave way to the pillar of cloud. The people were looking for the oasis Moses was leading them to. But by late morning the clans, families, and even whole tribes began going to their own tribal leaders wanting them to send runners to the front to find out from Moses what he was going to do about the water supply. The tribal leaders were doing their best to smooth over the turmoil that was beginning to churn in the hearts of the people. By mid-afternoon, even the tribal leaders were beginning to question Moses in their own hearts. They were able by that evening, to calm the people somewhat, by telling them Moses would know where to stop for water in the morning. With doubt creeping into their hearts, they hoped that what they told the people would be true.

Evening came and the people moved on even as the cattle, sheep, goats, donkeys, and camels began complaining in their own way. The small children had reached a point that they couldn't cry anymore. Their thirst had dried their throats to the point that making a sound hurt. The next morning as the sun came up the people began looking to their tribal leaders and demanded, "Send runners to Moses to find out where the water is." So, the leaders, unable to sway them to wait a little longer, began to send runners from every tribe. Joshua and Telok saw and heard what was happening around them, but they couldn't stop it. They had been asked to watch for physical trouble, not the unsettled questions of the people, and now the tribal leaders. They watched as the runners started out from the tribe of Asher.

Joshua and Telok were even beginning to have doubts about the direction the company was walking. Even though they didn't know this part of the desert it seemed to make more sense to stay alongside the Red Sea and catch one of the tributaries that led to the Sea. They each fought off the doubt within their own minds. It is in the mind that the battle is fought, and these two warriors knew that. "Maintain a level of belief and in that… maintain hope." Thought Joshua. "Or is it; maintain a level of hope and in that maintain belief?" He couldn't decide. He was having difficulty staying focused. Finally, he looked over to Telok, "I'm having a thought."

"Oh! What is it?" Telok curious.

"I'm thinking that we can make it to Acts and Klee by the end of tomorrow night?" Joshua said hesitantly with a questioning voice, unsure of what he was even saying.

Telok looked at his captain with a furrowed brow, "Are you sure you want to try and cover that much ground without any water? I know you want to see them, so do I, but this is not the way my brother; we need to keep our post." Telok did his best not to sound like he was scolding his best friend.

Joshua thought for a moment and lowered his head to look at the ground and then looked back over to Telok. "You are so right, my friend. I guess I was searching for something to take my mind off of water and the thoughts in my mind questioning even Moses."

"I, too, have been doing just that in my own mind. It is truly difficult. I don't know why the Lord God is leading Moses this direction but… this I do know." Telok stopped walking and looked at his captain. "I would rather be following the Lord and Moses, than trying to make it on my own."

Joshua looked back at his friend and smiled, "I'm sure being in obedience is safer than disobedience; in His care than in the care of the doubts in my mind." He laughed at himself and said, "And far better than in the service of the taskmasters of Egypt. And yes, I recognize you weren't a slave, but you were still ruled by a very selfish king."

~

Moses on the other hand was not laughing as the runners from all of the tribes had made their way to him. As each one approached him, he thanked them for completing the task of reaching him with the request from the tribal leaders. He asked each of the runners to walk with him for a while. The runners looked at each other and thought of how great an honor this was; to walk beside the man that had led them out of Egypt. Moses talked with them about how the journey was going and what they had learned so far. Timidly they each began to share. Moses could feel the excitement of the new life that had been born in each heart coming up out of the Red Sea.

He knew these teenagers would be the leaders of the future and he wanted to cultivate their interest and strengths toward being used by the Lord. Moses also knew that the demands being made were not from their generation, but rather from a generation that should know better: A generation that should at least have begun to trust the Lord just by watching His Mighty Handwork for them. And in that thought a cry went out to the Lord from his heart, "Lord, what shall I do with these people?"

The Lord spoke to Moses, and he heard His still small voice, "I AM The Great Provider."

He smiled and thanked The Lord and turned to his young students, "This is wh…what the Lord says, 'I AM The Great Provider'. Tell the people of each tribe to b…be patient with the Lord and they will see His mighty hand move again on their behalf."

And with a smile and hug for each boy he sent them back to pass the word from runner to runner until the truth of what Moses said reached each tribal leader. Moses looked at Aaron and waved for him to come and walk with him. As Aaron walked up Moses began the conversation, "Let me share with you what the Lord said to me."

~

Klee looked down at her brother and was surprised to find him awake. Acts looked at his sister and asked, "Are we still moving?"

"Yes, we are" she replied with concern in her voice.

"Why are my lips so dry and they feel like they're cracking."

She answered again with the same concern, "Yes they are."

He put his hand to the back of his head and felt the stitches. "Did this happen today?"

She reached over and pulled his hand away from his wound. "When the cart tipped over a handle from one of the gardening tools hit you right in the back of your head. We have been moving now for two days." Her voice raspy. "There is no more water, and the people are beginning to complain," she told him. Then she added, "They even demanded the tribal leaders send runners to Moses to… 'find out where the water is,' she said in a sarcastic tone bothered by the thought of what they had done.

Changing the subject, she asked her brother, "What did you see when you were out? What did you dream about?"

"Why do you ask?" Acts questioned.

"While you were out your whole body flinched, and moved like you were in a great struggle… almost like you were fighting someone."

Acts had to think a moment. He licked his lips trying to sooth them as he started to reach up and touch them and his sister popped his hand. He got the message and pulled his hand away from his lips. He began to answer her, "It was a fight. In my dream, I recalled in detail, the fight I had with Korah and Abiram only… I was seeing it from all directions. Some of it moved slowly allowing me to see even dust particles stop in the air. Other parts moved very quickly." He smiled, "And we won again!"

Klee asked, "Was it in all the colors as you have seen before?"

"No. It kind of stayed in blue and gray colors." Pausing, he thought about the other times he had passed out. "It did not feel like any of the other times. This was more like a dream I would have any night. In all of the other times before I have moved in a direction that seemed to teach me; show me something about our Lord."

"Maybe you needed to see the fight again; for the Lord to show you how brave you were." As she smiled at him.

"Yea… Maybe…?" He laid back down in the cart with his sister beside him and fell back asleep.

Klee looked up to see Naoon and the baby walking toward them. She smiled at her. "How is your brother doing?" Naoon inquired softly.

He is having trouble keeping up with the days and he still sleeps a lot" Klee replied.

"Does he remember anything of what happened?" Naoon said with concern.

Klee looked down at Acts and replied, "No. I had to tell him what happened, that we are still moving, and that the tribal leaders want to know when Moses is going to take them to water." She spoke showing her disagreement with their decision.

Naoon laughed softly and said, "I find it bothersome too." Klee was able to laugh with her. Naoon said, "I still haven't gotten to meet Acts while he is…. awake." This made Klee laugh again. "Maybe you can catch him awake tomorrow."

"I think I would like to meet her now" came a soft response from Acts.

"Well… in that case: Naoon…. this is my brother, Acts; Acts this is Naoon and her baby girl." Klee said with introduction.

"It is nice to finally meet you" Naoon said.

"I want to thank you for stitching me up. I went to feel of it, but I got slapped." Acts said with a half-smile that looked uncomfortable.

"Your head still hurts, I see" Naoon said. "Yes, it does!" Acts answered.

"Well, I hope that it stops soon." Naoon responded.

"Your baby is beautiful. What's her name?" Acts asked. "It's just 'baby' for now. I haven't given her a name. My husband was to name her, but he died before she was born. He never told me what he was considering." Naoon said sadly.

"I'm sorry to hear that" Acts said with empathy. "Well, I know that whatever name she gets will fit her." He seemed to speak more softly this time and within just a moment, he was back asleep.

Klee looked at Naoon and Naoon could see the worry on her face. "I have had only short conversations with Telok, and I know that he thinks very highly of Acts. I'm sure the Lord has many more things for him to do with Joshua and Telok." Naoon spoke with as much encouragement as she could.

"The Lord healed him before when he got hurt in a terrible fight." Klee told her. Naoon looked puzzled so Klee explained, "When Acts got hit in the head by Korah, it cut his head, but not as bad as this. Anyway, the Lord just healed his cut! I mean; one minute it was there and the next his head looked like the skin hadn't even been bruised."

Naoon looked back at Klee with her mouth open. Finally finding words she exclaimed, "He was just healed!?"

"It was amazing," Klee responded.

As the girls walked together Klee began telling her all about the whole ordeal and everyone involved. It was good 'girl time'.

Chapter 7

Bitter Waters

As the second day was coming to an end and the pillar of fire replaced the pillar of cloud, most of the people began to settle a little easier. The night helped them to focus, at least, on the next morning. It would be a new day, and they thought that the third day would be the day; the day they would find water. It was this thought that was shared between family and clans; even making it back to the tribal leaders and that seemed a comfort to them. But as they traveled through the night the march got slower and the spacing between the tribes began to fall apart. Joshua and Telok both noticed how the tribe of Asher was beginning to lengthen. They both saw it but neither one knew how to correct it; or if it really needed to be corrected since the attitude seemed calmer.

Every person was really starting to feel the ache in their muscles as the toxins began to become trapped in their bodies. With no water, their bodies were unable to flush the toxins out. Muscles in their legs were beginning to cramp. With no real excess of body fat on their well-defined muscles, Joshua and Telok were actually starting to feel it more than most of the other people. But in the mass of people there were thousands of men who had been in hard physical labor most of their lives and they too, had very little body fat. As the cramps began to hit Joshua and Telok they would have to stop and rub the cramp out just as everyone else was having to do. This was another thing that could occupy their minds and keep them from thinking about the hours they had walked. As the night passed so did the miles and the cramps seemed to be soothed by the cooler temperatures of the desert night.

In an effort to keep each other going, they tried to talk about something other than being thirsty, but their throats were so dry it hurt to talk so, most of the night was silent among the people. It had become a march of silence; at least for now. The morning, most likely, would bring attitudes to the surface.

~

Aaron had slipped behind Moses to walk with some of their own family and Moses took the opportunity to fellowship with the Lord.

"Well, Lord, it's just about to break dawn on the third day and I am surely getting thirsty." He began.

"I know my friend," the Lord responded.

"I hope you know that I am not doubting you; just trying to make conversation," Moses whispered back.

"The very fact that you want to have conversation with me brings me joy. I desire to have conversation with all of my children." The Lord paused. **"But there are very few that seek the level of relationship you and I have. In fact, my relationship with you is one of a kind."**

Moses combed back his long silver hair and thought for a moment. "I do love our relationship. I don't know what life would be like now if we weren't able to speak to each other daily. This time I have with You Lord has become my source of life; You are m…my life."

"And that, My son is the attitude I seek. That is the very drive that creates these moments that I can speak with you. Out of the mass of humanity I have created on this world there have been so few that have sought me this way."

"Who were they, Lord?" Moses asked.

The Lord smiled and began, **"Adam, Eve, and Able. Then Seth, Enoch, Noah, and Shem. There was a long length of time when generation after generation passed until Abraham. His heart and yours are very much alike. I spoke to him as I do you."** The Lord paused, allowing Moses to process the names.

He had not heard this history of his people although the name of Noah had been told to him as in only a story, not like he was a real person. Only a small bit of history was known to him, such as Abraham, but before that, he knew almost nothing. The Lord continued, **"After Abraham, it was Isaac and then, Jacob that I had fellowship with. His name I changed to Israel."**

Moses smiled and said, "I did at least know that."

"Israel listened to me, but it wasn't until the later part of his life. His heart became soft, and he allowed me to mold him into the person I needed him to be. I used his son, Joseph, to bring my people to Egypt. I have been quiet for over four hundred years now. You, Moses, are the first since that time and now I walk

with you as I did with your ancestors. It is your *thirst* for Me that brings Me to you. And it is, in this very time of thirst that I am teaching these people to have the same desire. I used Aaron to speak to Pharaoh, but it is to you Moses, I will speak through from now on and no one else. You, Moses, are my Servant and My Friend."

Moses could not stand it any longer and he stopped, got on his knees, and bowed his face to the ground in worship. He had never heard the history of his ancestors. This moment in time with the Lord was overwhelming! As the sun was breaking over the horizon it found Moses in a time of complete surrender to the God of the Universe.

This day would begin finding Moses on his knees knowing that, the Great I AM would supply what these people needed.

~

The third day had dawned, and everyone was looking for the deliverance they sought from their thirst. The Lord had created this thirst so that He could show them a small part of His personality. He would show them once again His provision and His love for them; which goes beyond human comprehension.

The pillars of fire and cloud had changed and now the people had awakened from their stupor of the night fighting cramps and trying to just stay awake. The sound of their voices began to grow so that even Moses could hear them. He walked straight ahead and as he walked up a small hill, he could see in the distance a reflection of the heat coming off the sand. Moses stopped and gazed in the direction of the reflection more intently. It was actually not heat rising from the sand, but water standing as still as a mirror. He couldn't just turn around and tell the people, it would cause them to react too quickly, and someone could get hurt. No… he had to seek the Lord's wisdom. He began walking again not giving any sign as to what he had seen.

"Lord, how am I to get these people to the water without causing a dangerous rush to it."

"Just keep walking toward the water and then when you are closer, lead them around the lake, but stay on the top of the hill. I will keep the people from seeing it until they can gather around it safely."

There were several small hills between Moses and the water and as he came to the top of the hill that led down to the shore he began to circle around the lake. It was very large, and Moses could see that most of the people would be able to gather around the shoreline in safety. The people just followed him as sheep would a shepherd. Even the animals kept walking not smelling the water. It had taken all morning, but by the time Moses had circled back to the point where he started, some of the people of the last tribe of Naphtali were able to see the people in the tribe of Judah. When the ram's horn sounded for all of the people to stop, they didn't understand why the entire company had made a circle.

Nahshon was standing facing the lake but looking at the other side at the people. They were standing on the hilltop with a gentle grade that led all of the way down to the water. He looked more intently at the reflection and suddenly realized it was…. Water!

He dropped his staff and walked slowly to the edge of the water. It was then that the eyes of the people began to open. They were looking at the water, but not trusting what they were seeing. No one moved except Nahshon. As he bent down, he pushed his hand slowly into the cool refreshing liquid. A smile appeared on his face as the word began to pass back through the families and whole company that they were finally to water. There was a great sigh of relief that could be heard by everyone. Several others slowly moved to the water and began to step in. Everyone else just stood back and watched to see if it was safe. Slowly Nahshon cupped his hands and then each person who had come into the water did the same. He pulled his hands back to his lips as did those around him. Almost at the same time, they all spit the water out as fast as they could.

The water was extremely bitter; so, bitter that they could not drink it.

Panic began to breakout across the company from those at the shore back to the outer perimeter. People began throwing sand in the air; falling on the ground, crying, and moaning as if being on fire. They all began to turn to Moses and Aaron with anger and expression as if set on killing them.

Satan smiled to himself, "Here is the moment I have waited for. They will turn on Moses and kill him and when his men come to his aid, I will kill them."

The people began shouting from all directions; "Why have you brought us into this desert? WHAT ARE WE TO DRINK?" As the entire company of Israel began shouting this over and over the panic grew.

Joshua and Telok were at a loss for what to do. Some of Salmon's family had actually tasted the water; his father being the very first. Salmon looked at his father and saw the anger grow on his father's face. In an effort to calm the growing rage, Salmon implored, "Father, just be patient. I am sure that Moses knows what to..."

His father did not hear his plea as he walked over to Moses and Aaron, "What are we to drink? We have walked for three horrible days in this desert. We have children on the verge of dying. WHAT ARE WE TO DRINK?!!!"

~

Moses and Aaron both fell to the ground on their knees. Moses pleaded with the Lord in what to do. In his heart, he heard the still small voice of the Lord, **"Calm yourself My Friend. Stand up."**

So, Moses stood, but Aaron stayed on his knees.

The Lord spoke to His friend, **"Now look over to your left by the water's edge. There is a stick almost as long as your staff. It is straight and balanced just for you. I prepared this stick for you long ago. It has been waiting on you for this very moment. Take it! Throw it into the water. Throw it as you would a spear to pierce the thirst of the people."**

Moses walked over to the stick and picked it up; feeling the weight and balance. More than half of the tribes were standing on the water's edge and the rest of the company lined the shore just behind them. The lake being lower, enabled the company opportunity to see what was happening. As the tribes nearest Moses gazed intently at his every move, they became silent. Joshua and Telok were on the edge of the people, watching just a few yards from the shoreline. Moses took the stick and grabbed a position on the shaft, holding it like a weapon; like a spear. This was something that Moses knew very well. He had trained with the best in Egypt, being part of Pharaoh's household as one of his very own sons. He looked at the spear for a long time, taking in all that the moment had to offer. He paid no attention to the people but seemed to be standing as if all alone; a lone warrior of faith surrounded by a sea of doubt. As he raised it to his shoulder the people were given the sight needed to see the expression on his face and the faith in his stance. Each person could see Moses so clearly, they thought they were standing just a few feet from him. He extended his arm behind him and taking two steps with perfect form, he threw the spear with all of his might. *The miracle of every person being able to see with clarity went without notice.* Every eye followed his actions. In anticipation, the people could not look away. As the spear was released it soared up in a high arch and flew far through the air. It almost seemed to be floating, so slowly, that time seemed to stop. As their eyes gazed at the stick, their mouths open as if they were just about to say something; they watched the spear disappear into the water; point first creating only a small ripple. Moses turned to Nahshon making eye contact with his. Moses said calmly, "Now… Go and taste what the Lord has provided."

Just as everyone was able to see what had happened, they now heard what Moses had said to Nahshon. Every eye now focused on him and watched him turn to walk back to the water. Captivated, the people could not take their eyes off of him.

Nahshon stepped to the water's edge. Stooping down, he cupped both hands in the water and lifted it to his mouth. Being the first to the water, Nahshon remembered the taste of the bitter water, but as the water touched his tongue a wonderful thing took place. The water was now sweet! It tasted better than the water in Egypt. The smile on his face suddenly began to register in the minds of the people that the water was now good.

As the people around the scene made their way to the water they began to shout and sing! The other tribes heard the celebration and knew that they had indeed reached water. Not just drinkable, but sweet, delicious water! Like a rope falling into water; beginning at one end and pulling the rest in by its weight, the people moved to the water's edge. Those who were first got what they needed; filling their skins and then, stepped back to allow others to approach the lake. The people spent the entire day filling water skins, water carts and tending to all of the animals. The lake was large enough to accommodate more than half of the tribes at one time. The site of seeing three million people getting a drink of water for the first time in three days was overwhelming and Moses could not stop thanking the Lord for such a wonderful miracle.

"Oh Lord, how wonderful You are; How amazing it is to see Your hand move in protection and in supply! You are faithful to meet our every need."

"And I will continue to meet every need, my Friend. Just Trust and Obey.

Chapter 8
Learning the Commands

It had taken all day for everyone, including the animals, to feel refreshed and satisfied. Moses stepped out several feet into the water so that he could be seen. He motioned for everyone to sit down and get comfortable. He looked all the way around the shoreline gazing at the people as if he were looking right into their hearts. And if it were known to the people, they would have understood that the Lord was giving Moses the ability to see them through His eyes in the spirit. He could see each and every person; read the expression on their face and understand their fears. The Lord was truly giving him the heart of a shepherd for the people. For what shepherd worth his salt does not know every lamb under his care? His gaze was so intense that the people felt it. His heart began to fill with love as he looked out among them and could see in his spirit, that they were but children; God's children.

The stillness was incredible. Not even the animals made a sound as they lay down filled with the life-giving liquid. Even though Moses wasn't speaking with his voice his eyes seemed to expose the truth of what the Lord God had done. Conviction began to burn in their hearts as the revelation became clear that the water had been made sweet for them to drink even in their unbelief. They again were filled with wonder of their new God. But their level of trust was only beginning. Would this God continue to take care of them, or would he abandon them somewhere along the way? They had seen first-hand what this God had done to the land of Egypt, and it caused a dreadful fear.

Moses pulled his staff up beside him and began to speak to them, "The Lord God is making a law and a decree to this people called 'The Children of Israel.' He has t...tested you. He has created a thirst in your body to show you the thirst that He wants in your very soul for Him. This is what the Lord says to you: "If you listen carefully to the voice of the Lord your God and do what is right in His eyes, if you pay attention to His commands and keep all of His decrees, He will not bring on you any of the diseases He brought on the Egyptians, for I AM the Lord, who heals you."

The miracle that had happened in the great valley on the other side of the Red Sea, before they crossed over, had happened again; every single person heard what Moses said as if he were standing next to them. And once again the miracle put every heart in wonder and amazement of this God they now followed. As they witnessed all that was happening, both Salmon and Acts immediately thought… which one had recognized the miracle first.

Moses looked at the entire company again. He paused for what seemed to be a long time, but it was only for a moment and then, he repeated what the Lord had told him: "If you listen carefully to the voice of the Lord your God and do what is right in His eyes, if you pay attention to His commands and keep all of His decrees, He will not bring on you any of the diseases He brought on the Egyptians, for I AM the Lord, who heals you."

Moses then led the people in unison, the command he had just told them. They repeated it several times until every adult and young person could recite the command. He smiled at the people and showed them that he was angry no more at their distrust in the Lord and the way they had acted upon reaching the water. Moses told them, "We are n…not going to camp here, but only rest tonight. I want you to ready your things for the sound of the ram's horn. In the morning, we will begin to m…move again. Gather around your banners at the first sound with your tribal leaders in the center of your tribe. Rest tonight and enjoy the goodness of the Lord." He paused a moment and turned to walk out of the water and all of the people turned to do as he had said. He saw Joshua and Telok and waved for them to come to him. Moses greeted them with a hug and asked, "Was there any t…trouble within any of the tribes that were close to you on the march here?"

"Not at all" Joshua replied.

"Good" Moses sighed with a smile. "The Lord has told me we are to k…keep moving on to Elim. In the morning, we will sound the horns for the people to move out." He put one of his strong arms around Joshua and the other around Telok; pulled them in tight and said, "I have missed you and I want you to know that I love you. Now did you c…come to a point of doubt in your hearts concerning the water?"

As he released them, they both turned to face him, and Joshua looked at his best friend and then back to Moses.

"Well, I guess… I kind a started to think it would have been better to stay closer to the Red Sea. Even though it made no sense it was just where my mind went." Telok added, "It was a test and to be truthful… I don't know how I would have fared if we had gone another day."

Moses thought for a moment and said, "I was just as thirsty as you and I… don't know what I would have d…done either." This brought a chuckle to each man and gave the mood some levity.

"Now we need to find Acts and Klee. I have b…been thinking of Acts these three days and anxious to see how he's doing." Moses told them. Joshua and Telok both gave a nod of understanding and agreement. Moses said, "I could see Ephraim's b…banner toward the south side of the lake as we circled around. They're not too far away."

Joshua and Telok had been so caught up in what was happening with Nahshon and the stick and getting water that neither one had kept up with where any of the banners were or where Acts and Klee were. Once they realized this, they both felt as if they had somehow let Acts and Klee down, but Moses caught them and said, "You are not to blame yourselves for how you felt reaching the water or that you didn't think of them right off. You were thirsty and the Lord was doing something truly wonderful, and you needed to see it just as much as the others. Now that all has been taken care of… go and find them. There was not a single thing happening that was more important than for you to see the lesson the Lord was instructing the people… and you. You were there and your presence gave hope and courage to those around you. The people w…watch you and your example was outstanding, and the Lord is greatly pleased with your actions."

Moses looked out over the people and said, "In the morning, I would like for both of you to get your ram's horns and sound the horns to begin moving. We will follow the cloud that the Lord has provided us. You have taught them well concerning the s…signals with the horns."

The men smiled at Moses; he was always very careful to not only thank them for what they did but praise them as well for the way they did their job. Moses continued, "I want you both to find your families and walk with them for a day and then I would like for both of you, Salmon and Acts to come to the front for a one-day meeting. I will walk with *'my four'* for a day and then you will go back and get Klee. Then, I would like for all of you to walk with me in the front until we reach Elim. If Acts is unable to come for the meeting day I will understand. The tribes are in good spirits, and I do not foresee any trouble." Moses continued, "And Telok… I know that Kemuel would like to see his son and… I think it would be good for you to check on Naoon and the baby." As Telok smiled, Moses paused for a moment and added, "We will be stopping at night now to rest. The people need that so very much."

Both of the men gave Moses a hug and turned to begin their duties, each holding the excitement on their faces of seeing those they love. From where they started, they could see the banner of Ephraim not very far around the lake's shore to the south. They gathered their ram's horns and quickly found Salmon. Telok and Joshua would sound the signal in the morning for the tribes to begin gathering around their banners.

They both gave Salmon a strong hug, but it was easy to see that something was bothering their younger companion. As they began to walk to the tribe of Ephraim it gave Telok and Joshua time to reconnect with Salmon. They could see the weight of what had happened on his face with the struggling grin he gave them.

Telok was the first to speak. "My young brother, what has caused such heartache that I can sense it in your spirit?"

The young man was timid in response. "My father was the first one to shout at Moses and I couldn't stop him. He wouldn't listen to me even when I pleaded for him to stop."

Telok stopped and turned Salmon to look up into his eyes. "Your father was acting out of survival instincts. Those instincts are a part of everyone, and they can make people do and say things that are not a part of their normal character. I am sure that he is dealing with his actions and that he feels embarrassed about them. Give him some time and I think he will want to talk with you about it." Salmon looked into his eyes and could see that Telok was speaking from experience. He thought for a moment and said, "You're right, Telok. I realize that I, myself was on edge as well. I will do as you suggest. Thank you."

With the mood repaired Joshua suggested that Telok find Naoon and the baby and then meet them at Joshua's parents. With the families traveling together they would be only one or two carts apart.

Chapter 9

Still Hurts

In the spiritual realm Satan, infuriated, slapped the minion closest to him and shouted, "A STICK! HE USED A STICK!" He turned and calmed himself.

"You…" Raising a fist to the sky, he spoke with complete disgust toward the Lord, "You turned the water sweet, taking the danger away because YOU knew what your precious people would do. They would have killed Your leader! Yet…" he smiled to himself, "They WILL turn on him. Given time, their weak human frailty will win, they will curse You and they will praise me!" He paused, "They will praise me in the gods I taught them to love in Egypt. Egypt is still in their hearts, and I will have their hearts and use them for MY pleasure." His voice could not convey the hate that filled his heart and the lust to be praised like the Holy One. He looked around and began to call out to his demons. "Go and find me the weakest of the humans. Find those who speak of Egypt with a longing heart. Remind them of what they had. Remind them of the meat and fruit they tasted every day. Prey upon their desires. Create lies and scenes for them to picture in their minds. They are so easily manipulated by sight, smell, and taste. GO, and find them and help them remember!" With the command given thousands upon thousands of demons began to move in and around all of the people doing as their master had said.

Satan turned and summoned a specific demon. He pointed to Acts and said, "This is what I want you to do." Turning, he very softly spoke his instructions, and the demon smiled at the opportunity.

~

The Angels of the Lord God watched intently with strong hands, on holy weapons, ready to protect the people from a deadly threat.

~

While Joshua, Telok, and Salmon were making their way to their families, Acts was still feeling the effects of the blow to his head. He was still very weak and dizzy and seemed to sleep a lot. The only time he had left the cart was to relieve himself. Klee had not left his side, and the stitches seemed to be holding the wound closed. There was no sign of infection around the wound and the swelling was beginning to go down. There had been little conversation because he really hadn't felt like talking.

Klee looked at her brother and asked, "Does your head still hurt?" "Yeah, but I think it's beginning to hurt less." Even though he tried to sound convincing his sister could tell he was just saying that to make her feel better. "I'm still dizzy when I stand though."

Klee looked at him curiously, "I find it very interesting that it is you who always has the dreams or the visions and you are the one to get knocked in the head; three times now! I just don't know what I'm going to do with you." A smile broke out across her beautiful face only making it more fun to be with her.

Acts smiled and replied, "Joshua is truly a blessed man." Klee gave him a small loving push, "You bet he is!"

Speaking of him I wonder when we will see them. I hope they can come before the company moves out. At least with the company around this lake, they won't have to come as far as when we travel in a line." Acts said as he surveyed the lay of the land.

"Joshua surely has you trained well as a strategist," Klee said proudly.

"He is a good teacher" Acts replied laying back and becoming quiet again.

Klee looked at him and spoke a small prayer in her heart, "My Lord God, will you please heal my brother, again."

~

The tribes were getting ready to move and Moses knew the pace would be slow; "There was no hurry. Arriving at the mountain would be on the Lord's timetable," Moses thought to himself.

He looked around and could see that Aaron was busy with some of the men. Moses began to speak with the Lord as he carved into his staff the account of 'the bitter waters'. "How far do you suppose it is Lord?"

"Not far My friend. And I do like the way you have kept up with all that has happened in your life on the staff I gave you."

Moses smiled at the Lord's comment. "I think the p…people need to have a record of what has happened. And I need to have in my hand the accounts of my LORD." Moses paused a moment, "I think the people have done well since crossing the sea. We have been on the move for what feels like a l…long time. I'm not trying to be a complainer," Moses stated.

The Lord began to teach Moses, **"It's not the time or the distance traveled, but the fellowship along the way. Your ancestor Abraham felt the same way sometimes. Every time he began to have a doubt or see that his focus was not where it should be he would look up to the stars and whisper My Name. I told him that his descendants would be more than the stars in the sky or the grains of sand beneath his feet."**

"And did that help him get his focus back to where it should be?" Moses asked the Lord.

"It would help him with his focus and just like him, your focus should be… On Me. Moses, I Am your future. Every day you spend with Me is preparing you for my purposes and a time we will walk together through eternity."

Moses' eyes widened. Such a thought was too wonderful to grasp. "Then… the day-to-day life I live is preparation; it is preparation for the time I will spend with you?"

"Yes. You are learning now what it means to trust Me. You are learning each day that you have the choice to act on your own or allow Me to guide you. This is a learning process and just as you learn this… so do My people. All of you will stumble and fall. But in these times of difficulty and doubt, I will always be there offering My hand of love and the opportunity of forgiveness; but the choice is yours each and every time. I do love you but, I also want you to understand that your actions have consequences. There is a harvest to both obedience and disobedience. This is what every child on earth has to learn and the closer you walk with me the clearer you see the rewards of walking in obedience."

Moses turned to look at the company of people called, 'The Children of Israel' and asked, "So, what am I to be teaching these people now?"

The Lord smiled on Moses His friend and said, **"'The Walk of Life - with Me.' You will begin to teach them how to place Me in** the forefront of their minds and how to be thankful. There is no better way to get your focus where it should be, than to be truly thankful in your heart and profess that with your mouth. They need to learn how to look at what My hand has done. And in turn, look to see what I can do if they will learn to obey Me. My laws may seem hard, but the yoke I will put on them is so much easier than the yoke of Egypt or the yoke of the evil one."

Moses thought for a moment and then shared with the Lord, "These people know what it is to have a heavy yoke. The Egyptian taskmasters were relentless in their drive to get work done. And most of the people have the scars to show for it. It's not the work of the yoke, but the giving up of what they have come to trust; even if what they have trusted all this time was a lie. The lie of: *'this is all life has to offer'*... which was slavery."

The Lord, God continued, **"They must come to understand the truth and the lie. Mother Eve learned this too late. When the Evil one, who is Satan, came to them in the beautiful garden that I had made for them, he approached them with a lie. He told them, that I did not want the best for them, but that I was keeping knowledge from them. 'Eat the fruit and you will be like God knowing what is good and what is evil'. He is a liar now as he was from the beginning. I say, "I love you." And he says he will love you also. But that is his lie?**

He has no love in him, nor can he love. He cannot speak the truth for the truth is not in him." Think on this; does the truth come from the creator... or that which was created and fell? What I speak is Truth and Life and these people must learn to choose what I have for them and also to trust that I want the very best for them. You will remind them of what I have done for them. You will always bring to light the wonders of My hand.

Your staff, the rod I have given you will tell the story. You have carved the burning bush and the number nine for the plagues. You have carved the 'Pass Over' and the people walking 'between the walls of water' in the rod. And now, 'the bitter waters'. As they look to see what I have done they will learn to expect what I can do. It is in this walk, that they will hopefully experience the Life I have for them."

Moses clapped his hands together in excitement in his fellowship and startled Aaron. As Aaron walked over to him Moses said, "Sorry, I didn't m…mean to do that to you."

Aaron relaxed and asked what he was doing. Moses smiled at his brother and said, "Aaron! Let me tell you what the Lord said." He put his arm around Aaron and began.

~

Joshua, Telok, and Salmon were coming up behind Joshua's father Nun, when his mother glanced back, smiled, and said, "Look, Hun!"

Nun turned around to see what she was looking at and when he recognized who was approaching, he put his hand up in the air and so did his son and two companions. The thrill in the tone of Joshua's mother got Klee's attention at once, and she popped her head up over the edge of the cart. As she looked to see, she squealed and began to climb out of the cart. Her face lit up as the morning sun. Acts was asleep and she managed to climb out of the cart without waking him. Stifling another 'squeal' wasn't an easy thing to do, but she performed it well. As Joshua closed the distance Klee ran to meet him.

Nun and Joshua's mom just took in the sight of their son and, soon to be daughter-in-law, presented in such a beautiful picture of young love. Even though they were not married yet, she and Acts were as much a part of the family as they could ever be. The fact that Joshua and Klee would be husband and wife thrilled their hearts.

Joshua picked her up and turned a circle with her in his arms. He put her down and tenderly kissed her.

Salmon walked over to the cart and peeked in on Acts. He could see the bandage on his head and watched as his breathing was even and slow and he could tell that he was resting well so, he did not wake him.

Telok began looking around for his father. Nun walked up to him and gave him a good handshake, a hug, and pointed, "Your dad and Naoon are over there just on the other side of those two large carts."

"Thank you," Telok replied, and he immediately turned and started for them. As he walked over to the cart, people from the clan would walk up to him and shake his hand, pat him on the back and some of them even hugged him. He was surprised at the way he was being greeted and he could see that no one saw him as Egyptian. When he saw his father's cart and Naoon sitting in the back he started to run but decided to walk instead. He wanted to allow his heart and mind time to take in the moment of seeing her before she looked at him. As he slowed his pace everything else faded away. The wind was gently blowing her hair out of her face and Telok could see her soft complexion. As he closed the space between them, she happened to glance in his direction. He could see her dark brown eyes. She could see him approaching like a warrior returning in honor and authority: His pace, deliberate and even. His eyes fixed on her; his face not in a full smile but, relaxed with a sense of determination. She could not take her eyes off of him or hide the elation she felt in seeing him. As he walked up to the cart Kemuel caught sight of him. He allowed his son to have this moment. Telok reached into the cart with his strong arms and lifted her out setting her on the ground as if she weighed nothing. They gazed into each other's eyes; shutting out the world. Telok finally looked over her shoulder at the baby girl sleeping on her soft bed. He returned his gaze to Naoon. As Telok looked at the baby this gave Naoon time to look deep into his light green eyes and she felt she could get lost in them. It was a very rare thing for an Egyptian to have eyes of this color.

Finally, Telok spoke, "It is more than 'good' to see you." "And it is more than 'good' to see you." She replied.

This was the closest they had ever been to each other in such a moment, but Telok nor Naoon felt any uncomfortable feelings. In fact, it felt so natural to them that they didn't realize they were so close. Kemuel gave a soft laugh that caught their attention, and he spoke to both, but mainly to Naoon, "Now that's what I was talking about. Being comfortable with someone is to be natural."

Naoon smiled as Telok, gave a look of question to his father and then to her. "She will explain it to you son." The comment had been from an earlier conversation Kemuel had with her concerning how she felt when she was with Telok. She had shared with Kemuel how she hoped Telok felt as comfortable with her as she felt with him. Kemuel had told her; he did and now he brought it to her attention.

The two relaxed and Telok walked over to his father and held his dad with a hug only a son could give. "It's good to see you, son." "It is good to see you too, dad."

Kemuel looked deep into his son's thoughts and asked, "So… what did you learn during our little walk without water?"

~

Meanwhile Salmon was feeling a little awkward not having anyone to talk to. He knew he was just as accepted into the family as Acts, but he just didn't really know what to do with himself at this moment.

"Gets you right in the o'l heart, doesn't it?" Acts commented as he pulled himself to the edge of the cart. "All this huggin' stuff can make you feel out of place."

Salmon spun around to find his best friend looking at him. He walked over to the cart and said, "Let me see it!"

"See what!?" Acts replied.

"The cut on the back of your head, I want to see if it is bigger than the last time." Salmon stated.

Acts complied with the request by reaching up and pulling off the rag wrapped around his head. He turned so Salmon could get a good look. Acts asked, "Well is it bigger… I can't really tell with my fingers?"

Salmon reached up to touch the edges of the stitches and heard behind him, "You better not touch that, Salmon!"

Klee had turned around to see what they were doing and with a big sister tone, she got Salmon's attention as well as Acts. Salmon spouted out, "I wasn't gonna touch the cut just the thread."

"I don't care! You two keep your hands off of it or I'll have to clean it again." That got Acts' attention because it wasn't fun getting the wound cleaned even with the tender touch of his sister. The wound was still very tender.

It was at this point that Joshua walked over to Acts and put his hand on Act's shoulder. He looked sincerely at his little brother and asked, "Are you getting better?"

Acts knew he must answer truthfully, "I really can't tell if it is any better. My head still hurts just as much as it did, and I still get very dizzy when I get up."

Klee put her hands on her hips and responded, "You told me you were getting better and now you say you feel the same." Her eyes flashed with sisterly rage, and she held her finger up and pointed at him and said, "You better start telling me the truth and not what you think I need to hear. Understand?" Acts looked back with eyes open wide and answered, "Yes, sister."

Salmon held his hand up to show Acts how long the cut was. With his first finger apart from his thumb and said, "It's about a whole inch or inch-n-half bigger than last time." This brought a laugh, and Acts replied, "Well this one hurts a whole lot more than the last."

Salmon responded, "Your eyes are kind of dark under them too." "Klee said, they were looking better though." Acts replied. "You mean they were darker than they are now?!" Salmon yelped.

Klee walked over to the cart and pulled Salmon aside; gave him a hug just as she would Acts and said, "That's enough admiring. Now let me put the bandage back on so it is a little more protected from dirt and young men." That brought a laugh from both of the boys and she, 'sisterly,' put the bandage back around Acts' head with just enough pressure to make her point. He lay back down against a big roll of colored blankets they had brought from Egypt and was asleep again within a few minutes.

As Klee turned to walk back over to Joshua, Salmon caught her arm and, in a whisper, Salmon couldn't hide his concern, "Is he gonna be alright?" She put a hand on his and said, "Now Salmon, do you really think the Lord is not going to take care of him? He's the only one of us who has visions of what the Lord is going to do next... aside from Moses."

A smile broke out across Salmon's face as she turned and walked over to Joshua. She grabbed Joshua's arm and looked into his eyes and said, "Now... I want to hear all about what happened at the lake. I was occupied with Acts and didn't get to see all of it. And there is something else we really need to talk about." She cut her eyes to Joshua's mother.

Joshua smiled and said, "OK. But Telok and I have to sound the signals for the first four tribes to move out. I'll tell you as we walk because Moses has instructed us to stay with the family for a day." Klee's smile dropped and she said softly, "And then you have to leave again?"

Joshua suddenly realized that he had left his sentence ending at the wrong spot and he began to fix it, "No! Well… Tomorrow we will go and meet with Moses for one day. That's what he said, 'one day' and then, we will come back, and I am taking you to the front with me. Moses wants Acts, Salmon, Telok, me, and you to go back to the front for the rest of the way to Elim." He paused and looked over at Telok and whispered to Klee, "And Naoon if Telok asks her." He watched as a smile returned to Klee's beautiful face. With her smile returned she popped him on the shoulder and said, "That's for stopping your sentence before sharing all of the information!"

He laughed and said, "I'll try not to do that again." He turned to look toward Telok's position, but he couldn't see him, so he got up on the cart and looked. When he found Telok he whistled, got his attention, and waved for him to come over. Telok picked up the baby and took Naoon by the hand and they started for Joshua.

As they walked up Klee smiled and said, "You look pretty comfortable holding that baby." Telok just grinned. Joshua stood holding two horns and then, Telok suddenly realized he had let his duty slip away, his attention being consumed with Naoon and the baby. He started to give Naoon the baby and Klee moved up and said, "I'll take her now." Klee turned to Naoon, and they began to talk as Joshua and Telok just looked on.

Salmon cleared his throat as Joshua and Telok looked at him. He smiled and said, "Don't you two have something you should be doing?"

They looked back at each other and Joshua stated, "Yeah…Yes, we… we better go sound the signal!" They turned and got into the back of Nun's cart and faced Moses' position. With strong tones, the signal was given and repeated by horns in the first four tribes. Within minutes the first tribes were moving; following Moses and the pillar of the cloud. Joshua and Telok looked at each other and Joshua asked, "What do you think… give them an hour and then start the second group?" "An hour sounds good. That should be enough space." Telok replied.

They jumped down out of the cart to find the girls just looking at them and Joshua asked, "What?" The girls looked back and Naoon said, "Oh! Nothing," as they stood admiring the men in their lives.

With all of the signals given, the entire company was now moving. At the end of the day, after the signal was given to stop for the night, the people began to cook, and the aroma of all kinds of vegetables and bread started to make its way all through the camp. On the three-day march to Marah, the company had not even stopped to eat because there had been no water, but now the smell of food filled the air. Even in this desolate place, the Lord provided grass for the animals to graze on. He never failed to pay attention to every detail concerning His Children. The people had water and food and for this moment in time, they were happy.

Telok and Kemuel had spread a blanket out for Naoon and the baby to sit on and she had offered to make supper, but Kemuel said, "No… daughter. I will serve you and you will enjoy it" given as a loving command which brought smiles.

Telok had been raised with children all around him and it was second nature for him to care for babies and small children. Naoon was surprised at how easy it was for him. It wasn't long before Kemuel had some breadcakes made with flour, honey, and some nuts he had brought out of Egypt.

Naoon watched them both and was amazed at the level of love Kemuel and his son had. She thought to herself, "It is like they have been father and son all of Telok's life.

Chapter 10
A Deadly Plan

After breakfast, Klee knelt in front of Joshua. "When would you like to have the wedding?"

"I will need to talk to my father first and then I would like to talk it over with Moses. I don't know when we will stop again to make camp that may last more than a day." Her eyes didn't stop sparkling nor did her face become downcast. She looked at him and said, "I think that's a wonderful idea."

It so impressed his heart to hear and experience her ability to let him lead and it only made his love for her grow. Klee had all kinds of questions about what needed to be done for the wedding, but she also knew that the chain of events needed to unfold. Joshua, Nun, and Moses needed time; time to see what the Lord would do and how far they would have to move. Only Moses knew how far it would be until they would camp for more than a day.

~

Naoon awoke to find Telok holding the baby. "How long have you two been awake?" Naoon asked sleepily. "Not very long; she's a morning girl" Telok answered looking into the baby's face. "Yes, she is. And she always wakes in a fun mood" Naoon told him.

Telok handed the baby to her mother and got up to help his dad get ready to move out while Naoon warmed up some of the breadcakes for breakfast that were left over from the evening before. Telok looked at his dad and said, "Joshua and I should be giving the signal anytime now for the company to move out."

"Yes, and I think we are ready to do just that." his father commented.

Telok noticed Joshua looking over at him, raising his ram's horn. Telok raised his hand in like greeting with his horn. They both blew a long and steady pitch. In only moments horns began to answer them in like manner and the company was on the move again. With everyone rested and the pace slow it would be a very good day of travel and fellowship.

Telok looked over at Naoon and held out his arms to take the baby. As she lifted the baby to him, she cooed and smiled. "She already knows who you are, and I think she likes you," Naoon commented. Telok looked at the baby in his arms and said in the high-pitched voice with which he only spoke to the baby, "She sure does know who Telok is." This only made Kemuel laugh.

Naoon mentioned to Telok, "Klee told me a little about the story of a fight with a man named Korah. It seemed horrible; something that should've never happened!"

"You're right! It shouldn't have." Telok replied. "How did you meet Acts?" she asked softly. Telok recounted the story to her, "They were leading Klee by a rope tied around her wrists." Naoon in surprise said, "Was no one even thinking of helping her?"

"No! Not a single person took any action. That amazed me; the lack of courage in the men around her." Naoon just shook her head in bewilderment. Telok continued, "Acts was able to respond in the way Joshua told him. We remained out of sight flanking Acts. When Korah jerked on the rope to spark Acts' anger, he didn't know that Joshua was within a few feet ready to end his life."

"Do you think he would've really killed him?" Naoon spoke with concern. "Yes! He would have killed him, but he didn't; he let Acts have control of the situation. Salmon, Joshua, and I joined in the fight, and during it, Acts was hit in the back of the head which caused a large gash. We got him and Klee out and that's when Joshua took them to be with his family."

"What happened to Acts' head?" Naoon asked. Even though she had heard the story from Klee she still loved to hear Telok tell it again.

Telok looked over to her, "The Lord Most High healed him." Telok continued with the story, "As Joshua and Klee walked up to the cart where he was supposed to be lying down; they found him standing beside it. Klee started to scold him, but Acts told her his head didn't hurt anymore and when he reached back to feel the cut, he couldn't find it. Klee pulled his head down to see for herself and sure enough the cut was completely healed."

Naoon thought for a moment and asked, "So do you think… it could happen again? Could his cut miraculously heal?"

"I don't' know… this time is different." Telok shifted the baby again. "It looks like he may have to heal the normal way." Telok lifted the baby to look into her eyes and said, "Let's go over and see how he's doing today."

Naoon smiled and took the baby from him. She had to pause in thought; the sound of them visiting someone together, like a couple, was such a pleasant and inviting feeling. She smiled and said to Telok, "That sounds like a great idea." He touched her shoulder as he turned to tell his dad. Kemuel smiled and waved. Naoon enjoyed his touch and the feel of his authority.

As they walked up to Joshua and Klee he asked, "How is Acts today?" Klee hugged Telok and replied, "His head still hurts. And he still gets dizzy when he gets up, but the wound is healing without infection."

Telok turned to Acts, "How are you feeling today, little brother?" Acts pulled up to a sitting position and answered, "I don't know; maybe a little better."

"And the dizziness your sister speaks of?" Telok asked. "I still get dizzy when I stand, and my head still hurts at times" Acts replied.

Telok turned to Salmon and put his arm around him and asked, "And… how are you, my friend?"

While the couples talked and walked Telok held the baby and talked with Joshua and Salmon with Acts staying quiet. As Joshua looked into the eyes of Telok he thought to himself, *He sure is playing the role of a husband and dad well… not actually being one… yet.'*

Telok couldn't help but notice a funny look on his captain's face, but he passed it off at the time. When Telok walked over to Naoon to give her the baby Klee walked over to check on Acts.

Salmon looked over at Acts and said, "He kind a sounded 'husbandly like' didn't he?'

"Yeah, 'husbandly like'" Acts agreed. Klee heard what they said, and she asked, "Is that even a word?" Salmon smiled and they both said together, "It is NOW!"

Naoon and the baby walked up to check on Acts. He did his best to smile and asked, "What's her name?" Klee and Naoon looked at each other and then Klee looked back into her brother's eyes and replied, "You have already asked her that; you don't remember?"

Acts looked at his sister and thought for a moment and said, "I don't. When did I ask her?"

"You didn't respond for a while and after Naoon stitched you up she came back over to check on you. I introduced you and you asked her what the baby's name was" Klee answered in a worried tone.

"Did she tell me her name?" Acts asked. "For now, her name is 'baby'. Naoon's husband died in Egypt before she was born, and he didn't tell Naoon what he wanted her name to be." Klee looked back at Naoon and could not hide the fear she had in her heart for her brother.

Naoon stepped up with the baby and let Acts look at her. She smiled at him, and he let her wrap her tiny fingers around his little finger. "Do you remember seeing her, Acts?" He looked at her thoughtfully and said, "It kind a seems like I did, but it feels like a dream."

"You have been sleeping a lot since the accident and I'm sure that even I would begin to get things mixed up as well. I think for what you have been through it is a wonder you remember your own name." Naoon tried to lift the mood a bit and encourage Klee and Acts at the same time.

Acts sat in the cart holding 'baby' and she began to coo and laugh with him. His countenance seemed to lift somewhat and both Klee and Naoon could see that she was good for Acts. Joshua and Telok walked over to see what the serious faces were about.

"So, what has you two in such a serious mood?" Joshua asked.

Klee turned to him and said, "Look at how good she is for Acts. His face is relaxed, and his eyes are clear. He is smiling with her and is not grimacing in pain." Klee looked into Joshua's eyes and said in a whisper, "He didn't remember meeting the baby. He didn't remember asking me what the baby's name was. I had to tell him everything again." She could not help but have tears well up in her eyes.

Joshua studied Acts for a moment and turned back to Klee, "This injury is not like the last. He has had much more pain, and his recovery might be slow, but he will eventually get back to being himself."

Klee looked at Salmon as he said with an encouraging smile, "Hey, he's the only one of us who has the visions of what's going to happen next... aside from Moses." She smiled and gave him a sisterly pat on the cheek. Klee turned back to Acts and asked, "Are you getting tired? I bet it's time for her to eat."

Looking a Naoon, Act's said, "She's fun. I would like to spend more time with her tomorrow if I could?" Naoon looked back at him and replied, "We will walk with you tomorrow for a while, how about that?"

"That would be great." He lifted her up to Naoon and got himself comfortable in the cart. Salmon looked over the edge of the cart and asked, "Are you going to forget me too?" Acts swung his hand at Salmon's face and just missed as Salmon ducked. The humor was good, and the time Acts had with 'baby' was very good. It wasn't but a few minutes and he was asleep again.

Klee looked at him and whispered a prayer, "Lord, please heal my brother.

Joshua looked at Telok and the baby, he gave a head nod directing Telok with his eyes to the baby; Telok's eyes opened a bit wider as he realized what Joshua was trying to say... though not saying it aloud. Telok shook his head 'no' very softly so the girls would not see the exchange of silent communication. Once, away from the girls for a moment Telok punched Joshua in the shoulder and said in a hushed voice, "What did you mean by that look?" "I was just thinking 'the baby doesn't have a name and it's usually the father or husband who gives the name. You could take care of that right now" Joshua said rubbing his shoulder.

"Well, what if we were not to get married... did you think about that" Telok said through gritted teeth.

Joshua looked back at him and asked, "Then... you don't want to marry her?" Telok stopped to think through what Joshua just asked. He did want to marry her... he just didn't know if it was too soon to even think about such a thing. "No... I do want to... or... yes!! I'm thinking about it."

He stopped and Joshua popped him on the shoulder and said, "It's all right brother... I do know what you are talking about. It will be just fine. I've seen the way she looks at you and when... ooowee... when you hold that baby she sure does brighten up."

Telok looked back at his best friend and questioned, "She does!?"

Joshua smiled and just nodded his head *'yes'* as Salmon watched them and said, "I sure hope Acts and I don't act this pitiful when we meet who we will marry."

Joshua looked back at him and said, "Oh… you will."

~

All the while, as this family walked in the joy of the Lord, Satan watched from a high point nearby. He looked at them as a lion would look; wanting to feed. His hatred for them filled his every thought. He had waited for these people to show just how quickly they would complain and demand their own way. They had water but the food supply from Egypt was starting to get low. This would be another good opportunity for him to put a plan in place. Satan already knew there was no food within a two-weeks walk. He began with the ones who already had an inclination for rebellion; Korah and Abiram were at the top of his list. There were those who would allow him to actually step into their souls and control them. These rebels were kept for special tasks. All he had to do was give a gentle push and they would follow their own selfish hearts. It was a complete mystery why the Lord counted these Israelites as more important than any other on the face of the earth. "What makes them so different?" he whispered to himself. "I will seek it out and then, I shall defeat the very plans… of the Most High."

Satan detested humans, especially those who walked with the Lord and wanted to follow Him! Satan wanted their praise and worship for himself. He was well aware of those who followed him through the worship of the Egyptian idols. Those he didn't care about. He saw all humans as weak and frail beings that could only survive within certain limits. Humans were easy prey for sickness and disease or injury; He stopped and thought of Acts. What made this one special?

Satan narrowed his gaze upon this weak human, Acts; this one boy gave him thought. He didn't understand why Acts was so sensitive to the Lord's leading, but because of that fact… he had decided Acts needed to be removed. The injury he had received had opened a wound in his head that would only need a little push, and his frail body would stop.

He called one particular demon over to his side. The figure was huge compared to a human; nine feet tall and bolstered massive muscles that were out of proportion for a body. He had long claws on the end of each finger. He held a long straight sword with a razor-sharp blade on one side and teeth like a saw on the other. It was wicked looking in color; stained with the blood of sacrifices. They were offered to his lord, Satan in parts of the land known as Canaan. The demon's name was, Qushunbab; which meant executioner of babies in the language of Dagon. He knelt before Satan with his sword across one knee, "What is thy bidding my lord?" His voice was a blend of several.

Satan spoke in a whisper to Qushunbab, "I want you to create a bleeding cut in the boy's brain where the injury occurred. There is a cut to the back of his head, and it will be of ease to put your claw tip into the wound and pull it open. That will kill the boy, who looked me in the eyes and was able to live. It will give me great delight to know that he died in front of his sister and the family that has taken them in. I do not want him to escape this time, do you hear me, Qushunbab? He must die… And I want it to be painful." Satan spoke with hate and disgust for Acts.

Qushunbab raised his head to gaze at his lord. His eyes were almost completely red with a slit in the middle that lay horizontal; like a stick floating in water. "It will be my pleasure, to do this great honor for yooou, my lord." Slowly dragging out the words as if asking for a reward.

Satan sneered, "After you have finished the boy, I will give you your own kingdom; To rule in my name! Qushunbab narrowed his eyes and stood with a smile on his hideous face. He bowed as he took a step back and then turned to survey the land and locate the boy.

Satan once again turned his attention to the people who followed Moses. One last gaze before he must leave to attend to other business. Although he hated humans, he also desired their worship. The Lord Most High desired their worship too, but the difference was vast between him, and the Lord God. Satan received worship from his own kind. Those who had followed him in the Great Rebellion in heaven were now subject to him in this world. He had been the strongest and most beautiful once upon a time, but those days had been so long ago. It was hard for him to truly remember the days of being 'holy'. Being worshiped, like the, Most High God were the thoughts that drove him now.

"Yes… these frail humans will worship me. All I have to do is give them time, for their very nature is driven toward sin. And it is in their sin, that they will be handed over to me… for sin must have payment. Sin can only be paid for with blood; I will demand their blood!" Satan continued.

The thought of their sin brought a smile to his face. The sin of man was from the beginning when all he had to do was raise a question within the souls of the first two; Father Adam and Mother Eve. It had been so easy taking the beautiful serpent and speaking through it; "The serpent was so willing to let me." He said seductively. He rarely needed to use tricks like that anymore; over the years, sin had come to be such a part of human nature that he could speak thoughts of any kind and lead most humans around like little puppies. Although he could not read human minds, because he was a created being, he had watched and studied humans every day since the falling away in the Garden of Eden. He had studied their facial expressions, words, and jesters. Those actions that tear down and crush the human spirit; greed, and eyes coveting things they shouldn't. Everything he had studied could be understood and influenced. Lust and pride were the easiest to work with. But now the Lord Most High had raised up Moses like great men before; men such as Seth, Enoch, Noah, Abraham, Jacob, and Joseph. He had known each one of them and remembered coming so close to pulling them into the traps he had set. So, close to killing each of them and also Moses as a baby.

He laughed slightly to himself. Even though, at the time he didn't know what would become of Moses, He simply influenced Pharaoh to believe there were too many Hebrew boys and one day they could overthrow him. In fear, Pharaoh ordered all Hebrew baby boys to be thrown into the Nile. He could not have seen how important this one baby would be. Watching Moses grow up as an Egyptian; Satan had created the desire in him to worship the gods of Egypt. Over time, Moses chose to identify with his birth heritage, the Hebrews. After witnessing an Egyptian taskmaster abusing a slave, Moses killed the Egyptian to save the Hebrew slave. In so doing, Moses would have received death for his crime, but he escaped to the back side of the desert. Satan seethed over the thought for a moment. He spoke softly to himself, "I will seize the next opportunity and kill him along with the people that follow him. Then, I will see what the Lord Most High will do... As for this boy called Acts, he will soon be dead." He laughed at his own trickery and turned to go to the country called Canaan, to receive worship from the humans there. It was full moon and time for human sacrifice from those who worshiped the god he had set up called, Dagon.

~

The Angels of God stood guard so the lives of His children could not be taken; only influenced. Even the Angels looked with great anticipation at the work the Lord was doing in the earth. But they wondered if the Lord would share His plans with His friend Moses. They did not fear the Lord's plans although it set Satan on edge. Satan was always looking for a way to entrap man not only in this life but in eternal life as well. But Satan and his demons were limited in their powers and to face an Angel was risky. One swing of an Angel's blade could send any demon to the pit; a place of utter torment, suffering; and waiting. Anyone cast into the pit only waited for the final judgment with no way out. It was an incredible place of fear that every demon of hell would do anything to keep from going. The Angels of the Lord Most High looked at the humans through the eyes of love; love given to them by the One, and Only True God; Yahweh.

Chapter 11
Recounting Visions

As the evening came to a close and everyone was asleep Acts lay awake looking up at the stars through the pillar of fire. For the first time, he realized and commented to himself quietly, "I haven't noticed that I could actually see the stars through the pillar of fire?" He was beginning to become impatient with himself concerning his healing. Getting back to normal without his head hurting was becoming harder to wait for than he ever thought. He reached back to feel the cut, wrenching from the pain even from gentle pressure. It did seem to be scabbing over, but it was still very tender around the wound.

He had been having dreams since the accident but had not told anyone. The dreams were all of past visions he had when he would pass out. They started with the dreams he had in the beginning, concerning the Snake of Mist. Moses called it the 'Death Angel' or 'Destroyer', but he still liked his name better. The first dream he could not remember, but the second one he could distinctly recall, bringing all of the color and terror to mind. He spoke softly as he recalled the dream, "It was a black night lit by the full moon."

Salmon heard him and sat up looking into the cart. He couldn't see Acts' face because he was lying on his stomach. He moved closer to the cart to hear Acts more clearly. Acts continued, "I could hear cries in the darkness, and they seemed so close I thought I could almost feel them."

Salmon now got on his knees and rose up to look at Acts. Salmon coming up over the edge of the cart made Acts jump. As Acts realized who it was, he said, in a hushed, but surprised voice, "What are you doing sneaking up on me like that?"

"I didn't mean to sneak, I thought you were talking in your sleep, and I wanted to hear what you were saying" Salmon replied apologetically.

After Acts calmed down a bit, he began to tell Salmon how he had been having dreams. "I can see all but the very first one."

Salmon looked at his best friend and said, "First what?"

"The first visions I started having… You know, when I would pass out." Acts tried not to be embarrassed, but he couldn't help it. "I was just talking my way through them again, and I guess it was a little too loud. I didn't mean to wake you."

Salmon got up into the cart, leaned back against the gate, and said, "That's okay, I wasn't sleeping very well anyway. So, tell me… I want to know. Maybe you telling me will help you remember; as you recall I was there for some of them."

This brought a smile to Acts as he began, "Well, the first vision started with the one I had back when we first left Egypt. Joshua and I were in the rear trying to see if anyone was following us."

Salmon laughed, "You were in the rear or were 'the rear'." He could see that Acts was not amused and got into a good position leaning against the wall of the cart, "Okay, tell me everything." excitement in his voice!

"Alright, but you're gonna have to keep your voice down," Acts told him. "Now what part did you hear?"

"You heard cries in the dark; you could almost feel them" Salmon responded.

Acts started, "In the dream, I could see a black smoke or mist moving through the light of the full moon. It was moving in and out of the shadows; the blood of a sacrificed lamb was dripping from the doorpost of the house. Then, I couldn't take in a breath as I saw this 'snake mist' coming closer to my family's house. It stopped and whipped its head toward me. I was paralyzed and couldn't move… It coiled like it was going to strike, hissing at me with yellow eyes. It jumped at me; its mouth open like it was going to kill me…" Acts turned to look at Salmon; his mouth open and his eyes wide as saucers as Salmon hung on every word Acts said.

"And then what?" Salmon whispered.

"And then, I looked up and heard Joshua saying my name and asking if I was alright." "Gosh! That had to be scary." Salmon said in a whisper… that was almost too loud.

Acts held up his hands to quiet him down some. Salmon looked around to see if anyone heard him, but he didn't see anybody moving and he looked back at Acts. "So… when was the next one; and what was it like?"

"Well… you were there for the next one. It was outside the tent of Eliasaph, and Elizur was there too."

"Yeah, I might have been there, but I don't remember a thing about it or what you said because I thought you were going to die or something" Salmon admitted.

"Now that I recall, you were a bit shaken. Well, this is what I saw, and I can't believe I can still remember this stuff so vividly." Acts said excitedly.

"I can see these dreams, but I couldn't remember meeting Naoon's baby. That kind of bothers me.

I know Salmon agreed. "Your memory will get fixed you just need to be a little more patient with yourself. Now tell me the next vision!"

Acts appreciated the encouragement and continued with his story: "Colors were swirling in my mind; faces were appearing and then fading away. The pillar of cloud floated in front of me. As I focused on it there were images flowing through my mind. The images eventually moved out of my sight, and then I could see Egyptian's whipping their horses in chase…"

"That is so neat," Salmon said, leaning forward. "And what else?" Salmon said in a lighter whisper than before. "That was all for that one" Acts told him. "The next was when we met with Moses: you, me, Telok and Joshua.

I remember the ringing in my ear was so loud that it drown out everything else. I saw a watery grave with dead men floating on top and under the surface of the water. The Snake Mist moved over the dead and seemed to be laughing. Then, I felt like I was lying on the bottom of the sea and the Snake looked at me but didn't approach. I struggled to move, and I felt so heavy. A hand came into focus reaching for me, but the person's face was hidden. I saw scars on the hands of this man. His clothes were so bright and white I had to look down, and when I did, I noticed the same type of scars on the man's feet as well. As my eyes moved up his body I saw the man's side; opened like a warrior in battle. I reached out with my hand to this man and as I took hold gripping his hand… the hand turned into Moses and then everything came back into focus."

Salmon swallowed and then blinked. "You were seeing what was 'going' to happen when we crossed the Red Sea. The Lord showed you what He was 'going' to do."

"Yea, but I didn't know it at the time, that's what made it a little scary for me." He thought a moment, "I don't know why the Lord let me see these things, but I'm sure He had His reasons."

"I think the next vision you had was when we were down in the deepest part of the sea on the way across." Salmon said. "Yep. That was a long one. It was when some of the people stopped to rest, and you gave them the instructions they would never forget."

Acts laughed quietly and then, grabbed his head in some pain. He managed to get the pain under control and then he began to tell Salmon;

"Faces of Egyptians whirled past me. People who held us in slavery all of our lives were sinking into the ground. I looked down at my hands and could see a stain on them. I thought it was mud and as I examined it more closely, I realized it was blood, and it stank with the odor of death. Like something that had been dead for days. I felt myself being pulled to the ground. The stain changed from red to almost black, and the stench grew so strong that I began to gag. I started crawling on my hands and knees, I saw small puddles of water that held scenes from my life, moments when I had made the decision to do something wrong deliberately: little lies told at different times, something I had taken without asking. I could see the attitude of my heart and it was black. A revelation dawned in my mind. Sin! It was the sin in my life that stained my hands and stunk so badly. I tried to stand, but something kept me weighed down. No matter how hard I struggled I was forced to stay on my hands and knees. I thought, *'was it the weight of slavery or sin that was holding me down?'* Was there a difference? Water started rising all around me, and I knew that if I didn't get up, I would drown. As I crawled in an effort to stand up, I came to the scared feet of the same warrior who had rescued me from the previous dream. As I looked up, I could see the warrior was holding a lamb, and its blood was falling onto my hands. I saw that the lamb's blood was washing the stain from my hands."

Acts looked down at his hands as he said it again quietly, "It was washing the black stain of sin from my hands." He looked up again and continued, "I could see that the warrior was extending his right hand to me, and again I could see the scars in the warrior's hand. I tried to look at his face, but it was like looking at the sun. As I reached for the warriors hand, He faded away and I realized it was the hands of you and Joshua.

This time when Acts finished Joshua spoke softly, "I remember you telling me about that. I have to say, that one I have given a lot of thought; Are my hands stained as well?"

"What's got you up so late?" asked Acts.

"I have been giving something a whole lot of thought." Joshua replied.

"Would it have something to do with my sister?" Acts smiled and then grimaced slightly as he put his hand to his head because it hurt.

Joshua turned to look him in the eyes, "As a matter of fact… It does. And I'm thinking… I want to get this wedding on the road. I'm going to ask Moses tomorrow when we get to him. I've already asked my dad, and everything is good."

"What's good?" A soft voice asked from behind Joshua. Klee had been awakened by all of the boys, soft talk.

Each of the boys looked at each other and agreed that they should be getting some rest. Klee stood there bewildered for a moment as she watched them all get comfortable. She smiled at them and understood they were just having boy time.

As Joshua settle back into a comfortable position and began to drifting off to sleep, he couldn't help but praise the Lord for this woman He was allowing him to marry. "Yep, I am a blessed man."

Chapter 12

Give Up The Past

Morning broke and Joshua was already up with his dad getting the team ready and storing the gear. Both, Salmon and Acts got up yawning and Klee awoke right after them. She started a quick breakfast of scrambled eggs and wheat cakes. As she was working, she looked over at Joshua and asked, "Did I hear you say that you had 'something good' last night?"

Joshua smiled and answered, "I do have something good… in fact you are more than good."

Acts and Salmon looked at each other and made faces that were as if they had tasted something bad. Joshua looked back at them and said, "Your days are coming and then, it won't seem so… icky."

They both said in unison, "Icky?!" as Salmon laughed, and Acts tried but he couldn't without having pain.

With everyone full of breakfast, Joshua could see that the tribe around him was ready to move out. He looked over to get Telok's attention and the signals were given at their proper time. Soon the entire company was on the move again.

Joshua looked back at Telok, "Are you ready to make the run to Moses?"

Telok answered, "Ready when you are Captain."

"Well let's get grab Salmon, the water skins and get started."

As Joshua turned to leave, Telok looked back at Naoon, "It will be only for a short time, and I will get back to you and the baby."

"I know you will. Say hello to Moses for me even though he doesn't know me." Naoon said in passing.

Telok raised his eyebrow, "Oh… yes he does."

Naoon looked surprised, "How does he know me?"

Telok gave her a hug and kissed the baby, "There is nothing that escapes his attention," as he turned to run and catch up with Joshua.

"A tuff 'goodbye?" Joshua asked.

"Kinda of. You?" Telok answered.

"Yea, but I don't think we will be gone too long this time." Joshua commented as they walked up to Salmon. "Are you ready?"

"Yes sir. But… it's going to be weird leaving Acts behind," Salmon said as he looked at his best friend.

Acts looked at each of his friends and told them, "I'll go next time besides the Lord, has me here for a reason." They each gave him a pat on the back and Joshua replied, "Next time then.

The three began with a fast walk, but soon felt like they needed to run and with the sound of their feet hitting the ground they fell into rhythm with each other.

The sound of their run attracted some attention from the people walking around them. The people waved to them as they passed through each tribe. They would stop quite often to fill their water skins and have brief conversations with people and the tribal leaders. They were able to ask about the health of the people and the water supply, although it would not be low for at least a week. There were some small arguments and disputes between some of the people that related to nothing really; just personality clashes, knowing that out of three million people there were going to be disagreements.

They also asked about the food supply. It seemed to be a growing concern with the people. Foods that had been plentiful back in Egypt, such as their vegetables, fruit, wheat, and other delicacies they were used to back 'home' as they put it, were now being used up quickly.

Joshua and his men also made mental note of the Egyptian idols that people were still carrying in their carts, but they said nothing about them. They made only brief conversations and would begin running again; listening to the rhythm of their feet which had a calming effect to each of them. It gave them time to think of what had happen so far on this journey and what the Lord still had to show them. It was a difficult thing to understand that this walk with the Lord was now a walk that involved the rest of their lives. They would never be under the rule of the king of Egypt again, they were now free… free to live in the vastness of the Lord.

~

As they neared the front of the company, they could see Moses and Aaron ahead a couple, hundred feet or so leading the people. Moses heard the rhythmic sound of their run and turned. Each of them were greeted with a big hug from Moses and Aaron. Moses took a step back and said, "Acts, was still not able to make the journey?"

"No sir. He is still in pain and the wound is being slow to heal" Joshua answered. "The stitches Naoon put to his cut are holding the wound and it is beginning to scab over but, it is still very tender."

"And he still gets dizzy when he gets up." Salmon added.

Moses pulled on his snow-white beard and said, in a thoughtful tone, "I will have to talk to the Lord about this; we can't have one of my top four men… d…down."

"I know, he would appreciate that." Joshua replied.

Moses turned and motioned for them to walk with him and Aaron. He asked how their families were doing and he looked at Telok and asked, "And, how are Naoon and the baby?"

Telok smiled, "I told her you would ask about her and yes, they are doing well. My father is seeing to that."

Moses asked Salmon, "Have you spent much time with Acts since you were able to see him after the waters of Marah?"

"Yes sir. In fact, he has been dreaming about all the other visions he's had on this journey."

"Dreaming the visions, he's seen before?" Moses asked thoughtfully.

"Yes sir. In fact, he told me all of them last night. It was really neat to hear him tell them; it was like he was a storyteller!" Salmon replied with excitement.

"Well… I'm sure he s…sounded like one!" Moses replied.

"I was able to hear the last one he told Salmon, and it was very thought provoking and… he did sound like a storyteller." Joshua added.

"I will have to hear these stories again for myself. It could be that the Lord is tying them all together. It could be that the Lord is setting him up to receive more of them… I'm not sure… but we will talk about it." Moses stated.

Moses turned the conversation to what was going to happen in the coming days. "We will be coming to Elim in two days where there are twelve springs and seventy palm trees. There is more than enough room for the people and the animals to spread out and rest for several days. I have been to Elim several times when taking care of the sheep for my father-in-law Jethro, and it is a beautiful place. It is so remote from other cities that its location is not known to very many people." He smiled and added, "You will like it… It is just the place for a wedding!" Cutting a quick look to Joshua. This brought a laugh from all of them as Telok and Salmon, both gave him a brotherly push. Moses continued, "We will talk about that in a little while, but first, I want to talk about the supplies; how do they s… stand with the tribes?"

Joshua reported, "The people are running low on the vegetables and dried fruit they brought out of Egypt. I pointed out that the animals we had could be used for food but, they seemed to focus only on what they were 'used to' back where they called, home. Wheat and corn meal are beginning to run low also The water is doing well.

As far as other things go, there are disputes between some of the people; petty things the way I see it." Joshua looked at Telok and Salmon and they nodded their heads in agreement. "The people still have some of the idols they brought out of Egypt and are continuing to keep them close; I don't like the attitudes it tends to influence the people in," Joshua added.

Moses studied the things Joshua said for a few moments and started to teach them. "The people are still unclear that Egypt is not their home any longer. Nor are the gods they worshiped while there. As the Lord leads and we follow, they must come to understand that we must give up everything to follow Him. HE is our 'LORD GOD', and we are His children, and He will provide everything we will need. If in that provision we don't get what 'we' think we need then, we must trust the Lord in 'His' wisdom. As our faith in Him grows so does our understanding, but to have only wisdom with no understanding… could cripple a person's walk.   And   to   have understanding with no wisdom could do the same." He looked at his men and could see they were having trouble with what he had said.

"Understanding that you have been invited to a wedding, of which we will have soon, and to wear grave clothes… Well, would be absolutely out of character for someone who attends by just using the understanding that they were invited. Now, if a person has understanding that he has an invitation and using wisdom, picks out what would be appropriate to wear and attend then, all is well. Same as when someone knows that a wedding is going to take place and they have the correct type of clothing shows they have wisdom in, how to attend a wedding. But, if that person has no invitation and no understanding of that fact… and they attend uninvited, that would be rude to the bride and groom." Moses turned to check and see if the boys were still on the same camel with him.

"Wisdom and Understanding are just two parts of a greater lesson; a lesson involving the rest of our lives. For me to even think that, I might arrive, in all of my learning would show that I have not learned at all. As I walk and learn so, shall you. You will learn and teach and then, you will learn more, and you will teach more. It is a pattern we will follow for the rest of our days. The Lord is so wonderfully vast that, we will never learn it all. It is a journey meant to fill our lives with wonder and awe." He paused for a moment and let them soak in the truth of what he was sharing with them.

"All of the people; including you, are beginning a walk with the only True God. Just as kids grow at different rates so do people with trust and faith. There are some days when I get up that I feel; and not only feel but know that I am the Lord's. Then… there are days that I don't feel like it; I don't feel like a child of the Lord God, but in my heart, I know that I am still the Lord's because He never changes. Our Lord has much to teach us, and I believe that soon, He is going to set us down and explain just what it means to follow Him both in mind, will and strength."

"So, why is it that some of the people still cling to these idols when the Lord has already shown how mighty He is!" Salmon asked.

Moses continued, "These people have been in a foreign land for over four hundred years. There is nothing written down and only stories told of how Joseph forgave his brothers and prevented Egypt from being swallowed by a famine. Joseph also told his brothers before he died to be sure and take his bones out from the land of

Egypt when they would leave, which we have done. I don't think they realized their exodus would take so long. All of this to say, the p…people have only heard stories of a God they had never met. This generation has had no other way practiced before them other than what the Egyptians lived. It is the only way they have known and now, The Lord God, has finally delivered us from slavery. He has brought us through the Red Sea and destroyed our enemy right in f… front of us.

Next, He brought us three days through a desert without water and then, made bitter water sweet. We are just beginning our relationship with Him. Our God is a patient God, but also, a very jealous God. Learning what is proper before Him and what is not, will be a daily journey in life. But I w…would rather be in His hands than the hands of the evil one; or an earthly ruler. Our God is a God who knows what we need before we do, He knows how to provide just what we need; when we need it. Learning to endure the whips of the Taskmaster's was not easy, but we learned how to respond in the correct manner in order to escape the whip. And the s…same will be with the Lord, except He won't use a whip" Moses said with a smile.

"Enough with the teaching for now… Let's talk about something fun… like a wedding!"

Chapter 13
The Fight

Acts had been lying around since Joshua, Telok, and Salmon left to go to the front for the meeting with Moses. He had partly been staying low because he didn't feel well and his head still kept hurting; but also, because they were going to the front without him. He remembered what he told them, "I'll go next time besides, the Lord has me here for a reason." Even though he spoke the words again to himself it brought no comfort, he still battled the depression he had already been fighting. His heart was… more tender to the Word of the Lord than most, even Moses had noticed that. He questioned his own heart at first, battling between believing that the Lord indeed, had him right where he was for a reason or that he was just… where he was because *'that's where he was'*. He also thought maybe he was just kidding himself concerning the Lord using him at all. After fighting with both sides in his mind he decided to speak what was in his heart, "Yes… the Lord does have me here for a reason. I do matter to Him, and I will remain steadfast in my faith despite what my vacillating emotions try to tell me."

He looked over at Klee as she held Naoon's baby. Naoon had come to walk with them just as she had told him she would, but right at that moment he didn't feel like he would be very good company for 'baby'.

~

Moving in and around the people Qushunbab, looked for the boy. He was chosen especially for this job because of his size and ability to do battle. He was not foolish in provoking the Angels, but he showed no fear either. He had been chosen for this mission and he didn't plan to fail the one he served. He found the boy in the cart and as he slipped close enough, he heard Acts declare with his mouth his faith in the Lord. He thought about how he was planning to making him regret those words.

The Angels of the Living God were not being taken by surprise. They had already moved in among the people and were cleverly hidden from the demon's sight.

"No matter," Qushunbab thought. "My presence has caused some fear I see. As well as it should." In his multi-sounding voice.

As the demon moved in closer to Acts; Acts suddenly decided to get up out of the cart he had been confined to since the accident and walk with his sister and Naoon. He slid to the edge of the cart and watched the ground pass under his feet. He let his feet drag just a bit. The dirt swirling from his feet made small clouds. Feeling alright, he slipped from the cart to a standing position as the cart continued to pull away from him. He felt steady on his feet and turned to start over to Klee and Naoon. His movement caught their eyes, and they smiled to see him up. He was walking up to them, but within just a couple of yards of reaching them…

Qushunbab reached out his clawed hand with the tip of his index finger. Just barely touching the skin on the back of Acts' head. As the tip of the claw came within just a couple of hairs from his wound Acts began to feel the presence of evil around him. Almost making his way to his sister and Naoon, his right hand went to the back of his head. Nun saw what was happening and stopped the animals from pulling the cart.

The demon had made contact and seemed to be pushing his talon into the wound. Acts went to one knee as Klee handed the baby to Naoon and ran to his side. As Acts knelt on one knee she steadied him. As the demon pressed his talon deeper into the wound Acts experienced more pain. He put his left arm over her shoulder and paused. Klee said nothing but put her right arm around his waist and watched and listened as her brother began to speak softly through agonizing pain. "I… will… not give in to this pain; I will… stand in my faith."

At that very moment, a large bronze-colored sword swatted the demon's hand away from the head of Acts. Qushunbab jerked his head around to see a pair of beautiful dark green eyes staring at him with great intent.

Qushunbab turned on his hooves to face this beautiful Angelic being. "I believe the boy said, he would not give in to the pain; that he would stand in his faith," Rend said, with a calm and even tone. Rend was the Guardian Angel that had been assigned to Acts. His height was a head shorter than Qushunbab, but that did not bother the Angel.

"This boy is mine. He has sin all over him and his sin must be punished!" Qushunbab spoke with a voice that sounded like there were four voices speaking from him.

"The blood of the lamb that has been spread on the door posts in Egypt is still covering him as his substitutionary sacrifice," Rend countered calmly.

The demon looked at the distance between Acts and himself. He studied the Angel and did not act without thinking things through. After deciding, he reached for the boy again.

Acts had been able to stand with his sisters help and now stood up, straight and tall. Klee asked if he was alright, but he said nothing more... the pain dropped him to his knees once again.

Nun had climbed down from the cart and was running to Acts. "Hold on Acts!" Nun yelled as he ran. The commotion got the attention of everyone who had been walking around them and they all started to run as they follow Nun.

~

In the spiritual realm, Qushunbab had been able to plunge his claw into the wound once again. He had caused a tear in the tissue of Acts' head that began to bleed on the inside and outside of his head. Rend brought his sword up to hit the claw away, but as his sword was coming up, Qushunbab turned to his side and brought his own sword down blocking the bronze sword of Rend.

The words came slowly from Acts but were very deliberate and as he spoke them, he seemed to be gaining strength. "I will not... give in to this pain; I will stand in my faith."

Rend spun to his left and brought his sword down on the demon's arm, breaking the contact he had with Acts. Acts opened his eyes. He looked into the face of his sister with Naoon standing right behind her. There was a moment of silence and for that moment there was no pain.

Qushunbab spun to his right moving him to the other side of Acts. Reaching out with his long arm, he extended his claw once again with more force. He planned to put his claw all of the way into the head of Acts. Rend brought his right foot up kicking the demon in his stomach, but it did not break the contact he was starting to have with Acts.

Acts once again brought both of his hands to his head in unforgiving pain. As Acts pulled his hands away, he could see the blood on his hands.

Rend turned to his left, bringing his leg around as if he were going to kick the demon again…

Acts, now stood to his feet and in a voice, clear and strong he declared, "I will NOT give in to this PAIN; I WILL stand in MY FAITH."

The entire family was now close enough to hear what Acts was saying.

Rend had swung his sword up from his hip, hitting Qushunbab in the upper part of his arm as it extended toward Acts. The cut was deep, and a sulfurous thick liquid poured from the wound in the demon's arm. Qushunbab flinched in pain but, he made no sound. His release forced by the Angelic Being held his attention. Qushunbab looked at Rend and declared, "You will be disgraced for this." He began to swing his sword around in circles down toward the Angels face. The Angel blocked each strike with strength that more than matched that of the demon. Qushunbab moved around in a circle inching his way back to Acts. Rend would counter, but the demon was a true warrior with the blade, and it had come very close to Rend more than once. Finally, Qushunbab was close enough to reach out and in this attempt, he planned to push all of his fingers into the open wound on Acts' head. He was going to kill this boy now and receive the glory his lord Satan would give him. As the tips of his sharp claw began to touch Acts, he suddenly found that he could go no further. The Angel was at bay for now; so, what was stopping him?

Using the strong shoulders of his sister, Acts began to stand up and as he raised himself to his full height, he lifted his head and looked up to the pillar of cloud. He said, with a strong even tone that could be heard by the family:

"My faith is in the Lord God Almighty and He is my healer." Gritting his teeth, as if looking at an enemy he would defeat, he spoke the words again. "My faith is in the Lord God Almighty and HE is my healer." The bandage around his head fell to the ground beside him.

The demon lost all contact with Acts and looked at the boy in disbelief. How could the boy keep him away; keep him from carrying out the mission for which he had been sent? This seemed impossible to the demon.

Acts looked down and studied the bandage for a moment and then, reached down and picked it up. Holding it in his hand he could not take his eyes off of it. Klee, Naoon, and Joshua's parents just watched him, as he held the bandage in his hand for a moment. With his right hand still holding to Klee… he slowly reached back with his left, his fingers tenderly searching for the wound. He began slowly and searched with more force not fearing the pain it could bring. His eyes began to open wide, and a smile broke across his face. Klee looked into his eyes as she reached up with her left hand and pulled back his hair.

Her eyes and mouth opened wide in surprise. She looked to Naoon and as she did Naoon began to understand something had taken place. She was behind Acts and as Klee had done, she too, combed his hair aside and searched for the wound, but it was not there. The stitches were in his hair, but not attached to his skin. As she combed her fingers through his hair the threads fell away. The very threads she had put there. She looked over at Nun and then, at Joshua's mother with amazement written all over her face. Nun and his wife walked over to inspect what the girls had discovered; the wound was indeed gone, and the scar served as a reminder of the battle.

It took a few minutes for the gravity of the situation to sink in and almost at the same time they began to lift up their voices in praise. Their praise heard by all of their clan brought everyone running over to see what the excitement was about. As each one looked and found what had taken place the news began to spread from clan to clan until the entire tribe of Ephraim, quickly heard what the Lord had done. Everyone knew of the accident and of the pain Acts had been in. Like a ripple in water caused by a single pebble, the news spread within a couple of hours to the front.

The look of defeat on the face of Qushunbab was evident to Rend. "You seem to have lost this battle. You should leave." Rend spoke with an even tone and not in a ridiculing way.

"I will leave when the boy is dead!" the demon shouted. In a fury, uncontrolled, he charged Rend. His wings pushed him through the air with great force; he lifted his blade to bring it down toward the head of the angel. Rend stepped to his left and brought his sword up at an angle deflecting the strike. The blade of the demon continued to the ground; leaving the demon completely vulnerable on his right side. Rend lifted himself with his wings as he leaned forward with great force, bringing his blade down, meeting the demon at the base of his head. In a flash, as his blade passed through, the demon completely went to ash and all of the particles fell and were swallowed up by the ground. The demon had been sent to the pit to await the final judgment of the Lord God. He would no longer be a threat to Acts. Rend turned to look around and he could see other Angelic Beings close by. Rend knew they would have never allowed Qushunbab to finish his work with Acts. He smiled at them, and they raised their weapons in respect, each turned to continue their watch over the people around them. Rend turned back to Acts and with a soft touch from the spiritual realm, he put his hand on the back of Acts' head. He wanted to let Acts know he was loved and protected.

In that moment, he felt the warmth on his head. He paused for a moment and smiled. He didn't understand it but, he just felt a peace all over him. Acts stood with his arm around his sister. Tears of joy running down his cheek as each member of the family and most of the clan came over to show their love for him and his sister. The praise continued for a good while and the Lord smiled upon all of them.

Rend spoke his own prayer: *My Lord God, You are always amazing and... unpredictable. I praise Your Holy Name!*

Chapter 14

No Understanding

Moses and the others had been walking out in front of the company of Israel and they all turned to see what the commotion was about. As they did two young runners stopped in front of Moses. They were out of breath, but even so they were trying to speak. The taller one spoke first, "Acts…" the boy swallowed, "got out of the cart…"

Joshua stepped up beside Moses and asked, "And what?"

As the boy tried to catch his breath the second boy picked up, "After he got out… he fell to one knee…"

Salmon and Telok now stood on the other side of Moses and Salmon asked, "Fell to one knee and what!?"

The first boy continued, "He spoke some words softly at first, as he put his arm around the shoulders of his sister…"

The suspense was beginning to build to a point that even Moses was having a hard time dealing with it, but he understood the boys had been running for a good distance and they all took in a deep breath with the young runners.

After just a few seconds the first one continued, "He spoke 'I will not give in to this pain.'" The boy said, still trying to catch his breath.

Salmon spoke with great urgency, "What!? What in great camels, happened?"

As the boy got his breath he continued, "He said, 'I will stand in my faith' and then, he spoke it again only louder."

The second boy was able to finish, "He spoke it a third time and the bandage dropped from his head and reached back to feel his wound."

Pausing only a moment, Telok to spoke, "Yes… and what happened." He could hardly contain his anticipation.

"And it wasn't there" the boy answered.

"It wasn't there!? What wasn't there" Salmon asked.

"The wound was gone! Only the scar remained" he replied.

Joshua looked over at Telok and both of them looked to Salmon. Moses never took his eyes away from the runners, suddenly Moses clapped his hands together which caused Salmon to jump. Moses pulled his hands up to his lips, "How Great is our God!"

Moses began to dance around lifting up praise to the Lord, while Joshua and Telok were still looking at Salmon. They were trying not to laugh at Salmon's reaction. When Moses began to sing it began to sink in, and Joshua, Telok and Salmon began to understand what this meant. They too, fell into praise with Moses. Soon they had the young runners in their circle, and they all lifted up their voices to the Lord.

Moses led them and they repeated, "Great is our God! He is worthy to be praised!! His mercies endure forever!!!"

~

Off to the south a wirier demon flew to the side of Satan who was receiving worship from the Canaanites. A human sacrifice had just been thrown from the top of a cliff called, "The Rock" in Caesarea Philippi.

The demonic imp slipped to the side of his lord, "I am sorry my lord, but the boy stood with so much faith that Qushunbab was unable to release the blood clot and kill the boy." Pausing for a moment the imp finished, "Qushunbab has been sent to the pit, my lord."

Satan stared at his imp and struck him, "If the Angel had not sent him to the pit, I would have. He took too long, and it gave the boy time to complete his declaration of faith. Now, I will have to plan another way in which to destroy the boy." Starring off in the distance. Hate filled his mind as he studied the situation. His expressions and how he used his words gave him strength. "He will not again escape… The Most High thinks me to be simple. I will set another trap that HE will not know. For I am craftier than HE."

He turned his attention back to the sacrifice being offered to him and took in the praise of the Canaanites. The time there was finished and now he would return to the people who followed Moses. He would take more time in planning his next attack so that it would be successful. As he turned, he stretched out his black wings and lifted himself into the air. Thousands of demonic warriors released their hold on the humans they were influencing and followed him. As their hideous forms rose into the air the sky turned dark.

~

As the news of what happened to Acts spread to the tribes forward, it also spread to those behind Ephraim. The message moved more slowly between these tribes, and it finally reached the ears of Korah and Abiram. These two had so enjoyed the first news of the accident and Acts being hurt. They had talked with each other of how it would have been so poetic if the boy had been killed by being hit in the head yet again. Korah looked at the man giving him the news and it angered him. "Healed!? For a second time this boy has been healed miraculously and for what purpose!? He is a boy and not a leader!! He possesses no position of honor and has no special talents. What does this new God see in him?"

Abiram stood behind him as he allowed Korah to vent his frustrations. After a few moments, he spoke in a soft voice. "It is true that the boy has no position of importance and… he is indeed not very bright. It does cause a puzzling picture when you look at him and see how this new God seems to take care of him. Could it be that He is putting him into a place so that he can fall from a… loftier height. It would only make you look that-much-better when your talents and your leadership are recognized by the people?"

Korah thought for a moment, "Yes… that sounds like something that could happen to only make us look better. To pull down the 'boy who was healed' would most certainly put us in a better light with those who choose to follow us." Korah's mind moved quickly, and he could see how good they would look as the leaders of the entire company of Israel. Pride swelled in his heart and as it did it completely blinded him to the very lord he was bowing to. It was NOT, the Lord God Almighty.

~

Sitting between Korah and Abiram were seven demons. They were laughing and playing them for the fools they were. They had been assigned to these men by Satan. They were feeding every ounce of pride the humans had in them. The one in charge of the small band spoke to the others, "They are so moldable with pride and arrogance it makes it easy to manipulate them.

They can't even see that they are out from under the protection of HIM."

One of the other demons asked, "Shall I go and get some of the other humans who are just as easy to influence?"

The leader smiled showing his teeth, "Yes… all of you go and collect other humans. Let's see just how much pride these two men will rise to." He stood looking into the eyes of Korah and was pleased to see the facial expression that showed hate for the young human. As the six other demons went off to do their jobs.

Although Korah could not see him, the demonic leader spoke to Korah standing right in front of him. "You will prove to be very useful in the coming days and we will receive much glory from our lord. He will certainly be pleased to watch the two of you strike at Moses and his weak followers who do his bidding."

The demon then moved over to look Abiram right in the eyes and spoke to his mind, "Can you see just how great you will be? All of the people will look to you for the answers of life, and they will want to give you praise, for being such a powerful leader." The demon could not keep from laughing. He could see his suggestions being considered by Abiram. His facial expression was showing pride and the desire to be praised by the people.

Soon the six other demons came walking back with nine people who thought of Korah and Abiram as great leaders; leaders with a plan and good ideas. Each one of them being influenced to think of themselves as possibly being given charge of certain people groups and receiving honor.

One of the men spoke to Korah, "I can hardly wait until you are in charge. Then, we won't be slinking away from these nations around us in which we know we out number."

"Yea!" said another.

One of the women walked up to Korah, "You look the part of a true leader. And having such a loyal and wise leader beside you, such as Abiram, only makes you look that much better."

Korah and Abiram took in all that the people had to say and with each comment their pride and arrogance only increased. Their pride creating a stench rising up from their hearts as revolting smell of decay; the very decay of their souls. The people did not even realize they were being led like animals.

~

Michael, one of the arch Angels of the highest honor, stood by his Lord and spoke softly, "My Lord God, shall we just allow them to disgrace Your Honor with such talk?"

"They don't understand what danger they place themselves in, but I will teach them all what I require of them and once they have learned; they will have no excuse. My Law will show them just how far they fall from the mark I have set in place. I want them to understand that they can only be saved by looking to Me.

They will have the choice of following Me or following Satan. If they are not My children, then they are his."

"But it angers me so, my Lord. They treat the good things You do for them as filthy rags. They do not give You the praise and honor You deserve. You are the creator of everything, and You hold this world's entire existence in the palm of Your hand.

"Quiet yourself My servant. I know your love for Me is great, but I want them to hear and learn from Moses and those I have put under him. I have good plans for these children of Mine. When the time comes, they will each stand in judgment for what they choose. Their eternity is in their choice, and they will have no excuse." The Lord God paused and guided the attention of Michael to the family Acts and his sister now belong to. "See how thankful they are. Their hearts almost burst with praise and love for Me. That is where I find Joy in My creation. Look at their faces, Michael. Look at the praise that lights up their very souls. True praise and thankfulness usher them into My presence and I love them."

Michael looked at Acts and Klee and then, to Naoon and the baby. She was dancing in praise with the baby in her arms. He laughed with excitement for them. Michael looked at them and asked, "And what beautiful plans do you have for them, my Lord?"

"Oh… They are going to be so happy with the family I will form through them. And that baby will have a name soon; I have placed it within Telok's heart."

"So… they will be married?" Michael expressed with joy.

"To you, My servant Michael, I will share My plans for them; but only you. Yes, they will be married, and the baby's name will be…" The Lord paused as Michael hung on His words. He smiled at his Angel friend… **"I will let Telok tell you when he gives the baby her name."**

Michael laughed, "That is so like You, Lord not to give away the surprise."

Chapter 15

The Advice

After all of the signals by the ram's horns had sounded, the Israelites had begun to settle down for the night's rest. Moses made himself comfortable beside the fire Joshua had made with the small stock of wood they had brought and found on their journey. Moses looked over at Joshua and asked, "Are you ready to get married?"

Joshua didn't answer right off because he knew that Moses was asking for more than a 'yes sir'. He looked up to the direction Klee would be settling down for the night; then he looked at Moses, "I think… that I am ready to have 'life with a wife.' She means more to me than anything in this world. The Lord is the giver of my life, and I am growing to understand more about Him with each passing day. But when I thank Him for all that He is doing in my life, she… is always at the forefront of my mind." He paused and after a moment nodded his head 'yes' and answered Moses, "And yes… I am ready to get married." That brought a laugh from Telok and Salmon.

"I know it is very evident to those who love you, me being one." Moses looked around the light of the fire at Salmon and Telok. "Tomorrow, we will make it to Elim, and I want you to go and get your bride and your family and bring them to the spring which has seven palm trees around it. It is at the eastern part of the oasis where I will set up my tent. There are two trees that bend toward each other, and it is there, I will meet you. We will begin the feast of celebration the next day. The feast will last a whole day. On the second day, you will have the men who stand with you posted right beside you. Klee will have the women who will stand with her. This will be the first wedding since we have been free; the first free wedding in over four hundred years."

"Wow! I had not even thought of that" Joshua commented, caught in amazement. "And now that Acts is well, he will be able to serve with a full heart and a strong body."

Moses chuckled. "As the t…tribes begin to file around Elim the distance will be short in getting back to your tribe and clan. I want you to return as soon as you can but, do not be in too much of a hurry." Joshua smiled and said quietly to Moses, "I don't think that it will take long at all."

~

The next morning before the pillar of fire was replaced by the pillar of cloud, Joshua had already got Telok and Salmon up to start back to the tribe of Ephraim. With the excitement in each man's heart, the run back would not take long. Moses had given them the news that the company would be to Elim just passed the noon hour when the sun was straight overhead behind the pillar of cloud. Moses called two men from the tribe of Judah to walk with him. He told them they would be giving the signal for the tribes to begin pulling into their positions around the oasis. With the springs of water being the central hub it would not be a long walk for anyone to reach one of the twelve springs. Moses had sent word by runner to each tribe where they would be camping at Elim.

There were to be four camps around Elim. Each camp was made up of three tribes. Starting with the tribes that would be camped to the north of Elim was the tribe of Naphtali; next to the springs. It had 53,400 fighting men. Proceeding away from the spring to the north was the tribe of Asher, which had 41,500 fighting men. On the outside edge was the tribe of Dan which had 62,700 fighting men. All three of these tribes had a total of 157,600 men of fighting age. These three tribes made up the camp of Dan. The land around the oasis had a gentle slope up to the top of the hill all around the oasis and that is why it could not be seen from any direction. This allowed the entire company to be hidden.

To the south was the camp of Rueben. The tribe of Rueben was the farthest from the spring, having 46,500 fighting men. Next to them was the tribe of Simeon with 53,900. The tribe closest to the spring was the tribe of Gad, with 46,650 fighting men. The total number of fighting men of age for the camp of Rueben was 151,450. Each tribe again was able to look downhill to the water.

To the west was the camp of Ephraim. It was made up of the tribe of Benjamin with 35,400 fighting men. They were positioned next to the spring with the tribe of Manasseh next to them. Manasseh had 32,200 fighting men. The tribe on the perimeter was Ephraim. This was the home tribe for Joshua, Telok, and Acts. There were 40,500 fighting men in their tribe. There were a total of 108,100 fighting men in the camp of Ephraim.

There were no landmarks at the top of the hill to give its location away to anyone passing by who did not already know of its existence.

And finally, to the east was the camp of Judah; forming this camp were the tribes of Zebulun camped next to the springs. In the tribe of Zebulun, there were 57,400 men of fighting age. The second tribe up the grade was Issachar with 54,400 fighting men and next to Issachar, and closest to the spring was the tribe of Judah. This was the home tribe for Salmon and in it were 74,600 fighting men which was the largest tribe. The total number of fighting men for the camp of Ephraim was 186,400.

Moses and Aaron camped to the east right next to the water. The rest of the Levites camped on the other three sides of Elim next to the water. The camp that was on the southern edge of the springs was the camp of Kohath. The camp of Gershon was to the west beside the water and the camp of Merari was to the north. These camps were made up of all of the Levites and the total number of men in these camps were 22,273. These positions were instructed by the Lord given to Moses.

~

The thought of being able to camp at Elim for more than a couple of days felt good to Moses. He knew that they would be at Elim for at least a week. He was excited for Joshua and was looking forward to the celebration and the joining of Joshua and Klee.

It didn't take long for the boys to make it to their families with Salmon being the first to see his. Salmon told his family that the wedding was going to happen at Elim, and he was excited to tell them he would be a part of the wedding. They told Joshua how happy they were for him and assured him that they would be there. When Joshua asked if Salmon could stay with him and Telok, Nahshon and Salmon's mother were moved at the fact that Salmon had become that important to Joshua.

Nahshon replied, "He is in your service now. We have given him over to you and to Moses."

This made Salmon walk a bit taller because he could not have been more proud of his father and mother.

Salmon, Telok, and Joshua immediately set out to find Klee and Acts. Salmon was so excited to hear all about what happened with his healing. Klee and Acts were trying to wait patiently, but it was becoming more difficult with each passing hour. "What could be keeping them so long" Acts exclaimed.

"They said that it would be a day and…" Klee looked off to watch for them and then continued, "It's… been a day." Her voice trailing off.

Naoon put her hand on Klee's shoulder and tried to ease the worry. "I feel very strongly that they will come today, and we need to be ready… so… what do we need to do to be ready?"

Joshua's mom began to help list off some of the things that could help keep Klee's mind occupied while they waited, "Well, you will need to try on the wedding gown that the women of our clan have prepared for you."

Klee's eyes opened wide and said, "You mean… the ladies have a gown ready for me?"

Acts had climbed into the back of the cart to stand so that he could see better from a little more height. Naoon placed the baby in the back of the cart with Acts and asked him to watch her. He had actually gotten used to having a baby around and said, "Sure, I'll watch her."

Naoon turned back to Klee, "We can put some blankets on ropes and tie them from Kemuel's cart to Nun's to give you privacy in putting on the dress." She turned to Nun as they kept walking and asked him if he had enough rope to make the idea happen.

"Yea… I've some rope and when we stop, I'm happy to get it out." Kemuel said proudly. Naoon smiled and asked, "Would you mind coordinating with Nun to tie the ropes to hold the blankets in place for privacy? Kemuel responded, "No problem." Raising his hand at Nun. As the planning continued.

As the morning and miles passed, they heard the signal to begin the tribes moving into position around the oasis. As the tribe of Ephraim got settled into their position on the outer edge, Kemuel pulled his cart up close to Nun's and they stretched rope from one cart to the other. The women threw blankets over the ropes forming a spacious room for Naoon and Joshua's mom to help Klee with the fitting. As the girls were taking care of the gown, Acts had climbed out of the cart leaving the baby asleep. He was moving up to the front by the oxen when he heard a familiar voice behind him.

"So… our new God healed the young warrior… again." The words sliding off with sarcasm. Acts turned around to find Korah standing beside the cart next to theirs. His voice smearing disappointment with each word he asked, "You've wormed your way into a small position with Joshua and Moses… have you?"

"Hello Korah." Acts replied flatly. The tone of his voice told Klee he was very serious. She pulled the makeshift curtain back just enough to see Acts and Korah standing several feet away from them. She reached over and grabbed Naoon's arm in alarm and said in a whisper, "That's the man who took me!" Naoon peered out of the curtain as well.

Acts continued, "Is there something you need Korah?"

"I just wanted to see for myself if the rumor was true and I guess it is… since you are climbing in and out of carts," Korah said playing with the words using a mockery tone.

Acts caught the meaning that Korah had been watching him for a least a short while; long enough to see that Joshua was not around, but with the presence of the clan so close, he knew Korah would never try anything here. As Acts spoke to Korah, some of the men in the clan had already noticed the stance Acts had taken to address the stranger and when they realized it was Korah, they moved in closer, but leaving Acts in control of the situation.

Acts asked again, "Is there something you need?"

Korah pulled the hood from his head and answered, "No… I just wanted to see; nothing else really. I was just wondering when the next mishap might occur with you; since there seems to be so much uncertainty surrounding you.

"Yea! I've noticed that too," Acts responded with a small laugh.

"You better be careful boy. The next one may just hurt you bad enough you won't pull out of it," Korah added.

"He better be careful about what?" Came a very familiar voice to not only Acts but, Korah as well. Joshua had walked up behind Korah and his voice caused Korah to turn quickly. Joshua asked again, "Be careful about what… exactly?"

Korah turned and looked Joshua in the eyes and since he was not causing a problem he answered Joshua, "Just wanted to see the miracle for myself." He felt like he could look back into the eyes of this warrior in such a stale environment. "I was just warning the young warrior," smearing the term warrior, "that the next accident could be terribly bad; even fatal, if he's not careful. It's… always good to keep people alert: not to be careless."

Joshua stared deep into Korah's eyes, and this made Korah uncomfortable. "It's funny you say that because the Lord keeps a pretty close eye on Acts. It would serve as a warning for anyone to be very careful in their actions that might… cause an accident because that person would have to go through the Lord to do it." Joshua looked over at Acts with a questioning brow.

Putting Korah in this kind of light had taken the situation well out of Korah's hands and so, he decided to take his leave. He held up his hands as he turned around to leave and said sarcastically, "It never hurts to warn somebody about accidents."

They all watched Korah walk away and Joshua turned to Acts and said, "Great Camels! I leave you for a day and you start drawing fleas."

This made everyone laugh as Joshua gave Acts a hug and asked, "So, where is your sister?"

"I'm over here!" She said in a high-pitched voice.

As they looked to where the voice was coming from, Klee put her hand out of the edge of the curtain and instructed, "You stay there. I'm trying on my wedding gown. I'll be out in a moment." Joshua turned back to Acts and asked quietly, "What wedding gown?"

"Your mom and the ladies of your clan," Acts stopped and corrected himself, "Our clan… have prepared a gown for her." He paused for a moment and added, "I haven't even seen it."

Telok put his hand on Joshua's shoulder and said in a whisper, "I wonder how many gowns they have?"

Joshua turned to look at his friend with amazement. "Do you mean…?"

"Well, I'm just sayin'… it has crossed my mind more than a couple of times these past days." Telok answered.

Salmon grabbed Acts and said, "I want to see where it was."

Acts turned his back to him and pulled his hair to the side and sure enough there was the scar to show that it really had happened.

About that time Klee and Naoon stepped out from the curtain; both greeting each one. Acts and Salmon turned to look at the baby and found her awake so, Acts picked her up and he said in a high voice, "Do you want to see your uncle Salmon."

Salmon punched Acts in the shoulder before he thought for a moment and smiled, "Uncle? That doesn't sound so bad now that I say it."

And as Klee and Joshua had their moment so did Telok and Naoon, but they were still a bit 'awkward' in just how much to share their affection; especially with others watching. They hugged and stood there looking into each other's eyes and Naoon said softly before Telok could speak, "I sure did miss your light green eyes."

"And I your dark brown" Telok replied.

Acts and Salmon were keeping the baby entertained while the hugging and stuff was going on. Joshua greeted his parents and shared with his family what Moses had said concerning the wedding. Joshua's mom ran over to him and kissed his forehead and then ran to Klee and kissed her forehead and said, with excitement, "We best be getting everything together… we need to get moving." She started getting a little food together. Klee grabbed her wedding gown and Naoon grabbed some things for the baby as Joshua began spreading the news with the clan that the invitation was open to all except for maybe Korah. That brought a laugh. It was within just a few minutes they were on their way to the springs at the east end of Elim.

~

Spirits were high; excitement filled the moments leading up to the beginning of the celebration with Moses. After arriving Moses started it off with a small speech of why they had come together for this celebration.

"Let's all celebrate the birthing of a n…new family. Joshua and Klee! Tonight, we s…start to prepare the way of their wedding!"

All of the family and clan of Nun began shouting and the women began singing with tambourines, small bells, and finger cymbals. Two of Joshua's cousins pulled out their harps, playing beautifully. The celebration also included some members of Salmon's family who were very proud for the young couple. After an evening of celebrating and everyone feeling the long walk, most turned in early.

Telok pulled on Joshua's shoulder and gave a small hand jester that called for him to follow. Joshua slipped out without anyone else noticing and asked Telok "Is everything alright?"

"Yes, my friend, everything is wonderful, but I am conflicted" Telok replied.

Joshua looked into his friend's eyes as he began to smile, "Are you conflicted concerning Naoon!?"

Telok motioned for him to quiet down and answered with frustration in his voice, "Yes!" he answered softly. "I see what you and Klee are about to do, and I know that it is what I should be doing with Naoon. I know in my heart that I love her... and I feel in my heart that she loves me, but I have not... told her."

Joshua squared up to his friend and replied, "Look... I have no doubt in my heart or mind... that Naoon loves you; because my friend it is written in every smile she gives you. With every small look stolen by her eyes for you... she says that she does." Joshua looked around and said, "Let's go talk to Moses about it..."

Telok stopped him saying, "No... he needs his rest. I will go talk with him in the morning; first thing."

"Do you want me to go with you?" Joshua asked.

"No... my friend, this is something I must do alone, but I will need to ask my father first." Telok's voice and face relaxed. "I just needed to tell you. It was just a strong feeling I had so maybe now I can get a couple of hours of sleep." They laughed at the moment.

Chapter 16

Proposal

In the spiritual realm, standing only a few feet from them were very large muscular individuals; it was two of the Angels assigned to Joshua and Telok. The one assigned to Joshua had brown hair with eyes so green they could not be described by any natural color in the world.

Semper looked down at Telok and said to Turion, "He is so taken with Naoon, and I can see why, she is a beautiful girl."

"Yes, she is" Turion replied. Tomorrow will be a great day for Joshua and Klee." Semper continued.

And it could be a great day for Telok and Naoon as well," Turion added.

Semper asked, "I wonder what name he will give to the baby?" Turion simply said, "I wonder as well."

And as Michael listened, he whispered to himself, "I too, wonder my friends." With a smile on his face and peace in his heart he returned to the Lord's side.

~

The next morning Telok couldn't wait any longer for his dad to wake and with a gentle nudge, his father came around, "Yes… what is it son?"

Telok answered, "I must speak with you dad."

"Alright son," Kemuel said as he got up with much interest after he had moved the sleep from is body. "Is there something wrong?"

"No!" Telok started. "I have been thinking about this for… what could be considered a while. I also know that Joshua and Klee's wedding has progressed the thought."

Kemuel, looking into the eyes of his son, said nothing but allowed his son time to form the sentences of the thoughts moving through his mind.

"It seemed to start at the very moment I met her. I looked into her eyes and saw a woman of deep commitment and a strong spirit. And when I saw the baby, it only called to my heart more strongly…" Telok paused for a moment looking into the eyes of the only man to have ever been a father figure in his life. He had listened to his wisdom and had watched his love in action to others, but more importantly to himself.

"I want to take Naoon as my wife and the baby as my own daughter; I ask for your permission." Breathing as if he had run a race, his dad let him catch his breath.

"I'm glad your mind is catching up to your heart son," Kemuel said tenderly. "I have watched both of you and from the very first moment I met Naoon… I wanted her as a wife for you. She is the image of what your mother was when we first met and walked in love with each other."

Kemuel paused, "I wish you could have known her." A tear in the corner of his eye caught Telok's attention. "Son, I want you to act upon what you have in your heart because I know your heart is good. I suppose you will need to talk to Moses about this."

"Yes Sir."

Kemuel smiled and gave his son a warm fatherly hug. This had come to be one of the most valued places on earth in Telok's heart; his father's hugs. After a few moments Kemuel put Telok at arms-length and said, "Go tell him; wake him if you have to." Telok smiled and said, "Thank you, dad." He turned and started over to Moses' tent. As Kemuel watched, in his heart, he praised the Lord for his son.

With the wedding and all of the family so close it was a short walk for Telok. He walked up to the tent of Moses. Just as he started to say something Moses said, from inside the tent, "Good morning, Telok."

Telok was taken a little by surprise. "Good morning, sir."

Moses commented, "I was expecting you today, just not quite this early… everyone else is still asleep."

Moses motioned for Telok to have a seat on a blanket by the door of his tent and offered him a drink of water. Telok took it and had a good long drink as if, drinking in strength to face the day. He lowered the skin and asked Moses, "You were expecting me today?"

"Yes, I was! The Lord and I had a talk about you just the other day."

Telok looked back at Moses in surprise; he never thought Moses to talk with the Lord about him. Moses continued, "It would seem you have strong feelings for Naoon."

"Yes, sir I do." Telok replied.

"Tell me… what is in your heart," Moses asked.

"Well sir, I told my father that from the very first moment I met her I could see she was a woman of deep commitment and a strong spirit. I was drawn to her in my heart like I have never known before. And, as I looked at her and the baby, I could only see me taking care of them, by the Lord's hand. And with Joshua and Klee's wedding it only increased the urgency I have inside to marry her and take the baby as my own." Small beads of sweat began to form of Telok's forehead as he spoke.

Moses looked at him and smiled, "You… my son, are as s… smitten as much as your best friend. I have watched you and I know your level of commitment. You are ready to die for those you love, and I also know that you went back into the sea to do just that. I saw your love for her… for me and for the Lord. This can be a time of celebration for two friends who have a bond that is closer than brothers born from the same womb. But there is something that must take place first," looking into Telok's eyes with the expectation of the answer he was waiting for.

Telok thought for a moment and the answer hit him, "But I need to ask her?!" "That is correct" Moses said with delight.

Moses paused and said, "With Joshua & Klee being the first wedding in freedom we might be setting in play some traditions that will be passed down from generation to generation. I find it e… exciting.

The Lord has brought you here to this place and has set aside Naoon for you and Klee for Joshua. It is no accident but, divine planning by a God who loves us. You have a good father and Joshua has a good father and mother of whom you will be able to lean on, to seek wisdom from and have someone always to confide in." He cleared some emotion that came to the surface with a small cough and said, "And me."

Telok smiled and nodded his head in agreement with Moses. He took another drink of water and got to his feet. "I guess I could go check and see if she's awake."

"Oh… I think she's already awake" Moses replied.

As Telok suddenly noticed Moses looking past him, he turned to see where he was looking and there was Naoon holding the baby; standing in the first hint of dawn as the pillars were changing; and she was beautiful.

"Go and ask her and come back and tell me if we are going to have a double wedding," Moses said with a smile already knowing that they would.

Telok walked back over to Naoon and as he walked up, he asked, "Why are you up so early?"

"It's the baby… she is a real morning girl." Naoon responded. "Why are you up so early?"

"I had something on my mind and needed to talk it out." Telok told her. "Is it very serious" Naoon asked.

"Yea... yea I think it is a serious matter." He paused to look at her and said, "I would like to talk it over with you if… that would be alright?" Glancing at the baby so that starring into Naoon's eyes wouldn't leave him without words. Telok moved in a little closer so he could feel the heat of her face. "I've had something weighing on my heart now for a while and I think it's time I shared it," he started.

She didn't speak but let him find his thoughts. "The wedding today has brought my heart to a point that I must find something out." He paused looking into her eyes and taking her by one hand and putting the other around the baby: An action that seemed so natural, he asked, "I would like for you to be my wife and the baby to be my daughter?"

Naoon step back just a bit, but not letting go of his hand and she said, "I too, would like to ask you something…?"

"What is it?" Telok asked with surprise.

"I want you to be my husband and the father of my baby?" She stated strongly.

Telok stood there looking at her and then he looked over at the baby and smiled, "I do want to be your husband and the father of your baby."

Naoon stepped in close and said, "Yes, I want to be your wife."

The two of them took all that was shared. There was nobody else in that moment; just Telok, Naoon and the baby as the dawn began to break. They stood together and looked up to see the pillar of fire begin to move aside and the pillar of cloud form. It was breath taking. Telok spoke softly but she could hear, "I thank You… my Lord God for the life you have given me and are continuing to give. I thank you for my beautiful wife and my daughter."

~

Close by to the south stood Turion and Semper, and two others who were assigned to watch over Naoon and the baby girl. As the scene below them unfolded, they heard the vows exchanged without ceremony and they could see the moment was tender and delicate. Turion commented, "Semper, I will have to say I wanted that to happen."

Semper held his sword across his right shoulder, his yellow hair covering part of the double-edged blade. He turned to look back at Turion with dark brown eyes that almost glowed and he answered with a question, "I wonder what name he will give to the baby girl?"

The Angel that watched over Naoon said with anticipation, "I hope he gives her the name soon; I think Axon is about to bust with anticipation."

Axon whirled about to cut a sly grin at Shadow. "Yes, I am… and can't help but believe the name will be most fitting for her." Shadow was the shortest of the four angelic beings, but extremely muscular and carried a sword that was eighteen inches long. He had black hair and eyes that were deep blue. As he looked back at Telok and Naoon he smiled and commented. "I love to hear His children pray. Those who want to know our Lord and obey Him have the sweetest prayers."

Axon wore a golden head band which held back his long sandy blonde hair. He was tall and thin for an Angel; well defined in his arms and legs with a lean look to his waist. His shirt was drawn in tight around his abdomen and his pants were loose around his legs and cut off at his knees. Axon carried a long spear with a broad double-edged tip that was fourteen inches long. The shaft would have been enormous for a human, but it was just right for an Angel. The shaft was twelve feet long and he could wield it as an extension of his own body. As he was watching Telok and Naoon he heard a sound behind him and spun about with lightning-fast reflexes. His spear readied for battle and this action caused the other three to draw their swords only to find Michael standing there. He grinned and said, "Gotcha."

They all paused and one by one they began to laugh. They had noticed the increase in active movement from Satan's demons toward the people and they had become very protective of their humans.

"So… will Telok name the baby today?" Michael asked.

"Well, you sure know how to keep your troops alert" Shadow commented.

"If Axon wasn't so jumpy I think we would have noticed you coming" Turion teased.

The others agreed and they spread their wings to gain tactical advantage in their mission to guard each child of God assigned to them; they settled in to watch the day unfold before them.

Chapter 17

A Small Spy

Telok and Naoon had been up for little more than an hour when Joshua and Klee joined them. "Good morning! Such a beautiful day for a celebration!" Joshua said with enthusiasm!

Naoon smiled at Joshua and said, "Yes, I would agree! I think I will go help Klee get breakfast started while Telok…" turning to smile at the baby, "Watches this little girl."

Telok replied, "It would be my pleasure." And as she turned to leave, he pulled her close and said, "I love you." And kissed her tenderly.

"I love you also." She whispered.

Klee greeted Naoon and asked, "Have you been up long?"

"No, not long. The baby loves her morning time." she answered looking back at Telok.

It looks like Moses is up. I wonder if he would like to eat with us." Klee asked.

Smiling at Telok, Joshua added, "Let's go ask Moses if he would like that? Telok got the message that Joshua wanted to talk with him, and he agreed, carrying the baby with him.

~

Lying in the sand under the cart next to the family, was a demon imp. He was listening to all they had to say. He followed Joshua and Telok.

Joshua asked, "Were there any developments last night?" This question elevated the imps interest. "What type of developments would you be referring to?" Telok asked with a tone that was teasing. "Come on… you know exactly what kind of developments. Did you talk with Moses and what did he say?" Joshua asked with great insistence.

"Well, as a matter of fact, "I asked Naoon if she would be my wife and for the baby to be my daughter. And then she asked me to be her husband and the father of her baby. It was so neat the way it happened." Telok said looking at his best friend. The imp suddenly realized he had news of great importance for his master.

"Congratulations my friend!" Joshua said with a slap on the back, "I have to tell you I think you two are so right for each other. So, when did Moses think was a good time for the wedding?"

Telok smiled and paused just for a moment and answered, "Tomorrow."

"Tomorrow?!… Joshua said with surprise! Oh! You mean… tomorrow with Klee and me?"

"Moses said, it would be nice to have a double wedding… that is if you two don't mind?" Telok replied with some apology for imposing.

"I know that I am honored, and I know that Klee will be too." Joshua said with excitement.

"None the less, I would like for you to talk with her about it first. We won't say anything about it until she gives her answer. And if she does appose… I will not take it in hurt… It will just mean we would wait until the next day," Telok said trying to give Joshua a way out if she wanted their wedding to be just that; 'their wedding'.

About that time Moses walked up and asked, "Getting all of the news, are you?" raising an eyebrow to Joshua.

The imp became very fearful within the presence of Moses, but at the same time he swelled with pride for being one of the few to every get this close to Moses.

"Well… so much can happen in just one night." Joshua answered.

The imp thought to himself, "I'll let them walk back to the rest of the family and see what else I can learn.

~

As Naoon and Klee worked with what was becoming the last of the food brought with them from Egypt, Naoon questioned in her mind as to what Klee would think of a double wedding. She kept the thought to herself because she wanted Telok to be in control of the 'asking' and knew that he would want it that way.

"Are you excited about tomorrow?" She asked with a sisterly tone and Klee liked it. "More than I can say." Klee answered.

"I am so excited for you," Naoon replied. "I have had one wedding and I thought that was nice, but to be able to have a wedding in freedom… That is something I would have never thought would have happened in my lifetime."

"I forget that you have been married. Being around you without a husband has set my mind to think of you as always being single. The baby just seems to belong here and to think that you had a wedding, and a husband is… well whole other story." Klee explained.

"The man I married seems like a lifetime ago. He was a very good man and worked hard for the taskmasters, but we weren't really free to live the way I had always dreamed my home would be. And then, getting pregnant and having the baby whirled by me so fast I almost couldn't believe it happened, but here she is." Naoon stopped a moment to think through what she was feeling. The emotion rushed upon her so fast that is took her by surprise. "The man and life I knew is only a memory now and seems so distant. Now I have met a man who is more than I could have imagined."

Klee touched her hand, "Telok is almost bigger than life."

The imp almost laughed but remained silent. *'Bigger than life,' he thought. 'Soon, my master will kill this human, who is bigger than life.'*

Naoon smiled, "Yes, he is. Our path is unfolding, and it is exciting for me, and I think it is exciting for him as well."

Klee started taking the food off of the fire and began filling the bowls. "For Joshua to trust someone as he trusts Telok…? Speaks mountains about his character. And now that I have met him and have seen his compassion and care acted out in front of me, it causes my heart to trust him with Joshua." Klee laughed and added, "And to see him with that baby is so 'out of character' for a warrior such as he."

Naoon laughed and added, "He does seem to have several sides to his talents."

~

The women of the family and clan walked up after breakfast. They began to talk, and it was good to hear them talk and giggling and to see everyone enjoying themselves and Naoon's baby. One of Joshua's aunts asked Naoon, "What is her name!?"

Naoon answered without hesitation, "Well her father was killed a month before she was born, and her name has just been 'baby' since her birth. I am hoping that she will be named soon."

Another woman of the clan asked, "And who will be the lucky man to name her?"

Naoon smiled at Klee and Klee answered for her, "I think it will be someone who will surprise all of you."

~

It was in the mid-afternoon when Joshua came over and took Klee by the hand and led her aside. "I need to talk with you about something," he told her.

"Is there something wrong," Klee asked with alarm.

"No… no there is nothing wrong; in fact, there is something very right!" Joshua said with excitement. She looked at him puzzled. He took her hands and said, "It's about Telok and Naoon."

Klee relaxed and her mood changed to a more curious mode. "What about them," she asked. Joshua looked around to see if anyone could hear and told her, "They are going to get married."

"You mean he has already asked her, and she didn't tell me!?" Klee said with surprise. Joshua explained, "She really couldn't tell you because that is more Telok's decision when and how to announce it."

Klee thought for a moment, "Well I can understand that, but still… I didn't pick up on it when she told your aunt that she was hoping her baby would get a name soon. It flew right past me," Klee said throwing her hand up by her head.

Joshua began to explain an idea: "Telok talked with his dad, he talked to Moses and then he talked to me."

"Sweetheart, what did he talk about?" Klee said, taking his hands to help him focus.

"Well… Moses thought… tomorrow…. would be a good day for their wedding?"

"Tomorrow… Oh! Tomorrow… Like with us!?" Klee said with great surprise.

"Nothing is set and if you want our wedding to be just with us… that is completely fine. They won't be hurt, and they will just get married day after tomorrow. I just wanted you to have the final say," Joshua completed breathlessly; leaving her with a way out.

She looked into his eyes and after thinking the situation over she began to smile and told him, "I think that would be wonderful! They are so right for each other…" Joshua smiled at her, "I know they are."

"Oh! What about a gown for Naoon?" Klee asked in alarm.

"Don't worry about that. I'm sure the family will have something that will work. I'm just glad that you are excited about it." Joshua replied.

"Well, why wouldn't I be excited?! A double wedding with best friends; it will be amazing!" Klee said hugging Joshua. She whispered in his ear, "I still get you, one way or the other."

Joshua smiled and whispered back, "And I get you." As he gently stroked her cheek. "Let's go tell them that we want them to have their wedding tomorrow with us."

As they walked back up to the crowd Acts asked, "And where have you two been?"

"Talking over some grown-up stuff," Klee answered with her sisterly tone and smile.

"A double wedding!?" The imp hissed. "I must get word back to my master." He whispered under his breath. He looked in all directions. Not seeing any of the enemy, he slithered out of the camp.

Joshua and Klee went over to Naoon and grabbed Telok by the arm taking them to the other side of Nun's cart. Acts looked at Salmon and asked, "What's going on?"

"I don't know," Salmon answered as one of the little girls of the family climbed on his back.

"I'm going to check it out." Acts said curiously.

Salmon now had another little girl climbing on his back and all he could say was,

"Okay."

Klee took Naoon by the hands and said, "I am sooo... excited! Joshua and I want you to be married with us. I mean... not to us... married at the same time."

Telok replied, "You mean it's all right with you... we won't be intruding on your wedding day!?" Joshua put his arm across his friend's shoulder and reassured him that it was no intrusion.

Klee told Naoon that they needed to find her a gown and this made them giggle. The baby smiled and giggled as well. Just about that time Acts cleared his throat to let them know he was listening. Klee whirled about and said, "Just what do you think you're doing?"

"Recon!" Acts answered. "I knew something was up and decided to find out what."

"Well, you better just keep it to yourself. We want to tell the family together," Klee fired back.

"Oh, I wouldn't dream of stealing my captain's thunder," Acts said smiling at Joshua. "Nor my other Captain's thunder either," he added. Joshua smiled and looked at Klee, "Our secrets safe with him. I don't know about Salmon though."

This brought a laugh from the group and Joshua asked, "When should we tell the rest of the family?" It was quiet for a moment and Acts answered, "Tonight after supper; that's when I'd do it." Telok agreed, "Yes, that would be a good time. Everyone will be satisfied with the food, and it will be quiet for a while." Klee looked at Naoon and they both looked at Joshua and he replied, "Sounds good to me."

After supper and the little children were asleep, Joshua got up to address the family. He was excited and cleared his throat to get their attention.

"Well, I am proud... we... are proud to have all of you come to be with Klee and I, on such a wonderful occasion. This is something we never thought would've happened... To be married as a free people."

This brought praise for the Lord from the crowd. "Klee and I are very blessed... as we all are, and we feel even more blessed now that we have come to know that Telok and Naoon are to be married as well. We have invited them to have their wedding with us."

The crowd was silent for a moment and then laughter and praise broke out. The men got up and ran over to Telok and began to congratulate him as the women immediately began planning the gown. The realization of the wedding being the first since becoming free people began to sink into their hearts. The women came and escorted Naoon off to the carts and Telok took the baby. Holding the baby gave the men a preview of what Telok looked like as a father and then they began to congratulate Kemuel on becoming a grandfather. The scars on his face could not hide the proud smile Kemuel had as he hugged his son and the men standing with them

Chapter 18
The Wedding

The slithering little imp approached Satan as he bowed several times before speaking. "My lord, there is news in the camp. There is to be a double wedding."

"The first wedding in freedom." Satan smeared. "Who are the grooms?"

The imp replied with a sinister grin, "It is the Egyptian traitor and Joshua, my lord."

Satan got up and walked to the edge of the rock he was sitting on and peered down at the camp of the Children of Israel. His hate and desire mixed. He said, in a quiet voice, just loud enough that the small imp could hear, "I have a plan, and it will take some doing, but I think I will be able to eliminate these families altogether. I will go about it in a way, which will show that I am in control and NOT Him!" He turned to the imp and said, "Now go, and find out as much as you can of the plans, they have in leaving this place. Do not come back without word." The small imp bowed and backed away and was gone to fulfill his master's desire.

Satan turned his attention once again to the camp and focused on Naoon's baby. "She will make such a sweet sacrifice in worship to me."

~

After breakfast Klee and Naoon slipped away to look at their wedding gowns. They were beautiful; made with the finest colored linens from Egypt. The colors were brilliant, and the cloth was made of silk and wool woven together. Naoon looked at the women and said, "I don't know how to thank you for such a beautiful gown."

"You thank us like any girl of our family would… you just say… thank you." Joshua's Aunt replied.

Naoon smiled and looked at each one of them and to Klee and as tears began to well up in her eyes, she said with a breaking whisper, "Thank you."

~

Meanwhile, Joshua looked at Telok and asked, "Do you have something to wear other than that?" Telok replied, "What do you mean 'other than that'. You still have on the same thing you always wear."

"Well, I have something that may surprise you," Joshua said. Reaching around the corner of his dad's tent, he pulled out, not one, but two wool and silk cloaks that were as white as wool could be made. "Dad pulled these out last night when everyone was busy. He said he got them from the Eunuch that was over the Queens maidens or something like that before we left Egypt." "They certainly look the part of a wedding. I think we will look better than good," Telok commented.

Nun came from the other side of his cart and said, "Why don't you boys try them on… Let's see what you look like after a bath and your hair clean. I'll bet the girls won't even recognize you in the ceremony," Nun chuckled as he directed them into the tent. They didn't argue!

After the bath, each one felt like a prince. As they were finishing the final touches, Moses called out to the family and got everybody's attention. "We will have the ceremony this evening j…just as the pillars change. The men will not see the women until then. I will sound a soft signal on the ram's horn for everyone to gather under the two palms that bend down and touch each other; beside this first spring."

Everyone gave a sign of understanding. The girls stayed on the other side of a carts that was several over so that there would not be a 'chance meeting' before the wedding. They kept themselves entertained with the baby and Klee looked up at Naoon with a sudden realization, "The baby gets her name today!" Naoon paused and smiled, "Yes… I have been thinking of that all day."

"I just know that Telok has a wonderful named picked out for her," Klee said as she looked into her little face.

~

Joshua looked over at Telok and asked, "So… do you have a name for the baby?"

"No!! I haven't decided on a name. I want it to be special, but I want it to cause remembrance of what the Lord did here today," Telok said with frustration.

Acts looked over at them and said, "I know what I'd name her." Telok looked at his young friend and said, "I sure could use some help here!" "Her name should bring to mind the Great thing the Lord is doing today and where it happened… I'd name her 'Elim'." "What does 'Elim' mean?" Telok asked.

Moses walked up and answered, "Place of Renewal."

A smile broke out on Telok's face as he replied, "That is wonderful! What better way to begin two new families than at this; 'Place of Renewal."

Joshua looked at Acts and commented, "That 'whack' on your head gave you some sense little brother."

"I'd like to think that too, but I still have hesitations," Salmon said smiling at Acts.

Moses called Joshua and Telok over to talk with him. "I would like for you both to move up with me as we travel from here. While you are in your honeymoon state, I will have Acts and Salmon move your tents. Nun, his wife, and Kemuel are welcome to travel with us as w…well." Moses looked to each of them, and they responded with, "Yes Sir."

Acts caught Telok by the arm and said quietly, "Concerning your daughter… You would have thought of her name on your own… I just helped you."

"I thank you, little brother. I will give her the name and honor you in my heart for it," Telok replied with a smile. "Okay, but don't tell anyone else. It's just between us guys," Acts instructed as he looked at Joshua and Salmon. He knew Moses wouldn't say anything.

~

The time had finally arrived. Joshua and Telok took their places beside each other under the two bent palm trees.

Joshua said out of the side of his mouth to Telok, "You would have been standing beside me anyway." Telok smiled and answered, "I know my friend and the honor would still have been mine."

Acts and Salmon stood to the left of the grooms facing Moses. They were prouder today than any other day in their life. Moses turned and motioned for the girls to be ushered up next to the grooms. The women separated and as Joshua and Telok looked at their brides for the first time in their gowns, they were both overtaken with emotion and gratitude to the Lord. The women of the family sang a song of marriage and love that had been passed down from previous generations. When and where it came from was a mystery. Nonetheless, it was beautiful and moving.

Moses stepped up in front of the two couples and began to speak, "This is a great day in the Presence of the Lord. He has planned this day from the foundation of the world. His eyes have been on each one of you all of your lives and now... He is choosing to bless you with each other and make you into one family. He is the One who set marriage into place, and He is the One to keep it... if you will only love and trust Him. He will teach you how to love each other with His love and how to meet each other's needs. Ladies, the Lord has designed each of you specifically, to be the 'help mate' to your husband. Men, as husbands, you will be the security and provider for your wife as the Lord has designed you to be.

Standing in front of your family and friends as free people; this being the first w...wedding since being delivered out of captivity. He has led us and you to this place and now I ask you, Joshua and Telok, do you accept the responsibilities given you to protect and cherish your wife; to provide and love tenderly; and stand before the Lord as their covering mate? Do you, Joshua, take Klee as your wife; and Telok, do you take Naoon to be your wife?"

Joshua and Telok joined hands with their brides; Each looking into the eyes of the woman they loved. With voices strong and deliberate they said in unison, not planning it that way, "I do accept the responsibility."

Even though they said it together they didn't even notice it. Moses smiled to himself and turned his attention to the girls. "Do you Klee and Naoon accept the responsibilities of caring for the home and seeing to the needs of your husband; do you accept the responsibility of lifting your husband up to the Lord each day and choose to follow your husband wherever the Lord leads him?"

Klee looked into the eyes of Joshua and said with strength and commitment, "I do accept these responsibilities."

Naoon paused a moment and looking into the light green eyes of Telok and repeated, "I do accept these responsibilities."

Moses motioned for Joshua's mom to bring the baby to Naoon. He looked at Telok he asked, "Do you accept the responsibility of becoming the father of this baby girl; to raise her in the presence of the Lord as your own?"

Telok looked into Naoon's eyes and then to Moses and said, "I do accept the responsibility."

"Then have you decided a name for her?" Moses asked.

Telok looked at Naoon and to the baby. He paused so that he could take in the moment. The family was almost leaning forward in anticipation of the answer to the question. He looked to Joshua and Klee and turned to Moses and asked, "May I ask a question of Joshua and Klee?"

"Certainly," Moses answered.

Naoon also turned to face them as well. Telok asked, "Will you both accept the responsibility of becoming 'Parent Warriors,' who will stand to protect her and help guide her in becoming the woman of God she is to be as we raise her?"

Joshua looked into the eyes of the man who had started out as an enemy to him Telok had become not only a man of their nation, but a man of honor, after the Lord's heart, and had become a brother to him. Joshua turned back to Klee, who had tears flowing down her face and was unable to say anything at that moment.

Joshua looked back at Telok and said with commitment in his voice, "We do accept the responsibility of becoming 'Parent Warriors' for your daughter."

Telok turned to Moses and said, "Her name is to be…" he paused again. And with a strong voice he proclaimed; "Her name will be… Elim… for it is here that we found a 'Place of Renewal,' before the Lord."

At the sound of her name, the people began to shout and clap their hands. As the people continued to shout, Moses turned back to the young couples and leaning toward them a little, proclaimed: "You may now kiss your brides."

Joshua took Klee and pulled her in close. He leaned down and kissed his bride with great compassion, tenderness, and with a tear. She wiped the tear from his cheek and said, "I love you, my husband." And with a little break in his voice, Joshua answered, "I love you, my wife."

Telok stood in front of Naoon and took her face with both of his hands and pulling her close he kissed her tenderly. It was the kiss that Naoon had waited for all of her life. The memories of her past life faded away as she began a new life with Telok and Elim.

The happy couples would stay in two special tents. The men of their clan had stocked the tents with waterskins and the last of the dried fruit from Egypt that their families gave in love for the newlyweds. There they would spend two days in seclusion to share and learn more of each other. After a few minutes of the crowd celebrating, the heart of Naoon broke open into praise and she sang a song with a voice that captivated everyone present. Her voice was clear and low in tone; able to reach down into the very hearts of the people. She brought the song to a high tone that cut through the air just as a cool north wind brings a fresh feel on the face of someone who had been working in the field in the hot Sirius sun. She lifted the people in joy and led them into a great time of praise and thanksgiving to the Lord.

Chapter 19

Given Responsibility

As Acts and Salmon enjoyed playing games with the younger children, Salmon looked over at Acts and noticed him quickly step around the corner of a tent. with Acts gone, the children moved off to play another game. Salmon, curious, went over to investigate what Acts was up to. When he rounded the corner, Acts turned around and looked him in the eyes and then his right hand went to his right ear. As Acts fell to the ground Salmon caught him and laid him down easily on his back. "I've got you brother."

~

The mind of Acts began to move along a line of time, like following a rope. It seemed to be a long line, but then, he reached a stopping place. It was a scene in which people were angry. The movements were fast; alternating with slow. Like someone turning very quickly to look at him. Then suddenly seeing their hair swinging slowly around their head as they turned.

As he looked out over the crowd he could see faces, but he didn't really recognize any of them. It appeared they were shouting, but Acts couldn't hear them. He could see their facial expressions of anger, their mouths moving, and could read some of the words they were saying. "What are we to eat?" Acts scanned the crowd until he focused on Moses. The crowds were waving angry fists and continued shouting at Moses and Aaron.

His mind moved along the line of time again. Stopping, Acts looked and found himself on his hands and knees. The very thing that the people were shouting about had become a weight on his back. It was the weight of food. He could feel the weight and knew what it was, but he could not get it off of his back. It began to crush him and as his arms began to give way to the weight; his head hung low to the ground in struggle. As he tried to push against the growing weight, he looked to see the scared feet of the Warrior.

Suddenly, he could see the Warrior from behind as if he were watching from a different vantage point. The Warrior took hold of the weight of food and lifted it off of his back. He set the entire weight of food onto His own shoulders. Acts could feel the relief of great weight. As he looked up to see the Warrior, once again he saw the scars on His hands. He paused to stare at the scars and as he did the Warrior reached down to help him to stand. Acts began to stand and try to look into His eyes, but the Warrior turned to walk away. He was carrying the weight on His shoulders. Acts wanted to say something; wanted to thank Him, but he could only watch.

The line of time moved again. Now Acts was watching Moses and Aaron standing in front of the people. Moses raised his hands to the level of his shoulders and the crowd fell silent with every eye on him. Moses raised his hands above his head, the Warrior appeared above him, but Acts still couldn't see his face. The Warrior began to rise above the crowd. The crowd couldn't see the Warrior. Acts didn't know how; he just knew they couldn't. The Warrior held His hands out and food began to fall from His hands. The food fell on the people and Acts could see that it calmed their fears. Acts tried to look and see the face of the Warrior one last time, but as he looked up it was Salmon's face that came into focus.

~

Salmon didn't say anything but held his friend as if he would a fallen hero. Acts began to clear his mind, and he asked Salmon, "Was that one very long?" Breathing heavy, like he had run hard for a short distance.

"It was awhile; not you're longest... but it was close" Salmon replied. He helped Acts sit up and Acts commented, "Boy! Am I thirsty?"

As Salmon got up, he looked Acts in the eyes and said sternly, "You stay put." He paused a moment and then repeated, "Stay... put!" He went and retrieved a waterskin and was back within a minute. Acts took a long slow drink and thanked him. Salmon waited for Acts to get his thoughts together because he knew from past experiences... it took a few moments for Acts to get back to himself.

"That one was different. I never felt any fear, even though there were some things that should have caused a lot of fear," Acts said scratching his head. "I'm glad you were here Salmon. I don't like the thought of having that happen by myself."

Salmon looked at his friend and asked, "Are you ready to tell me about it?" "Yea, I need for you to hear it so that I can keep it straight in my head," Acts told him.

As he shared the events Salmon sat in complete amazement; as would a little child being told a magnificent story. When Acts finished, Salmon felt an urgency in his heart and suggested they go and tell Moses. Acts agreed and Salmon helped him to stand. After Acts got his balance, they started the walk over to Moses' tent. As they approached, Moses could see by their faces that something had happened. He felt in his heart that no one was in danger and concluded Acts may have experienced another vision. Reaching the tent, Moses motioned for them to sit down on a blanket he had spread out for visitors. He gave each boy a piece of dried fruit and a water skin for refreshment.

As Acts looked to Moses, he began to recount the vision. "I moved through time like following a rope. I don't know how long I traveled really because I stopped a couple of times along the journey."

Moses just looked at his young companion and let him develop his thoughts. Acts continued, "The people were shouting, but I couldn't hear them. I could however read some of their lips."

"What were they s…saying?" asked Moses. "They were asking, "What… are… we… to eat?" Moses paused and thought for a moment and asked Acts to continue.

"I started moving again. I saw you and Aaron and realized the people were shouting at both of you. I didn't know why… All of a sudden, I found myself on my hands and knees. I could feel a huge weight on my back. I was beginning to be crushed and I lowered my head to the ground to use more strength. The more I pushed the heavier the weight became. And somehow, I realized that the weight had become the very thing the people were shouting about; it was the weight of food. As it began to crush me, I brought my head up and I could see The Warrior."

Moses sat back quickly; he asked, "Was it the same Warrior as before?"

"Yes. When I saw His feet, the weight began to lift. I could feel him lifting the weight off of my back. I felt such relief. He reached down and helped me to stand. As I began to rise, I tried to look at His face, but He turned and started walking away from me with the weight of food on His shoulders. I wanted to thank Him, but I couldn't speak and then I moved along the line of time again. I could see you and Aaron with the people. I watched you raise your hands, and the people fell silent. You raised your hands again; higher and I could see the Warrior above you. As He began to rise above you and the crowd, I understood that they couldn't see the Warrior. Food started falling from the Warrior's hands onto the people. I could see that it calmed them and as I tried again to see the Warrior's face… it faded into Salmon's."

Moses studied his young friend and after a few moments, he asked, "Were you ever afraid?" Acts thought for a moment and answered, "No."

"I can see how this m…might coincide with the food supply dwindling. Everyone I have talked to is running out, and at the m… most we have two or three days left among the entire company. I can also see how the Lord will supply. He always does." Moses slowly turned his head and looked off into the distance for a moment and said in a low voice; "He always does."

Salmon added, "He provided a way of escape from Pharaoh, He provided a way across the Red Sea. He provided an incredible miracle when the walls of water came crashing down on the Egyptian Army. And He provided us with water. I don't think He's about to quit now!"

Moses smiled at the faith of Salmon. He could see how he had grown in his faith from the beginning of the exodus until now. Moses reached down and got a drink of water; wiped his lips and said, "You are right Salmon… He will provide and it appears we may be going into another time of testing. We are to start getting ready to leave Elim…" Moses paused to think of Naoon and Telok's little girl's new name and he smiled and repeated her name, "Elim."

Moses continued, "We are to travel into the Desert of Sinai which derives it n…name from the mountain called Sinai. I know for a fact that this desert is harsh. It will have no mercy on us, and we will have to depend on our God… There is no other way."

Acts and Salmon studied Moses as he said, "When the two days of seclusion are finished concerning our two young couples, it will be time for us to leave. I know as well… they will want to hear all about this recent vision. All of this is nothing to worry over… but… Acts…" He paused to look into Acts' eyes, "I think it would be best to only tell them. The vision was n…not frightening to you, but it would most certainly cause fear in the people. It boggles me that you have such keen sight in your visions. I don't begin to understand why the Lord speaks to you as He does, but I am not going to question Him about it."

Moses switched to a conversation of planning. "So, this is what I want you two, to do… I want both of you to s…sound the horns to call the runners; from every tribe. When they arrive, you will give these instructions: Tell the tribal leaders to begin preparations to leave and that I want them to be ready to pull out on the morning of the third day. We will leave in the same manner we have always moved, tribe after tribe.

When we stop each tribe and clan will stop where they are. We will not make camp the way we are now until we reach the place the Lord tells me. We will remain in a line until the signal is given to camp as we did here at Elim. Tell them to start raising their banners on the second day so that the people will know where to focus their attention concerning the location of the tribal leaders. They don't need to know the destination and if they ask, tell them the Lord is leading us with the pillar of cloud and fire. Ask for an estimation of the food we have and return with the answer by the morning of the second day."

Moses looked at the boys and could tell they needed some reinforcement of the instructions. "So… to recap; we are leaving three mornings from tomorrow; I want the tribes to be ready by the end of the second day; we will move in the same order and camp in a line until the signal to move again is given; and I want an estimation of the food by the morning of the second day. You are to get these instructions out as soon as you can."

When the boys smiled, he knew they understood. Moses added, "I need you two to be strong and courageous; do not falter in your faith even if those around you do. Keep looking to the Lord and everything will turn out as the Lord plans. There is no safer way."

The boys looked into Moses' eyes and said, "Yes sir." He gave each of them a hug and said, "Now go get the ram's horns from Aaron."

As they began to walk off Moses shook his head and said to the Lord, "They are becoming men, but still so young in stature."

"I know my friend, but I have given them the strength and faith to follow your instructions. They will complete the task. I AM about to do great things."

Moses fell in worship to the Lord as the boys walked off. He could only thank the Lord for even speaking to him…after all… "Who is man that You, O Lord, are mindful of him?"

It didn't take the boys long to find Aaron and as he handed them the horn's, he paused to just look at them a moment; he commented, "I am so proud of you boys… Uh! Young men…" spoken apologetically. They laughed as he corrected himself. The boys thanked him and turned to search out a spot to sound the signal to call the runners.

Salmon tugged on Acts shirt sleeve and pointed to a rock over by the spring nearest Moses and Aaron's tents and Acts agreed. They both climbed up on the rock and got comfortable. Looking to each other Acts said, "One." Salmon said, "Two." And they both said 'Three' and began to sound the signal for the runners to come from every tribe.

The sound of their signal was repeated like a ripple in water by the other tribes. All of the people knew what the signals were, and no alarm was felt by them. Everyone out to the very edge of the company heard the horns in reply within just a few minutes. They got down from the rock and stood there for a moment feeling good about what they were assigned to do.

Acts looked at Salmon and asked, "You want to go get something to eat from Joshua's mom?" Salmon replied, "Yea! Because Joshua's mom cooks like my mom." As they began to walk over, Acts looked at Salmon and said, "I wonder how the 'marriage seclusion' is going?"

Salmon had to laugh because of the way Acts said it and he just shrugged his shoulders and said, "I don't know… how's it supposed to go?"

"I don't know! I never have given it any thought. We'll have to ask them when they get back," answered Acts.

Nothing else was said until they saw Joshua's dad and greeted him, "Hello Nun." "Hello boys," Nun answered back. "Do you think we could ask your wife for something to eat" Acts asked. "You can ask her, but we are getting mighty thin on the supplies. Everyone's getting low on wheat, flour, and oil. But you boys go ahead and ask. I'm sure she'll find something for you."

He smiled and turned to go work on his cart. Abruptly stopping, Nun turned around to ask, "If you sounded the signal for the runners does that mean we will be leaving Elim soon?" Both of them answered at the same time, "Yes sir."

"Okay, then I guess I'd better get this axle fixed," he said as he turned and got back to work.

They looked at each other and turned to go find Joshua's mom. As she saw them coming, she pulled two honey bread cakes out from under a towel and had one in each hand for them. "You better enjoy these because this is the last of the wheat. I had just enough to make supper, and these were extra. I suppose I knew in my heart you two would come asking for them." She laughed a little as she said it, but all the boys could do, with their mouths full, was smile with expressions of complete satisfaction.

Chapter 20

Back Story

It didn't take long for Acts and Salmon to devour the bread cakes and get a drink. They filled several skins full of water to have ready for the runners and headed back to the rock from which they sounded the signal. Resting for a few moments, Acts laid his head down on the rock and Salmon got concerned; and then he heard Acts say, "Gotcha!"

Salmon did not appreciate that and told Acts as much, but Acts still found it amusing. A few minutes later the first runners began to arrive. Acts and Salmon handed them the water. They would wait for the others before giving the instructions and the runners were grateful for the rest. It would take a while for all of the runners to make it.

As they sat there with the other boys they made note of their ages; they were about the same age or slightly younger. Acts began talking to the boys to find out more about them. As the conversations started the runners began sharing how they looked up to Acts and Salmon and what a privilege it was to get to meet them. It made Acts and Salmon feel a bit uncomfortable. They did not see themselves in that light. It even humbled them because they knew they would not be where they were without the Lord leading and directing them to such a place of service. Acts explained how the Lord had moved in his life and Salmon shared as well. As they talked about the miracles of the Lord and the wonderful things that had happened, the time went by quickly and it seemed only a short time for the runners of the outer tribes to arrive. They gave them a few minutes to relieve their thirst and catch their breath. Acts then started with the instructions.

~

"These are the instructions given us by Moses. You will pass them to the tribal leaders: The tribes are to begin getting ready to leave Elim and they are to begin raising the tribal banners on the second day. Tomorrow morning will be the first day."

Salmon continued, "We will leave the morning of the third day." He emphasized again, "Tomorrow being the first morning. The tribes are to move in the same manner we have been moving but the path will get slim. It will be important for the runners to be spaced so that word can travel quickly. When the company stops for the night, the tribe and clan will camp where they are. There will not be room for the company to gather as we have here at Elim. When Moses reaches the place for the company to gather, we will sound that signal. Salmon turned to Acts.

Acts took the cue and continued, "If the tribal leaders ask about our destination; you are to tell them, 'We are going to follow where the Lord leads us with the pillar of cloud and fire.' Moses wants to get an estimation of the food supply and return with the answer by the second morning." He paused. "Do you have any questions?"

None of the young men had any. As Acts and Salmon stood, so did all of the runners. They told them goodbye, shook the hand of each runner, and made sure he was told 'how good a job he is doing". They each thanked Acts and Salmon and began the run back to their individual tribes.

Acts and Salmon looked at each other and Salmon commented, "Were they looking at us like… we… were important or something?" Acts watched them leave and replied, "Yea… I don't quite know what to think about that."

They turned to walk toward Moses' tent, in silence. As they reached Moses, he greeted them with a hug and asked, "How did it go?"

"Just fine," Salmon answered. Moses turned to look at Acts, "I asked both of you." Moses said with a bit more emphasis.

Acts thought for a moment and answered, "As we sat and talked with them… it seemed as though they looked up to us… like we were something more than we are."

Salmon added, "They are the same age as we are and yet they treated us like we were older or something."

Moses had a small laugh and tried to explain to them what had happened. "You two have been placed into the position of… of warriors; under the command of Joshua. Joshua is my s…second in command and because you serve with him, you serve me.

The Lord has placed me in command over the entire nation of Israel. There is probably not one young man in the entire c…company who doesn't wish to be where you both are. You both have been placed where you are by the Lord Himself. Your unique relationships have been forged by the Lord's design. For them it is an honor to be the runners and to have the orders passed on to them by Acts and Salmon… the servants of Joshua, the servant of Moses… that is why your encounter with them was… uncomfortable for you."

Even as Moses said it, Acts and Salmon still had a hard time looking at themselves that way. Their attitudes in service had been from the heart. To notice the way people looked at them was not the important thing. They just wanted to serve.

Moses smiled at them and told them 'not to worry about it. Just keep serving the way they had been.' Moses could not help but admire the young men for their humility and passion.

Since they had in their hearts the desire to serve. He decided to give them something else to do. "I hear that Nun is having to deal with some problems concerning carts in the tribes around him, why don't you go over and see if you can help him in any way?"

They eagerly jumped up looking back at Moses and said, "yes sir" as they took off. Moses didn't know if they were excited about helping him or seeing if Nun's wife had one more bread cake hidden away.

~

By the morning of the second day, runners were arriving with reports of the food supply. Each one of them gave the same report: only small amounts were found in each tribe. Moses hugged each boy and after they had rested a while he sent them back to their tribes.

Acts looked over at Moses' staff. It was also referred to as the 'Rod of God'. He wanted to ask Moses about the carvings on it, but he didn't know if this was the right time. The day was coming to an end and the time for leaving was approaching fast.

Moses turned to Acts and Salmon after the last boy left and said to them, "The food supply is shorter than I had anticipated. The land we are going thru is very harsh and the p…people are going to be tested again. The Lord wants to show them what is in their hearts. The Lord doesn't test us because He doesn't know what is in our hearts, but to show us where we stand in our faith and love toward Him." Moses continued, "We are headed for Mount Sinai. This is the very mountain I was on when the Lord spoke to me from the Burning Bush.

He paused a moment, looked at them, and asked, "I have never told you that story, have I?" They looked at each other and replied, "No sir."

Moses said to them, "Well, let me get the last of the dried fruit I have, and we will share it as I tell."

They sat down on the blankets as Moses shared the fruit and then reached over and took his staff. He pointed to the top of the staff at the first carving. It was the image of a burning bush with a hand in it. He began, "I will tell you in more detail sometime, but let me get to the mountain without a lot of the story up front." He told them how he had fled the land of Pharaoh even though he was raised in Pharaoh's house. He had to escape because he had killed an Egyptian Taskmaster for beating an Israelite.

"I went into this very same desert, and I met s…seven sisters, who were keeping their father's sheep. While I was resting at the well the women came to draw water and began filling the trough, for they were shepherdess'. I watched some m…men come to the well and begin to disrespect the women and make fun of them, driving them away. I could not just stand and allow this type of abuse. With all of my military t…training I easily overcame the men with a staff and a spear and sent them on their way (with a few bruises I might add)." This brought a chuckle from the boys. "The women went home and told their father, Jethro, what had happened. Jethro is the priest of Midian. I was invited to stay with them and… I… s…soon fell in love with Zipporah, his oldest daughter." He looked at them and said, "You didn't know that I was married, did you?"

The boys just shook their heads 'No' and Moses laughed. "There are many things you don't know about your leader." He refocused and began again, "We were married and soon I was a shepherd just as my wife and father-in-law. For f…forty years I was a shepherd and one day while leading the sheep far into the wilderness, I came to Mount Sinai. I looked up at the mountain and saw a flame. It was a color that I had not seen before.

I went up the mountain to investigate and found a burning bush. Strangely, the bush was not being consumed by the flame! As I approached the burning bush a voice came from the middle of the bush. The voice called my name twice, 'Moses, Moses' and I said, 'Yes, here I am.' The voice told me to not come any closer but continued, 'Take off your sandals for you are standing on Holy Ground. I AM the God of your fathers – The God of your father Abraham, the God of your father Isaac, and the God of your father Jacob.' When I heard this, I covered my face because I was afraid for my life."

Moses paused a moment because the boys were sitting there looking at him with eyes wide and their mouths open. "Do you boys want a drink of water?"

Without taking their eyes off Moses, each grabbed a water skin and took a big drink and then when they lowered the skin Acts said, "I was getting so thirsty."

"Me too" Salmon replied.

"Well, you were sitting there with your mouth's open that's why!" Moses responded with a laugh. "Do you want me to k…keep going?"

With great enthusiasm, they both said, "Yes sir!"

So, Moses continued, "After I took off my sandals, I came a little closer and heard the Lord speak to me again. **'I have certainly seen the oppression of My People in Egypt. I have heard their cries of distress because of the harsh treatment of their slave drivers. Yes, I am aware of their suffering. So, I have come down to rescue them from the power of the Egyptians and lead them out of Egypt into their own fertile and spacious land. It is a land flowing with milk and honey, and it is occupied by several different nations. Look! The cry of the people of Israel has reached Me, and I have seen how harshly the Egyptians abuse them. Now go, for I Am sending you to Pharaoh. You must lead My People out of Egypt."**

Moses paused, "But I told God, *who am I to appear before Pharaoh? Who am I to lead the p…people of Israel out of Egypt?"* Moses reached over and got a skin and took a big drink.

"What did the Lord say to you," Salmon asked with concern.

"Well, I tried to convince the Lord that I was *nobody,* but He wouldn't let me go. He said to me, **'I will be with you'.** To have the God of the universe tell you 'He will be with you,' was amazing! That meant something to me. Never had ANY god from Egypt EVER spoken to me, much less tell me that they would be with me. But I wanted out.

Then, The Lord said, **'and this will be your sign that I AM the One who sent you: When you have brought the people out of Egypt, you will worship Me at this very mountain.'** I still tried to get out of it again, if I go to the p…people of Israel and tell them, 'The God of your ancestors has sent me to you,' they will ask me, 'What is His name?' What should I tell them?"

The Lord told me, **'I AM… Who I Am. Say this to the people of Israel: Yahweh, the God of your ancestors – The God of Abraham, the God of Isaac, and the God of Jacob – has sent me to you. This is my eternal Name, My Name to remember for all generations.'"**

Moses looked at the boys to see if they were blinking. They were so captivated. As he paused each grabbed a water skin again and took a big drink and Acts asked, "What did He say next?"

He told me to go and call the elders of Israel. To tell them, **'The Lord, the God of your ancestors'** and He repeated them, **"The God of Abraham, Isaac, and Jacob – has appeared to me. He told me, I have been watching closely, and I see how the Egyptians are treating you. I have promised to rescue you from your oppression in Egypt. I will lead you to a land flowing with milk and honey."** I listed off all of the n…nations He had told me that were living in the land. **He told me, 'The elders of Israel will accept your message. Then you and the elders must go to the King of Egypt and tell him, The Lord, the God of the Hebrews, has met with us. So, please let us take a three-day journey into the wilderness to offer sacrifices to the Lord, our God.'**

Moses leaned over and got a drink, and the boys could hardly wait for him to get back to the story. He wiped his mouth and took in a deep breath just to mess with them and then he got back to it.

"The Lord said, **'But I know that the king of Egypt will not let you go unless a mighty hand forces him. So, I will raise My hand and strike the Egyptians, performing all kinds of miracles among them. Then at last he will let you go. And I will cause the Egyptians to look favorably on you. They will give gifts when you go so you will not leave empty-handed. Every Israelite woman will ask for articles of silver and gold and fine clothing from her Egyptian neighbors and from the foreign**

women in their houses. You will dress your sons and daughters with these, stripping the Egyptians of their wealth.'

And that is just what we did."

"Yea! My mom got all kinds of cups and cooking stuff from the Egyptians she was friends with," Salmon said.

Acts sat in thought for a moment and said, "I don't think Klee and I got out with much. Our family did not share with us. They took everything." He paused a moment and said, "But we got so much more with our new family. Joshua's mom got all kinds of cloth, gold and silver and other stuff… it filled their cart."

"And it fell on you," Salmon said laughing.

"Yeah, it's probably good that it wasn't a solid gold rake handle," Acts said as he laughed. After a few moments of lightheartedness Acts looked at Moses and asked, "Then what happened?"

"Well, I tried to get out of it for a third t…time, but the Lord just wouldn't have it. I told the Lord, *'What if they won't believe me or listen to me?* What if they say, 'the Lord never appeared to you'?" Moses said lifting his hands as though he were reliving the scene. "Then the Lord asked me, **'What is that in your hand?'** *A shepherd's staff,* I answered.

The Lord told me, **'Throw it down!'** So, I threw it down and it became a cobra. I jumped back." As he said it Moses threw his arms back and it made the boys jump. Moses continued, "The Lord told me, **'grab its tail,'** so (even though I know you don't grab a serpent by the tail) I reached down and grabbed its tail, and the snake became a shepherd's staff in my hand again.

'Perform this sign and they will believe that the Lord, the God of their ancestors – the God of Abraham, the God of Isaac, and the God of Jacob – really has appeared to you. Now put your hand inside your cloak.' So, I put my hand inside my cloak" and Moses demonstrated it before the boys. "When I pulled my hand out it was white as snow with leprosy. I began to panic, and the Lord told me, **'Now put your hand back into your cloak.'** So, I put my hand back into my cloak and when I pulled it out again, it was restored. The Lord told me, **'If they do not believe you… and are not convinced by the first miraculous sign or the second take some water from**

the Nile River and pour it out on the dry ground. When you do, the water from the Nile will turn to blood on the ground.'

But once again, and for the fourth time, I pleaded with the Lord, *Oh Lord, I am n...not very good with words. I n...never have been, and I'm not n... now, even though You have spoken to me. I get tongue-tied and my words get tangled. I am slow and hesitant.* Then the Lord asked me, **"Who makes a person's mouth? Who decides whether people speak or do not speak, hear or do not hear, see or do not see? Is it not I, the Lord? Now Go! And I will be with you as you speak, and I will instruct you in what to say."**

"So, I pleaded with the Lord a last time, 'No, Lord, please s... send someone else.' At this, the Lord became angry with me. **"What about your brother, Aaron, the Levite? I know he speaks well."** In Fact, He is on his way to meet you! He will be delighted to see you. Talk to him and tell him what to say.

The Lord seemed to calm His anger at me. **"I will help both of you as you speak, and I will instruct both of you in what to do. Aaron will be your spokesman and speak to the people for you. Then you will stand in the place of God for him, telling him what to say. Take your shepherd's staff with you and use it to perform the miraculous signs I have shown you."**

"That is how I came to be the leader of Israel. I didn't w...want to be. I desperately wanted out of the position, but the Lord had prepared me for this all of my life. I know what it is like to b...be of the very house of the king of Egypt. My Egyptian mother was the daughter of Pharaoh. I was trained by the very b...best warriors; schooled by the teachers and generals of the armies of Pharaoh. I knew how his house worked. I knew what they considered important and what was not. I loved my Egyptian m...mother and her family. They treated me as their own. My brothers were as much family to me as your siblings are to you. Or like you two and how you are toward each other now." He smiled at the boys.

"My Egyptian mother died while I was on the backside of this desert. I learned, a couple of years before I left, that my nursing m... mother and her family were not only Hebrew but my birth family. I grew to love her as my real mother whose name was Jochebed and my father's name was Amram, and I became close to my sister Miriam and Aaron even though I was of the house of Pharaoh. And when I killed an Egyptian to s... save a Hebrew I disgraced my Egyptian family and the house of Pharaoh and that is why I had to get out of the country because they would have m…made an example of me."

Moses paused a moment and returned to the call of the Lord, "I think that when the Lord told me to take off my sandals at the burning bush because it was 'Holy Ground.' He was setting me apart. He was bringing me into His Presence. He was teaching me how to approach Him. When He told me to throw my staff to the ground, He wanted to show me that it would not be by anything m…man would think of to deliver his people. I was to depend on Him and Him alone."

Moses picked up his staff and turned it to show the boys the carving on the top of the staff. "This is the burning bush." It was very detailed with the flames and hand in the bush. He went to the next carving that started down the shaft. "This is the number nine in Hebrew on this side and in Egyptian on the other. These are the nine plagues." Moses was very good at carving and the carvings were clear and smooth. Pointing to the next he said, "This is Pass Over." He looked at Acts and said, "You will recognize this as the tenth plague!" The carving had a door frame with a drop of blood over the door entry on one side. The 'Snake of Mist' or the 'Destroyer' was on the other. It looked just the way Acts had seen in his vision, and it surprised him. Moses noted the look in his eyes.

As Moses pointed to the next Salmon said, "That is the 'Walls of Water! The crossing of the Red Sea!"

"Yes. It is Salmon!" He smiled at him. "And the last one… for now, are the "Bitter Waters. I'm still working on it."

He slapped his hands on his knees and said, "I want you boys to get a good night r…rest because tomorrow will be a busy day getting everything ready to move." He smiled at them and mentioned, "Also, Joshua and Telok will be back, and they will want to hear all about what has been going on."

The boys stood and as they started to leave, Acts turned back and said, "Thank you for sharing that with us. I know parts of the story were hard. I know what it's like to *not* have a mom. Even though Klee tried to take her place… it just didn't seem the same. We kinda grew up together and I know Klee missed her too." He smiled and turned toward Nun's cart.

Acts got comfortable leaning against the wheel of the cart and Salmon found a place over against some baskets that allowed him to press into them. Salmon said, "I keep forgetting you didn't have a mom. I can't even imagine what it would be like to not have my mom."

"Well, I understand that, and I wouldn't want you to go through it. Besides, I have a whole new family now. Complete with a mom and dad!" Acts replied.

"Boy you've got that! Joshua's mom can really cook, and Nun can fix just about anything. Helping him with that axil today, I learned some things I didn't know. They really… are… your new… family," Salmon barely got out the words just before he fell asleep.

Acts looked up at the stars through the pillar of fire and spoke softly, "Yes, we are quite a family." He smiled and drifted off to sleep.

~

The next morning was the end of the 'days of seclusion' for the two newly wed couples. As they walked up to Salmon and Acts the couples could see they were still sleeping. Joshua and Telok couldn't help themselves. They appeared beside the boys without a sound and began to yell, "ANTS, BIG ANTS!!" The boys frantically jumped up brushing off their clothes and dancing around. Nun just about busted his gut laughing and so did Klee and Naoon. When the boys realized that it was just a big joke they laughed in a mocking manner and Acts said, "Yea, Yea you got us this time, but paybacks are coming!"

Joshua smiled and patted Acts' shoulder and said, "I know little brother and that would only be fair." Klee and Naoon gave the boys a big hug and Klee said, "I missed you guys." Naoon asked, "Did anything happen while we were gone?"

Acts looked at Salmon and then looked at Joshua and Telok and said, "You did miss another vision!"

Klee turned Acts toward her and said, "So what was it? I want every detail."

Chapter 21

The Key

As Acts began to recount the vision, Salmon would make sure he got all the details straight. Joshua, Klee, Telok, and Naoon were captivated. Joshua looked at Acts and asked, "Was it the same warrior as before?" Acts answered, "The very same one."

"And you have told Moses?" Telok asked.

"He heard the whole thing" Salmon answered.

"What did he say?" Klee asked.

"Well… he's still kinda thinkin' about it. He just said, we will treat it as a warning, and he mentioned that we should keep this in the family." Acts moved his arms in a circle and repeated, "I mean… in this family." Everyone took the meaning and nodded in understanding.

Salmon added, "Oh! There were the runners!" "What runners?" Joshua asked.

As Acts and Salmon got the men caught up on what was going to happen Klee and Naoon greeted the rest of the family. After getting through the greeting, Joshua's mom pulled the girls aside and said, "OK! I want to hear all about your time away," smiling as she said it. Klee and Naoon looked at each other and began talking; one following the other. It was 'girl time' at its best.

With the girls being busy, Kemuel walked up and gave his son a hug and got in on the conversation with the guys. Acts and Salmon did a good job of explaining all of the instruction that Moses had laid out. Joshua and Telok seemed impressed as they recalled the information.

~

In the back of the company, Korah and Abiram were again, stirring up the people in the area around them. Satan had been waiting for such an opportunity and dispatched his demon warriors. They were to move in and around the people to increase the number following the two humans. All the enemy had to do was to cast a few questions into the minds of the men and show them a little doubt and their human nature would do the rest. He whispered into Korah's thoughts,

"Is it going to be enough food or is Moses leading all of you to your death? It is just about time for a real leader like yourself to step up and point out the failures of Moses."

Korah agreed with his thoughts and the demon could see by the expression of his face that the bait had been taken. Korah turned to Abiram and said, "It won't be long now. The people will start to get very hungry and that is when we will take a stand and point out the failure of Moses and his 'so called,' leadership. Moses will be removed from his place of 'honor', he said smugly, and we can walk up and present the best ideas on how to lead the company. We will take the best parts of the land by force. We are enough to fight and to win; this is the old story we have always been told… the Lord promised us land and this land in the hill country looks pretty good."

"The Canaanites and Hittites are in control of this country, but with the numbers we have, I think we can overcome them and maybe even make them *our* slaves," Abiram replied.

As the demonic ranks scattered throughout the people, they would promote the fear of running out of food and raise doubts in the people's minds concerning the leadership of Moses.

~

By early morning Joshua and Telok were ready to go. All of the tribes were ready to pull out the next morning when the horns sounded. This would begin another time of testing. This had been a good place to rest and now they were to travel toward Mount Sinai as God told Moses. He didn't know exactly how far it was, but they knew The Lord was their guide. Again, it was not the distance traveled, but the journey.

Moses knew these people. He knew what different types of personalities existed such as Korah, Abiram, and Dathan; as well as others. Out of three million people there were those who only left Egypt to escape the slavery of Pharaoh.

Moses also knew he had to ready himself for this next part of the journey. He paused in his heart a moment and reflected on the days walked without water. It had been hard on him just like the rest of the people. He was not immune to the difficulty, but he also understood going without water was vastly different from going without food. This would be very difficult. He smiled and spoke softly, "It is safer to be in Your will, O Lord than any other place on earth."

Aaron walked over to him and looked at Moses' staff. "The carving of the 'Bitter Waters' is looking pretty good."

"It just needs a few finishing touches." Moses began.

Acts and Salmon were busy helping the clan with final preparations. Salmon said "It's only a couple of miles to my family. I think I will run out to them and see if they need any help."

Acts looked at his best friend and asked, "Would you like some company?" Salmon looked at him and smiled, "Anytime my friend!"

They found Salmon's dad had everything taken care of. Salmon asked his mother how the supplies were holding up.

"Well..." She began. "What we have is enough for tonight's supper, but the morning breakfast leftovers will be the last of it." She looked worried as she said it and then she added, "I hope Moses knows where we are going because the food situation is not only looking grim, but it is looking dangerous."

Acts and Salmon looked at each other and acknowledged her fears. They began to look around at the rest of the family and clan and they could see worried expressions on many faces. It struck an uneasy feeling in Acts and Salmon. Neither one said anything at that moment. Salmon waited a few minutes and added, "Isn't it amazing how the Lord has directed Moses in leading us? I look back over the past couple of months and I'm overwhelmed at what I have seen. And to watch Moses throw that long stick like a spear into the bitter waters of Marah, making it sweet to drink was so powerful. Acts and I have been with Moses, and we have seen his faith in action."

People of the entire clan began to gather around to listen.

Acts added, "The Lord is leading Moses and Moses is so faithful to listen and follow His instructions. There is no need for worry; the Lord knows what He's doing even if we don't. He has every single detail worked out and all we have to do is trust Him."

The family looked back at these young men and could not doubt their faith in the Lord or Moses. They could all see that being under

Joshua's command had taught them well. The family could see growth both in leadership skills and the courage to speak and they marveled at the young men. It seemed the moment they entered the camp and started to speak the level of faith in the family increased. Acts and Salmon didn't really notice it, but Nahshon and Salmon's mother did.

Acts just smiled at his best friend and watched him. 'He was quite the speaker,' he thought to himself. As the two began walking back to the front Acts looked over at Salmon and could feel Acts' intense stare at him and Salmon asked, "What?!"

"Oh... I was just thinking of how good a speaker you are." Acts replied. "I watched your family listen to you as you told them about the Lord and Moses. You had their complete attention as well as mine. You spoke with power because it came from your experiences, and it was compelling in how you presented your faith."

Salmon turned his gaze forward and commented in a low tone, "I really didn't even notice."

"That is a good thing; because you would have probably got your tang tungled."

They both laughed and Acts said, "Let's run. I feel like running." As they picked up the pace their feet fell into rhythm and soon, they were relaxed in mind. Each found thoughts of what the Lord might do to solve the problem concerning the food. Each one also knew that the Lord would probably do something they could never think of. They made it back to the front just as they were getting ready to bed down. Not much was said, and emotions were... level. All of them knew the coming days would be hard not only on their bodies, but they also knew their faith would be challenged as well. There wasn't any fear... it was more along the line of questions in each heart.

Questions such as: "Will I be able to stand on my faith? Will my body take control and force me to do actions I wouldn't normally do? How will I respond to other people as they waver in their faith or even abandon their faith completely? Can I stay strong for my family? It was these types of things that each person battled within their mind. Moses said it would be another time of testing... not testing for the Lord to find out what was in their hearts, but testing so *they* would know themselves what was in *their* own hearts.

Moses already knew that they were having questions and he prayed for the people, "Lord, I lift up Your people to You and I pray that You will give each man, woman and child… what it takes to come out on the other side of this test, a person who will trust You even more." He paused and smiled, "I… trust… You!"

~

The next morning came quickly, and everyone was up seeing to last minute details. Moses called for Joshua. "Gather your men. I want each of you to have a ram's horn. We will sound the signal when your men meet us here."

Joshua turned to go get them and Aaron looked at Moses commenting, "Joshua is a natural leader."

Moses looked back at his brother and agreed, "He is surely a leader called by the Lord." As Moses watched Joshua call his men he thought in his heart, "Now *there* are my F…Four."

Joshua walked up to Moses with Telok at his side; Acts and Salmon right behind them. Moses smiled and gave them each a hug and said, "It is time."

Each one took a direction and began to sound the signal and as they did the same sound was transferred from tribe to tribe until it reached the outer edges of the whole company and within minutes the entire company was moving. It looked like a slow dance with each family getting positioned within their clans and families forming into larger groups and all of them moving with the banners of their tribes. Moses stood and watched for just a moment; Turning he grabbed Aaron's arm and said, "My Brother we are going to s…see the Lord's hand in ways we cannot even imagine."

Aaron smiled and answered, "It is your faith that continually amazes me, little brother."

Moses patted his brother on the back and replied, "Thank you… for being the big brother who spoke to the King of Egypt with s… so much eloquence. We make a pretty good team." They had a quiet laugh together.

Salmon poked Acts and asked, "I wonder what they're talking about?" Acts looked and replied, "They're probably trying to figure out the 'warning' the Lord gave us."

"Yea… that would be something to talk about all right," Salmon said thoughtfully.

~

With all of the people on the move the dust began to rise and whirl about in the wind, lifting high into the air. As it reached the edge of the pillar of cloud shade, it changed color in the sunlight. Pausing, Acts looked up and pointed it out to Salmon. That got Joshua and Telok's attention and Joshua asked, "What are they looking at?" Telok replied, "Acts is probably seeing another one of the Lord's miracles."

As they turned to keep walking, they looked at their wives who were walking behind the cart with Elim in the back asleep. It was casual conversation and soon everyone fell into the rhythm of the walk. By the end of the first day everyone was ready to stop and get some shut eye.

The next morning came quick and soon the company was on the move again. Moses and Aaron were out in front following the pillar of cloud. It was at the end of the second day that the demons work began to show in the people, and they began gathering around Korah and Abiram. The demons stirred the people just like a hug pot of burnt stew starting with Korah's location and working outward as it would to the edges of a boiling pot. The people were beginning to respond to the doubt and questions the demons were throwing into their minds. They hurled the thoughts like rocks thrown at a target. It was quiet, but effective.

Satan rubbing his leather like hands and claws together, spoke softly, "These *children of Israel*," spoken with hate and disgust, "are so easy to manipulate. I will relish their praise when the time comes."

In the sea of people, the Angels of the Living God were disguised and watched as the demons moved among the people. Their orders were to watch and not interfere with the demons as long as no harm came to the people. The demons were unaware of the Angel's presence. The demons thought they were being clever and going unnoticed by the Angels but The Lord's will… is *always* hidden from Satan and his minions. They never for a second knew anything about the Lord's intentions. The Lord was using them to show the people what was in their hearts *and the truth*... would present itself in a matter of time. It was at the end of the second day that people began sharing with each other the fear they had about the food. The fear began to wound their faith.

Moses could feel what was beginning to happen and he told the Lord, "Lord they are beginning to doubt and have fear."

"I know my friend," the Lord responded.

"I'll have to tell you, Lord it is making me pretty uncomfortable," Moses added.

"Being uncomfortable is not such a bad thing, Moses. It keeps you on your toes and helps you watch and see how I will work. It can also make life more rewarding. I AM watching over you. Don't worry. I am teaching these people to lean on Me and not on their own understanding."

Moses took in a deep breath and replied, "I know that I sound like a child at times; in fact, most of the time. But that is how I feel. The way the people grumble, grabs my attention and that pulls my focus away from You. They see *Your* actions through me and that causes me to have pause. I see You as my life and I do not want to have any pride well up in my heart or cause them to stumble. You are everything to me and I don't want to displease You."

"Pride is something humans deal with on a daily basis. Pride is very offensive to me. It is what Satan used in the garden that led Adam and Eve to fall. It is Satan's pride that caused his fall from Heaven. Pride is a killer. And left unchecked, it will destroy you. But I am teaching you each day how to hold onto my hand; through the 'uncomfortable' times. It is love, Moses, which casts out fear and it is pride that casts out faith. I am teaching you how to walk in that faith and away from pride. Several times a day you can move your thoughts back to me by just whispering my Name.

I gave one of my names to Hagar who was Mother Sarah's servant girl. Sarah struggled to believe me when I said that she would have a son and because she felt "incapable" when I took some time to bring My promise to fruition. She gave Hagar to Abraham so that he could have a son through her.

While Hagar was pregnant with Abraham's son, she ran away from her mistress, Mother Sarah. I came and spoke with Hagar concerning her and the baby. I shared with her my name 'El-roi,' which is 'The God Who Sees Me'.

Moses, I do see you. And I love you and now, you have one of My Names."

Moses clapped his hands together and pulled them up to his lips. He began to dance around and sing to the Lord from his heart. He sang speaking the Lord's Name over and over; "El-roi, El-roi, The God Who Sees Me." He had walked a little ahead of Aaron and as Aaron watched him, Moses turned and called him to his side. His elation was contagious and soon Aaron was dancing with his brother. They walked and praised the Lord and after a while Aaron looked at his brother and asked, "Where did you get that name?"

Moses looked back at his brother with tears in his eyes and exclaimed, "It is One of the Names of our Lord God. He g... gave it to Mother Sarah's servant girl, Hagar, and now He has given it to me." He clasped his hands together and breathed out long and slow. "As I was walking with Him… he told me… 'He sees me.' He gave m… me His Name… El-roi. I was completely overtaken by what He said."

Aaron stopped walking and said to Moses, "Sarah's who?"

Moses had forgotten that what the Lord was telling him had never been written down and most of the history of the Hebrew people had been lost over time. The stories tried to be shared, but as the generations passed so did the stories. Aaron looked at his brother and said, "It just amazes me how sensitive you are to His voice."

Moses continued, "The Lord was talking to me about p... pride and how to keep it in check in my own life. I spoke to Him about how I did not want to get in the w…way of His will. He told me that if I wanted to get my pride in check all I n…needed to do was whisper His Name... The God who sees me."

Moses looked around, "Here is where we will stop tonight. Have the Four," meaning Joshua and his three warriors, "Sound the signal to stop here." Aaron turned and walked back to Joshua and said, "Moses would like for his 'Four' to sound the signal to stop." Joshua looked back at Aaron puzzled. Aaron answered his silent question, "That is Moses' name for you and your men, 'The Four.' It's kinda catchy," Aaron said with a laugh. Joshua smiled and repeated, "The Four." As he turned to get the attention of his men he repeated it again, "The

Four." He thought about it a moment and decided that he liked it. As his men came to him, he told them to get their horns; it was time.

~

In a matter of minutes, the signal was passed, and everyone began to prepare for the night's rest. The company had been resting in more of a linier line due to the terrain and not the way they had before camping at Elim. Korah and Abiram had been watching the people and they were convinced that the tribes immediately around them were beginning to see things their way. So, with the darkness upon them and everyone beginning to bed down they began to share with those in their vicinity, the plans of taking the hill country for themselves. They would take it by force and even make those who occupied the land, their slaves. As the hunger in their stomachs grew the plans of Korah and Abiram had begun to look like a logical step to take.

Korah emphasized, "Moses doesn't really know where we are going and therefore, he doesn't know the way." As Korah spoke, the demons milling around the people would speak words of reason into their minds; making Korah seem like a wise and a good leader.

This only brought pleasure to Satan as he watched his plan working; the only thing that would bring more pleasure at this time would be a plan for the death of the young human, Acts; but he had yet to come up with a plan. He would never admit that to any of his minions. It puzzled him; he was determined to figure out how he could get to the young man. But he could be patient and would keep looking for the right time. He had already picked the three demons from his army that would carry out the deed. He smiled as he relished the thought of killing him. It made his mouth actually water to dwell on the thought as he sat back beside the rock from which he watched the boy ever so intently.

That night it was harder for people to go to sleep. The hunger grew inside them and in the children. When children do not sleep those around them do not sleep and this only compounded the stress. The demons of Satan were working all through the camp; not just around Korah and Abiram. They were casting 'thought rocks'; questions into people's minds, as quickly as they could because they knew the humans would eventually fall asleep and they wanted to cast as many doubts as possible. *Does Moses really know where he is going?*

What will we do for food? How long is this journey? Has he thought about the children?' These questions and others played heavily on the human frailty that was being led into a wilderness. It was a wilderness that seemed to have no plan of survival. This uneasiness seemed to only play into the confusion and stress of the people.

~

As difficult as it was for everyone to try to rest, it was just as difficult for Acts and those around him. Their stomachs growled as much as anyone else. He listened for Elim to cry out, but because she was still breast feeding Naoon was able to keep her satisfied. It was hard on Naoon's body to produce milk under such harsh elements.

Telok was a good husband and would get her water when she needed it. He would hold Naoon and stay awake with her when Elim was awake. Telok was very sensitive to her feelings and that made her feel more secure.

Joshua was just as intent on seeing to Klee's needs. There wasn't really a lot to be said; still they reassured each other by seeing after each other's needs, but also to the clan that traveled around them.

Acts looked over at Salmon, who had, within minutes of stopping began helping Nun inspect the cart to make sure everything was working well. Salmon had a real heart of service, and it didn't matter if it was handing down instructions from Moses or working on a cart axial, his heart was always concerned with helping others. That was one of the things about Salmon that made Acts proud to have him as a best friend.

Acts looked up toward Moses' tent and could see him slowly walking around and could tell by his body posture and hand gestures that he was talking with the Lord. Moses was a very animated person; he used his whole body to convey his thoughts. That was one of the things that made it so fun to listen to him.

Acts lay his head back on a blanket and looked up listening to the sound of his own stomach talk to him. He began to think about this 'test' they were in. He included himself in the thought because it wasn't just the people of the company, it involved him as well. Just because he was given the vision didn't mean he was excused from the test. He felt the hunger and the pain as much as the next person. What he did have was the knowledge that it was... a test. It was a test given by the Lord. And he knew that the Lord would never hurt His children for the fun of it or out of spite. Moses had taught them of God's love and how His Hand was watching over them. His hand was not placed in a position to smite. But still, the hunger was there, and it did cause other thoughts to creep in without the help of a demon. The human frailty always questioned anything that denied it what it thought it needed. That is what brought the most concerning question to Acts: 'What were Korah and Abiram doing with all of the questions and fear of hunger that would only fuel the plans they had against Moses and Aaron?' He knew they would most certainly use this time to gain a following and that could prove to be dangerous, not only to Moses and Aaron but to him and his family as well. It was this thought that caused him to stay awake just a while longer. He knew these men had a great prideful desire to have a position of leadership and to be praised. The thoughts swam a few moments in his mind as the sleep he needed overtook him. The questions and the wondering faded.

~

The morning of the third day began the march to the destination in the Desert of Sin that God had shown Moses. The people seemed to get up in a mood that was sharp toward each other. As Joshua and Telok looked around at their clan they could see and hear husband and wives biting at each other with their words. And the scowls on their faces spoke much of what was happening on the inside of each person.

Naoon and Klee were walking together and began to notice the mood of the clan as well and it made them feel very vulnerable for some reason. Naoon got Klee's attention as she watched one of Nun's cousins almost hit his wife when she asked a question. She spoke in a low tone, "Klee, did you see that?"

"Yes," Klee said just as quietly. "I thought he was going to hit her. I have never seen that type of action… ever… demonstrated in any of Joshua's family."

"I want to guard against that so much… I don't ever want to treat Telok like that," Naoon said with a break in her voice.

"Me neither," Klee answered. "But again, I can't see Joshua or Telok acting that way toward either of us." She paused for a moment and added, "I know they are only human, and I know we are newly-weds, but I can't help but see them as being stronger than some of the other men in the company."

"I agree…" Naoon replied. Klee lowered her head to look down at the ground and told Naoon, "I will have to say I have had questions in my heart that I can't find answers to…"

"What are they?" Naoon asked with a concern in her voice. "I can't help but ask if we really know where we're going? I mean the hill country looked green in the upper elevations. Why aren't we headed there instead of… into more wilderness?" Klee told her in a quiet voice; with some embarrassment.

Naoon thought carefully before saying a word, "I don't think questions are dangerous if we are able to tie a rope around what we know has happened and use it as an anchor. You know as well as I do what we saw the Lord do in Egypt. You know how He has treated us since and just because you have questions does not erase any of what His loving Hand has done. You and I will have many questions. I think the way to approach these questions is to keep a tight grip on that rope of what we know in our hearts. I can see that sharing with each other is a way of maintaining a good grip on our faith, and even when our grip weakens, we will be able to hold on and encourage each other during those times. I will hold on to you and I know without a doubt you will hold on to me."

Naoon's words spoke nourishment to Klee's heart. It was in moments like this, the bond between them grew stronger. The hunger within them weakened as they found strength in sharing with each other.

~

Telok looked over to where Joshua was walking and could see him talking with his father. He walked over to them and said, "I was having a thought." Joshua and Nun smiled at him and Joshua asked, "I know you have good thoughts… so what is it?"

"Do you remember the questions we had during the first test without water?" Joshua nodded his head 'yes' and Telok continued. "I know we have learned from that, and I began to think of what made us able to… to stand in our faith. I believe that it was in sharing our struggles and encouraging each other." Nun nodded and commented, "I had questions of the same nature."

"We were all having the same types of questions, but we were timid in telling each other; not wanting to question Moses' leadership. Once we did share with each other it seemed that our faith joined, and we were able to reaffirm our trust in Moses and what the Lord was doing," Joshua explained.

"It was in the actual act of sharing that helped us break down what was going on in our minds. The questions were there… but being uplifted from our brothers, our hearts were able to hold to our faith," Telok added.

Nun asked, "But this test… this time is different?"

"Yes… because we know that it is a test." Joshua thought for a moment and decided to tell his dad about the vision Acts had and how it related what was happening now. As Joshua recounted what was told to them, Telok gave his approval that the context was accurate.

Nun thought about it for a moment and said, "Well that puts a new light on the subject. To know that it is a test can certainly bring about a new perspective. I'm sure that if most of the people knew of the vision that would also reassure them that the Lord has not abandoned us, and He is still leading us through Moses."

Nun paused a moment to think, combing his fingers through his long black and gray hair and said, "I know that our walk with this 'new' God has only been birthed for little more than a few months. And trust does not come easily with me because I have seen and experienced the failures of the gods back in Egypt. To pray to them and watch one of your own family die at the hands of forced labor leaves me with some 'trust issues'. To tell you the truth, my heart was, before we had this talk, starting to doubt Moses in a big way. And now that we have shared our thoughts with each other I have a tool with which to help heal my broken trust. Being able to share my thoughts and have someone, like you two men, will help keep me accountable in holding true to my faith." He chuckled and said, "It is amazing what a few words can do."

Chapter 22
Totally Unexpected

The faith of the company of Israel as a whole was not standing well. Satan had, through the work of his minions, fueled doubt in many others besides Korah and Abiram. Through the walk of that day, man's human nature had not only sprouted, but was beginning to show the fruit of that doubt in their actions. The rest of that day seemed to speed their pace. Their anger was evidence of the conflict they were having inside.

Moses had given the instructions to sound the signal and stop, but there was a large crowd that kept walking so they could approach Moses. The place where Moses stood was on an elevation that allowed him to watch them approach. Joshua quickly called to his men. As he grabbed his staff from his father's cart the others did the same. They formed a line in front of Moses and Aaron and watched as the crowds gathered. Moses looked into the faces of The Lord's people and had compassion for them because he knew that this time of testing was not easy for them. He was experiencing the same hunger and could completely identify.

Suddenly Acts' vision became clear to them as they each realized they were watching it unfold before their eyes.

Korah and Abiram had moved all the way from the middle part of the company to a position in which they were able to step in front of the crowd to challenge Moses. Korah surveyed his position and could see Joshua and his men ready to defend if needed. The size of the crowd gave Korah the courage he needed to approach Moses even though Joshua and his men were within striking distance.

Korah wasted no time with greetings and stated, "Have you led us into this wilderness to die?" This brought a loud response from the crowd.

Dathan voiced, "If only the Lord had killed us back in Egypt." The crowd again responded fueling the three men on.

Then Abiram spoke out, "There we sat around pots filled with meat and we ate all the bread we wanted. But now you have brought us into this wilderness to starve"

This brought a response from the crowd which prompted Joshua and his men to perceive an actual level of threat: if a man stepped forward, they *would* be stopped. The noise and the men throwing dirt in the air did not move Moses. He studied the crowd for a long moment and looked straight into the eyes of Korah and then Abiram and finally Dathan. The stare caused them to become very uneasy and they began to look away from the penetrating eyes of Moses.

As Moses surveyed the situation, he heard the still small voice of the Lord calling him to pull away and have communion with Him. Moses looked out across the crowd and decided to keep a little distance socially, for that moment. He called Aaron to his side and told him to tell the people: "The Lord is calling Moses to discuss this matter. All of you will wait until he has returned from speaking with the Lord. No one is to leave. As Aaron spoke the words of Moses, the crowd became extremely uncomfortable which in turn made Korah and Abiram the same. They had not taken thought that the Lord would call Moses to speak with Him.

Moses turned and walked away from the crowd while Joshua and his men stood their ground. Their stance confident; showing no fear and Joshua spoke a warning to the crowd: "No one is to approach Moses or Aaron without an invitation." Moses smiled at Joshua as he turned.

Several yards away from the people the Lord began to speak to Moses,

"Look I am going to rain down food from the heavens for all of you.", speaking the words as if telling Moses that it was because of him specifically. He then gave Moses instructions concerning the food from heaven.

"Each day the people can go out and pick up as much food as they need for *that day*. I will test them in this to see whether or not they will follow My instructions." Again, He was going to show them what was in *their* hearts so they would have a clear understanding of their obedience or failure to His instructions. Moses stood with the Lord and received the rest of His instruction concerning the food from heaven. As soon as the Lord was finished, Moses turned and called Aaron to his side. He shared with Aaron all the Lord told him. They both turned back to the crowd and Aaron began to lay out everything.

The news of the crowd going to meet with Moses had already been making its way through the entire company of Israel. The people, not having anything better to talk about, gave fuel to a fire that spread as if the wind were feeding it. The talk among the crowd was like a low roar and as Aaron began to speak, the people in the crowd became quiet. Aaron gave the instructions first to the crowd in front of them and then he raised his eyes to the rest of the company of Israel. And as he did, once again, he could be heard by the entire company as if he were standing next to each individual. This miracle alone served as witness that the Lord himself had given the instructions to Moses and Aaron. No one dared question the instruction for fear of what this new God of theirs would do.

~

Aaron began, "By evening you will realize it was the Lord who brought you out of the land of Egypt. In the morning, you will see the glory of the Lord, because He has heard your complaints, which are against Him, not against us. What have we done that you should complain in regard to us?"

Moses added, "The Lord will g...give you meat to eat in the evening and bread to eat in the morning. Take instruction how you are to gather the food that our Lord supplies."

Aaron turned back to the crowd and continued: "Each day you are to gather enough food for you and your family. There will be exactly what each person will need. Do Not keep any of the food for the next day. You are to go out each day and gather what you will need for that day only.

On the sixth day, you will gather twice as much as usual and prepare it because the seventh day is to be a holy day of rest, dedicated to him. By this you will know that it was the Lord Most High that brought you out of the land of Egypt."

Moses raised his staff and said, "See the Glory of the Lord!"

As the people turned to look at where Moses pointed, every person in the company could see a cloud off in the distance in the same direction they had been traveling. The cloud boiled and moved with great power of lightening and fire as though it could reach out and touch any person in the company. The sound of the cloud could be felt in their very core.

It was terrifying to the people, but to Acts it was the Glory of the Lord he had longed to see. His heart began to pound in rhythm with the lighting in the cloud. At that moment, he could only pause in his heart to praise the Lord! As the lightening flashed, Acts could see in the cloud the form of a Warrior with a sword in His right hand and His stance ready for battle; His size as tall as the pillar of cloud; His sword glistened with all of the colors in a rainbow. The cloud moved with such force and power that it shook the ground under the feet of the people. The people where frightened beyond words and could not speak. Acts took in every second and looked with longing eyes to see the Warrior more clearly. Acts' gaze was so intense that it caught the eyes of Joshua, Telok and Salmon. And then they noticed the people. They could see how the people wanted to cry out in fear, but no one made a sound. The people somehow found comfort to have Moses standing in front of them; between them and the Glory of the Lord appearing in the cloud.

Moses turned back to the people and raised his other hand and pointed, "Now… watch, and see the wonderful provision of the Lord God who brought you out of the land of Egypt."

As the people stood there, a vast number of quail began to fly into the camp and cover the ground. At once the crowd of people dispersed and every grown adult began to collect the number of birds for their family and prepare them. In only a couple of hours the aroma of food began to fill the air.

Joshua walked over to Moses and Aaron, "Klee and Naoon have prepared the meal, and we would like for both of you to join us." They agreed and joined the two new families; each of them enjoying the sweet fellowship.

Acts kept looking in the direction of the cloud and finally Salmon asked, "What are you looking at?" Acts blinked a few times and then suddenly understood what Salmon was asking and he replied, "I can't get over the amazing site in the cloud. It was the most wonderful thing I have ever seen: Even better than being on the cliff after we crossed the Red Sea."

"It was almost… a little scary to me," Salmon commented back unsure of his feelings.

"I could see the 'Warrior' in the cloud. He was standing ready for battle with a sword in his right hand. The sword was made up of every color of the rainbow; it was awesome!!" Acts shared with passion.

Salmon looked back at Acts and asked, "Was it the same 'Warrior' you have seen in your visions?"

"Yes! I believe it was." Acts answered. "Are you sure? The cloud was rolling and moving so much…" Salmon squinted.

"I couldn't see the scars in his hands or feet, but I just felt it was Him," Acts stated with a slight degree of defense. Deep down, he knew that Salmon was just trying to understand what he was talking about.

"Wow! I wish I could have seen Him too!" Salmon said with a bit of disappointment. Acts looked at his friend and asked, "You didn't see the 'Warrior'?"

"No," replied Salmon. Acts looked back at his friend and told him, "I am sure that you will see Him one day."

In the distance, Klee shouted with a loud voice, "Acts… Salmon… come and eat."

"Now that is a lovely sound." Acts told Salmon. "You bet it is." Salmon said slapping his knees as he jumped up.

The food and fellowship together was exceptionally good as they all sat around eating the quail, roasted over the fire. Moses couldn't help but reflect back through what had happened. The vision Acts had was so very clear now: "Food was falling from the Warriors hands." He spoke this to himself as he looked across the fire at Acts. Moses smiled as he looked at the young man who was… *so very sensitive to the Lord*. He thought back through the instructions the Lord gave. They were so very specific and he questioned in his heart, "Will they obey or not?" After a moment, he passed the thought to the side of his mind and went back to enjoying time with the families.

That evening all the people of Israel went to sleep with full stomachs. There were some who even fell asleep pondering on what the Lord had done that day. But there were the few, like Acts, who fell asleep in the awe and wonder of the Lord. It was in those few, like Acts, Salmon, and the family that the Lord would speak to as they slept. And in those dreams, He would expand their faith to walk in a way that was pleasing to Him. Those were the hearts, willing and ready to receive what the Lord had to offer in their obedience.

~

The next morning Acts was awakened to being feverishly poked by Salmon; "Come on Acts! Come and see the ground! It looks like frost."

As Acts found his way out of the sleep he was enjoying, he looked around, and could see what Salmon was so excited about. He looked at Salmon and then to his sister and asked, "What is it?"

The rest of the camp was acting in the same manner and as Moses came walking up, he laughed and said with a loud voice, "It is the 'B... bread of Heaven' that the Lord said He w...would provide." He looked at Acts and said, "Pick up a piece and taste."

Acts reached down and took a piece and ate it. His eyes opened wide as he proclaimed, "It tastes like honey wafers; only better!" Salmon reached down and took a piece and laughed and said, "It's delicious... It tastes better than honey wafers!"

As the wind blows coming from one direction and moves across the land, so the sounds of people tasting the bread moved across the company. People began to pick it up holding it in their robes. Those who wanted a sizeable portion got it, and those who could only eat a little ate all they wanted. Every person had the exact amount they needed for the day.

Acts said, What is this food from the heaven's called? I've never seen or tasted anything like it before.

Salmon looked at Acts and said, "That's what we should call it... Manna, meaning... What is it!?"

Acts, replied with his mouth full, "Manna... I like it!"

And so, Salmon gave the name, Manna to the delicious bread and soon every person in the company was calling the 'Bread from Heaven' ... Manna.

As the day passed the manna on the ground melted away but there were some people who still did not trust the Lord to provide as He said and kept extra, hidden... trying to keep it for the next morning. The evening came and brought quail for all to eat just as it had the day before, but when they awoke, they found the manna full of maggots and it had a powerful, rotting stench. The smell was overwhelming and caused people to gag. Moses, realizing that some of the people had tried to keep it, became very angry. And in his anger the Lord allowed the entire company to hear and feel his anger.

"DID NOT the Lord give you specific instructions? DID HE NOT spell out to you just what you were to do? The Lord will give us our daily bread. He will provide EXACTLY what is needed for each day." Moses paused, taking in a deep breath, and then let it out. He looked out across the mass of humanity; his initial anger passed, he began to speak with a calmer attitude, "Learn… LEARN to t… trust Him. The Lord, God is so intense in His love for you and even more powerful with His care for you… but you must trust Him. He is The Lord, The One and Only God who brought you out of the land of Egypt."

~

Moses and the people continued to move for a couple of days before preparing for a day of rest. The Lord faithfully provided all they needed in the way of food. Moses was leading them in the direction of Mount Sinai. The terrain was very rough and some of the passes were very narrow. While walking in the wider spaces Moses would walk slowly so the rest of the company could catch up. In the evening and on the days, they didn't travel, the people would come and bring all of their problems to Moses for him to resolve. They would come all day to the tent of meetings and Moses would patiently listen and then pronounce the decision that needed to be made. At the end of those days, Moses was completely drained, and the family began to worry for him.

As the days went by, the people began to notice the water supply starting to dwindle. Some began to question in their hearts as before. The thirst they felt at Marah was still on their minds, and in their fear, the salvation of the Lord was not. Many of the people only understood living from one moment to the next, failing to see the faithfulness of the Lord throughout their journey.

Finally, on the eighth day of moving they came to Rephidim which is not far from mount Sinai. At Rephidim they found a dry pond and several empty wells. The people turned to Moses and began to grumble with anger. The tribes closest to Moses again, decided to march toward him and as before Joshua and his men took their place to defend Moses and Aaron. As the people walked up, they were shouting, "Give us water to drink!!"

It was not Abiram or Korah this time and Nahshon was holding his tongue as well, but nonetheless the people began to shout with one voice; *Give us Water to Drink*!! Some of the men even tried to make their way through Joshua and his men.

Joshua took his staff and bending toward one of the men, moved his staff behind the man's knees and pulled his legs out from under him. The man hit hard on his back and all the air in his lungs rushed out. The other men immediately stopped. Joshua stood over the man until he got his breath back and said in a calm voice, "Please do not approach Moses or Aaron without an invitation." The statement was heard throughout the crowd. Even though he spoke in a calm voice the command was still very strong.

After the man was able, Joshua put his hand out and helped the man up. Joshua looked at him and said, "I'm sorry I had to do that." The man just looked at Joshua and said, "Me too."

The crowds began to yell again but Moses said, "Q... QUIET!" and the command got their attention. With his voice raised a little louder and with confidence he spoke to the people, "Why are you complaining against us? And why are you once again, testing the Lord?"

But tormented by thirst they continued to argue with Moses. "Why did you bring us out of Egypt? Why are you trying to kill us, our children, and our livestock with thirst?"

Moses turned his back to the people prayed earnestly to the Lord, "What am I to do with this people, they are ready to stone me?"

The Lord said, **"Walk out in front of the people. Take your staff, the one you used when you struck the water of the Nile, and call some of the elders of Israel to join you. I will stand before you on a rock at Mount Sinai. Strike the rock, and water will come gushing out. Then the people will be able to drink."**

Moses turned to Aaron and said, "Call the elders of Israel and the tribal leaders who are in the first five tribes and tell them to come to me now."

So, Aaron said to the people, "Send runners to the elders and tribal leaders who are in the first five tribes. Tell them they must come to meet with Moses… Now!"

At once five runners were sent out and passed the word to the next until the very words Aaron had spoken were given to the tribal leaders of the five tribes: Judah, Issachar, Zebulun, Reuben and Simeon.

It took half of the day for all of the tribal leaders to reach Moses. These tribal leaders were Nahshon who is Salmon's father, Nethanel, Eliab, Elizur and Shelumiel. There were also several other men who were considered elders; men of good standing.

Because they had been invited by Moses, Joshua and his men let the group pass through. As they walked up, they began to spout out the demand for water. Nahshon was the only one to hold his tongue for he was not in agreement with the other tribal leaders as they approached Moses and Aaron. Moses looked at them and said, "Silence!"

They became quiet and then he continued, "You will accompany me to a place out in front of the company of Israel." Moses turned and grabbed his staff and began to walk with nothing else said. Joshua and his men stayed in their positions between their leaders and the rest of the crowd. Moses and the men walked for at least a half mile and then Moses looked into the distance toward Mount Sinai, raising his hand to stop the elders for a moment. He stared for only a moment, but to the elders, it seemed longer; no one said anything. Moses smiled because he could see the Lord standing on a rock just out in front of them about a hundred yards. The grade was steep up to the rock and the men were getting winded. Moses stood there in awe of the Lord and in his heart, he praised Him and thought, "If only Acts were here." And then suddenly remembering the men who had walked with him he turned and said, "We must go a little further." And he turned to continue walking. As they approached the rock, they could see it was a huge boulder. The men began to question where Moses was leading them because all they could see was this enormous rock.

Moses turned to the men and said, "Stand now… and see the wonderful provision of the Lord God Almighty who brought you out of the land of Egypt."

He turned and with his staff, he struck the rock just as the Lord had told him to do and water came gushing out from a crack that had appeared at the top of the rock. The flow was so fast and full that it created a powerful river within moments. As the water flowed right down the center of the company of Israel, it widened and soon it was more than twenty yards wide. The people began to shout and dance around! As the water flowed past them, so did the praise and laughter. One tribe after another began to experience the refreshing water flowing from the rock. As they tasted the water it was purer than anyone had ever had. The water flowed through all of the company and then was taken in by the land as it passed the last of the animals that traveled with the tribe of Naphtali. Moses named the place Massah Meribah, which means to 'Test and Argue,' in the pure form of their language. For it was in this place they tested the Lord and argued with Moses and Aaron.

The water would continue flowing from the rock until they left that place.

~

Moses turned to Joshua and pulled him to his side to speak with him quietly. "I tire of these people and their whining. Now that the Lord has given them water, I would like to visit the rear of the company while we are camped here at Rephidim. We will be here for a few days and it will give me some time of rest, away from the front." Joshua understood what Moses was talking about because he was tired of the whining just as much as Moses.

Moses instructed, "I want you to get your men…"

Joshua could not hide the look of disappointment on his face as Moses spoke the words. He did not want to leave Klee at this time. But Moses already knew what his warrior was thinking, and he continued, "I want you to also get your wife, and Telok's wife and daughter ready as well; you will all be going with me."

The look on Joshua's face relaxed and a smile replaced the anxiety.

"I will also bring Aaron and Hur with me. We will only stay two nights and then we must return to the front to lead the company to Mount Sinai." Moses finished.

Joshua was so happy that the family would stay together. Moses only smiled at him as he turned to go and get the others ready for the trip. Moses spoke to the Lord, "He is such a newly wed."

"Yes, he is my friend," the Lord answered him.

Chapter 23

Taken

Off in the distance to the north, Satan sat, observing the Israelites. He had watched as the Lord confounded all of his plans thus far, which only increased his hatred for the humans. He had worked it out so carefully. They were running out of water again and he had made sure the only water to be found at Rephidim had been dispersed into the ground. He had planned for them to find absolutely no sign of water anywhere and his demons had prepared everything, just as he ordered. But then, "the *Holy One* produces *water* from a *rock*!?" He could never have imagined that would've taken place. Now he would have to plot a new way to kill Moses and disperse the people. He also stared with malice at the young man, Acts.

If only the crowd of *'new followers'* had been able to advance and carry out all the things he had told his minions to place in their minds, These so called *'LEADERS'*, deaths would have been sealed. But *Joshua* had to step in and foil all that would have taken place. Now Joshua's death had become as important as Moses and Acts. He smiled and leaned back against a rock and said to himself, "You will never fore-see what I have planned in the coming hours, *O Most Holy One*." He spoke the Lord's name with as much disgust as he could muster. "The humans were bedding down for the night; they wouldn't be going anywhere," he whispered. After a few moments, he turned to slip off into the night. He stopped to look back once more at the pitiful humans and then to Acts, Moses and Joshua; he sneered with a growl thinking of their demise as he disappeared like a flash of lightening.

~

Michael watched as Satan slipped away and spoke to Semper, the angel assigned to protect Joshua, "The enemy is forming a new plan. I don't know what it is, but I know that we are to be ready. The Lord is allowing him to move in places we cannot see or even go at this time. We will have to completely trust the Lord God just as the Children of Israel are learning to do."

Semper didn't say a word but nodded in agreement. His personality was quiet and calm but try and hurt the one he loves or has been assigned… well, that would bring out the warrior side and complete wrath that comes from a holy anger.

Michael looked down at the company and watched as each family lay their heads down to rest and he loved them with the Love of the Lord. He looked over to Semper and said, "Go and take your watch place beside Joshua and his wife and I will go and meet with the Lord."

Semper spoke; his voice soft and a deep tone, "I will keep my post and all will be safe." Then with speed unimaginable to a human, he moved within just a few feet from Joshua and Klee. He took his eight-foot-long doubled edged sword and cradled it in his powerful hands; His watch steady and ever moving in all directions. He glanced over to Turion and Axon who were given the privilege of guarding Telok and Naoon. They nodded their heads in acknowledgment of his presence. Shadow was standing right over Elim. His deep blue eyes staring into her beautiful face and then he looked up at his brothers and said quietly, "Isn't she beautiful?" They responded with smiles and Shadow began to look in all directions to guard this beautiful baby girl. He would not fail. None of them would.

~

Satan went to a part of the region where a certain war lord was camped; his name was Shyhestany. He was a descendant of Amalek who was the grandson of Esau.

Esau was the twin brother of Jacob and Jacob's name was changed to Israel; from which the company of people delivered from Egypt got their name, "The Children of Israel" because they were his descendants.

Shyhestany was the leader of a nomadic people who made their way of life by raiding anyone traveling through that region.

The Amalekites originated from the land that was given to Esau. It was called the land of Edom. They were powerful warriors, trained for battle from childhood and were very cruel people. They worshiped a Canaanite god called, Agog. The god they worshiped was not a god at all, but a prince of demons set up by Satan to keep watch on that region.

As Satan approached Shyhestany in the form of a human traveler, Agog the demon prince, bowed low in the spiritual realm giving Satan all honor. Satan appeared to be a wealthy man and had many gifts to offer Shyhestany. Shyhestany looked at the lone traveler, but for some strange reason, he did not question why he was alone or why he was traveling in that region. Satan in his disguise, told him of a people who had the 'wealth of Egypt' in their carts. That there was much to be gained and all they had to do was to attack the tribe at the rear of the company.

"They will be camped at Rephidim for a few days and the people are spread out. There is a tribe in the rear that is not keeping up very well and there are many who are tired and weary from their travel. Their god has been harsh on them, not giving them water until just before death or food before they faint with hunger. By the time the other tribes begin to turn and come to their aid, you and your men will be gone with many riches and women… who were beautiful in form to be taken along with the gold and silver. And the water carts were already hitched to well taken care of animals."

Shyhestany listened and was taken by the traveler's knowledge and gifts. "How far are they from us at this point?" He asked the traveler.

"You can be in position within a day and a half depending on your men and just how fast you want to get to the 'ripe pickings' there is to be had. You have time to plan your strike." Satan spoke with a calm attitude to appear as if there was no hurry in his mannerisms. "These people have been slaves all of their lives. They are led by a madman who thinks he hears from one god." This brought a laugh from Shyhestany.

"The fame of your people will be known by nations and your name, Shyhestany, will be famous for taking down the people who are led by this man. He will be in the rear of the company of people within the next day. There you will be able to kill him and those who stand around him. Taking their lives will bring much glory among the surrounding nations who worship Agog, as you do. The men who stand with this "madman" are young and inexperienced in battle. It will only be good practice for your men. I am sorry they are not the warriors you would find a challenge." He paused to allow the emotions to build in Shyhestany and then he finished, "But killing them and taking their women will be gratifying none the less." Satan spoke with all the skill used to influence kings and leaders, since the Garden of Eden.

Shyhestany heard and completely soaked in all that Satan had offered him. "If you attack early in the morning hours, as silent as a serpent, you will be gone before anyone will know you were there. The women of the people rise first as the men lay sleeping, unaware of their surroundings." Satan finished, knowing he had given just enough information.

Shyhestany immediately turned and sent for his commanding officers. Satan looked at Shyhestany and said, "I can see you have planning to do so I will take my leave. Please keep the gifts I have offered as a pledge of my devotion and honesty to you."

Shyhestany smiled and replied, "Of course, my friend. Is there anything else my people can do for you?"

"There is nothing. Thank you." Satan bowed as much as he hated to bow before a human… but it was all in the act to win the small rulers confidence.

As Shyhestany turned to meet with his men, Satan moved off into the night to a place in which he could observe Shyhestany and his men. He did not want this plan to be undone. He sent for Agog, who immediately came to his master's side. "What is thy bidding my lord?"

"Send out scouts to see if any of the Holy One's *misfits* are in the area." Satan was talking about the angels of the living God. "Send word to me as soon as the scouts return." He smiled to himself. He had planted the seed and now to let man's nature see it through to the end.

Shyhestany had explained everything to his men and within a half day, they began to move toward the Children of Israel just as the afternoon began. They walked the rest of that day and camped. They would be in position to watch the Hebrews for the next evening. They would wait for the early morning hours and approach under the cover of night. The Amalekites' thirst for battle began to grow as they anticipated the taking of life and the thrill of blood.

~

Moses and his party had arrived at the tribe bringing up the rear of the company early in the afternoon. He enjoyed greeting the people of the tribe of Naphtali. He, and his 'Four', fellowshipped with the men as Klee and Naoon entertained with the women.

Everyone was so excited to meet the 'Newly Weds' and Elim was as beautiful as ever. Ahira, the tribal leader had asked Moses and his party to camp with the families at the very end of his tribe. He knew that these men would only have this opportunity to meet Moses, and he valued his men in the rear. Moses had agreed and so everyone with Moses slept in tents provided by Ahira.

It was late in the evening when everyone settled down and the people went to their tents. The party had been good for Moses and his men. Klee and Naoon both mentioned it to their husbands, and they agreed that this had been a good 'break' for them as well. Sleep came quickly as they were all exhausted from the walk and evening of greeting and celebration.

~

As Shyhestany and his men approached the company of people, they could see that an enormous cloud of fire hovering in the sky above stretched from the front tribe to the very back. He and his men stopped and wondered at the sight. They could use the light to secure the items they came for. Also, with the light from the pillar of fire, they could see and calculate the distance between the last tribe and the beginning of the next. It seemed to be at least two miles in distance; a distance that would take longer to run in the sand than on a harder ground.

He and his warriors knew well the strength it took to run in this sand. He turned to his officers and ordered, "Just before Orion's belt passes over head we will move in silence, as serpents." The men knew the night sky well and Orion's belt was a constellation of stars used to helped in determining time.

"Secure the water carts first and then move to the carts with the treasure. Check the content and make sure there is gold and silver before trying to move them. Check the cloth, if it is truly from Egypt, it could be worth more than silver. As the women begin to wake and move, look for women that will bring the most price. If anyone gets in the way kill them quickly." As he looked to each of his men, they all gave a nod of understanding and at once they went to tell their squads the orders that were given.

Shyhestany's men began to move on the company at least two hours before the people would begin to stir. In the camp, they began taking water carts; moving many of them within minutes. They were very skilled, without making a sound and they had moved twenty water carts out within an hour.

The Angels of the Living God had been given the orders not to interfere unless a life was at stake.

After the water carts, they began checking the contents of the others. As the pillar of fire burned some of them would stop and stare in amazement, but soon got back to their task. And then out of nowhere something began to fall from the sky. Each man held out his hand and caught a flake or two and examined it. One of the men put a flake in his mouth and his eyes widened. Nothing was said as every man in the raiding party began to taste the manna. Every one of the men belonging to Shyhestany's company stopped and stared at the sight and wondered what it meant. Shyhestany thought to himself, "What magic is this that feeds such a people? I must find the sorcerer who conjures this spell and have him cast it for my people." After thinking about it for a minute he then reasoned, "It must be a sorceress. For only a female god would think to do such a thing: Perhaps one of the guests who had arrived the evening before?" He smiled to himself and looked to his men and gave a hand signal to watch the tents of the guests. "Keep checking and as soon as they appear move on them quickly." The little king said quietly.

Everyone was sleeping soundly until Elim awakened Naoon. She quickly quieted her by feeding her, but the sound did not escape the attention of Klee. It was about that time that Naoon came out of her tent carrying Elim. As she stretched and yawned, she began to look around at the manna and she bent over to take a piece when her eyes caught something odd. She stood and looked more intently. Looking around she could see footprints in the manna. And then she noticed details of their camp were different. "The water carts are gone!" she spoke softly. Just as she spoke the words, Klee came emerged from her tent. She looked over at Naoon and could see on her face something was not right.

She was just about to ask what was wrong, when two men appeared from around the sides of the tents. One grabbed Naoon, first putting a knife to her throat. She held Elim close, and the baby made no sound. Klee stifled a scream realizing it would put Naoon and Elim in more danger, so she became as a statue. The other man put a knife to Klee's throat and motioned for them to begin moving to the north side of the tribe. As Naoon and Klee walked they looked around the tents and could see hundreds of men moving and leading carts and other women out of the tribe. The women were getting up to begin gathering the manna for their families. None of the women being taken said anything for fear of their lives. The men of the camp thought nothing of the sounds, only that of the women moving about to start the day.

~

An hour after Shyhestany and his men had left the camp with their captives, Acts, suddenly sat straight up. Salmon, who was several feet away from him sensed his action and sat up with him. "Is something wrong, Acts?"

"Yes!" He began to get up and move outside the tent. He could see that something was very wrong as he began to put together what was missing. He looked and could see many footprints in the manna that were leading to the north side of the camp. Moses had told them to bring their horns in the event there arose a reason to use them, and there was. Acts reached for his and motioned for Salmon to do the same: they both began to blow a single loud tone. The people came rushing out of their tents in alarm.

Joshua and Telok were out first and as they ran up to Acts, they didn't have to ask; they could see that carts were gone and then they began to look around for their wives. Telok yelled for Naoon and Joshua ran around the corner of the tent yelling for Klee. They met back where Acts and Salmon were standing. Joshua looked at the people and could see the chaos that was beginning to take over as they realized they had been raided.

Then he heard the voice of Moses. "Acts…! Sound a two-pitched tone. Joshua and Telok, you choose men from the clans and tribe who can fight. Begin to pursue them. I will take Aaron and Hur with me to the top of that hill." Moses pointed to the northeast. It was a hill that was taller than any they could see. He felt the Spirit of the Lord and said, "I will station myself on top of the Great Hill which overlooks the country to the north. You will f…fight and win because the Lord will give us the victory as long as I raise my hands to Him holding the staff of God."

Joshua and Telok only nodded and then Joshua told Telok, "You take Acts, and I will take Salmon. As you see a man able to fight, point at him and command him to follow with whatever weapon he has. We will meet at the very north edge of the tribe as soon as possible; then I will give instructions."

Telok and Acts began to move as the last word fell from Joshua's lips. As they ran through the camp each pointed at men and soon, they had 380 men gathering around Joshua within just a few minutes. Some of the men had swords, spears, and staves. Some were experts with slings. While others had grabbed gardening tools such as an ax, sickle, or pick. There were even a few men who were very good with bows. Joshua looked at the men gathered and pointed toward the hill that Moses was in route to. "We will go out and fight and we will win because The Staff of God will be held up before the Lord for us by Moses. Do not be afraid but be of good courage. I want us in four groups: The men who have bows will be with me. You men to my far left make a group of one hundred, you men to my immediate left form a group of one hundred and you men to my immediate right…" And before he could say the words the men to his right began to form a group of one hundred. Leaving a group of eighty men standing in front of Joshua.

He told each group of one hundred to put ten men into ten groups with one man responsible for his ten. "This will be a fast way to keep up with each man." With urgent, yet precise instruction he said, "Telok will take the first group of one hundred and move a half mile to the west. Acts will take the second group and move one mile from this position to the west before turning north. Salmon will take the third group and move a half mile to the east and then turn north. I will take the group of eighty, with those carrying bows, and move straight to the north in the tracks of the enemy.

As we approach the raiding party, my group will begin the attack. As soon as the enemy turns to engage us, Telok's group will come from the west to flank them. As Telok moves toward the fight, Acts, your group will move past the enemy so that you can move on them from the north. Salmon, your group will move on them from the east just after Telok and his men move from the west. Give my group time to be fully engaged in the fight before you come." As he looked at Acts he said, "You must wait until both of our groups are fully engaged and then you will move around the enemy and attack from the north." Joshua looked around at all of the men and asked, "Are there any questions?" Not one man spoke, but all of them raised their weapons.

"I know that many of our loved ones have been taken including my wife and Telok's wife and daughter." His emotions were hard to put aside but he continued. "The Lord God will keep our loved ones safe so that we can do what we need, to get them back." He paused and looked intently at the men and his stare seemed to only fuel the energy of the righteous anger that burned in each heart. Joshua finished and all of the groups began to move into position. He looked to the hill where Moses, Aaron, and Hur would be. He could see that they were about a quarter of the way up the hill. He looked back at the men as they moved out and calculated the amount of time it would take to reach the raiding party. He spoke softly, "They have the water carts and other carts filled with valuables… they also have to lead their captives, who will no doubt, cause them to move slower…"

Joshua turned and looked back at those of the tribe who would not be going out to fight and felt compassion for them. They were as much in turmoil as he for those taken. Turning back to the north he began to move his men of eighty and thought, "We should be able to catch up to them just before noon. Moses should be in place by that time and then we will crush them."

His heart thinking of Klee only gave him more courage as he led his men to the north moving as fast as they could. The run was hard, and it took longer than they wanted, but as Joshua topped a small hill, he could see out ahead of him dust whirling in the air. He held up his right arm with a fist and the men came to a halt. He shaded his eyes and could see the carts and some of the people, but they were still too far away to pick out individuals. He thought to himself, "I didn't think they had taken so many of our people; the group seemed to be much larger than expected." He waved his arm, and they began to walk instead of running to save strength for the fight.

As they inched closer, Joshua motioned for them to stop; they were within a few hundred yards. The enemy's backs were to Joshua, and they were moving as fast as they could, pushing and pulling the carts and the people. He couldn't see Klee or Naoon, but he knew they were there... somewhere.

~

Shyhestany had decided that one of the women, either Klee or Naoon, was the sorceress and he had claimed both for himself. He had much lust in his heart for them and couldn't wait to get them back to his camp.

Klee looked over at Naoon and could see she was having trouble keeping up while holding Elim. Elim was crying because she hadn't been nursed in a while. Naoon looked over at one of the other captives who had very dark skin. Klee did not recognize the woman and realized she had not been traveling with them. She was beautiful and her eyes were black as coal. She started to help Naoon walk; to help her keep up, but one of the men guarding the captives slapped her and she fell to her knees. Klee shouted to Shyhestany, "We won't be as pleasing to you if we fall and faint on the way." This caught the ear of the leader and Klee continued, "Please put this woman and her baby into a cart."

Shyhestany looked back at her and told her to, "Shut up!" But Klee kept on until he turned and walked back to her and slapped her with the back of his hand. She fell to the ground, her lower lip bleeding. The woman with dark skin started to move toward Shyhestany and in that moment the guard took his spear and put it all the way through the young woman. Her eyes met with Klee and her face seemed to be at peace with her attempt to help her. As she fell to the ground her body became motionless. The guard pulled the spear from her body and looked at Shyhestany. His commander seemed pleased with the way the man had acted in protecting him. Shyhestany then turned to Klee. Her face etched with terror and sadness. As a tear began to fall from her cheek, she looked directly into the eyes of Shyhestany; which was not usually permitted. As she looked into his eyes she said, "Please... put the woman and her baby into a cart."

Her eyes were beautiful, and they spoke to Shyhestany, and he thought to himself, "She must be the sorceress from the courage she speaks with. And the compassion she has for this other woman and her baby. She even cares for this one who is now dead. She will be the one to cast the spell for me or she will also die." He turned to two of his men, "Put the woman and her baby in that cart." Pointing to a cart with room in the back. He looked at Klee, "There! Are you satisfied?"

"Thank you, sir." Klee answered. He began walking away and Klee spoke gritting her teeth, under her breath, "And thank you for the reason my husband… and Naoon's… will not let you live." As she spoke the words, she looked over at Naoon and could see the same horror that had struck her heart at the death of the woman with beautiful, dark skin. Tears flowing down her cheek as both of them realized these men had no respect for life at all.

Naoon looked at Klee with fearful memories of losing all of her family in Egypt to men who lived by the same code as the ones leading them now; The men in Egypt and these men knew there were always more people just over the next hill. And they would take whatever they wanted. The fear of that life started to overwhelm her, but as she looked over at Klee, she could see a woman of great strength. Klee looked back at Naoon and tried to give her a small smile, but her lip split open, and Klee flinched with pain. Naoon grimaced as she watched Klee and then mouthed the words to her, "Thank You." Klee nodded her head and turned to start walking again holding her lip as it bled for a little while longer.

Naoon looked down at Elim who was now quiet as she was fed. Naoon spoke softly to her, "Your daddy is coming, and he will take all of us home." She looked off to the north, where they were being taken and could see only a vast wilderness. Then she turned and looked back to the south. She blinked as she saw some movement. "But was it just the dirt blowing in the wind?" She raised her hand and covered her eyes for shade and could see a small band of men heading toward them. She immediately wiped her face with her hand so that the men following her didn't see her looking… They thought she was moving her hair from her eyes. Her heart filled with hope, she looked over at Klee. Klee had one hand next to her mouth and could see that she was in pain from the back-handed slap. Klee looked over at Naoon and as she did, she could see Naoon's eyes telling her: *THE MEN WERE COMING.*

Chapter 24

The Battle

Joshua brought his men to a halt as he looked ahead, and he could see someone lying in the sand. He covered his eyes, and he said softly, "It's a body!" He glanced at the men directly next to him and said, "We will move slowly up to the body. It could be a decoy to throw us off if they've seen us." They moved with silence; just as a lion, stalking prey. As they approached the body, they could see that she was a woman of dark skin and beautiful in the face. They could also see the wound created by the spear. Each man felt in his heart a tremendous sadness but also relief that she was not one of their wives or daughters. Joshua, getting their attention, looked at them in the eyes. Knowing there was nothing more they could do for her, he turned to get back on track; not only in movement, but in mind as well.

Joshua moved slowly up a small hill and as he looked over, he could see that he was within fifty feet of the men in the back of the raiding party. These men were the scouts who were moving slower so that they could see if anyone followed. Joshua looked at his eighty men and with hand signals had them spread out to actually… encircle the scouts of Shyhestany. Just as the first scout turned to move to the north from his southern position behind his people, Joshua rose up and grabbed the man around the throat and pulled him to the ground without a sound. As he put his weight against the back of the man's neck, his arm under the man's chin, a small pop could be heard. The man's neck broke. He then raised his head up for a quick glance at his other men. One by one, thirteen enemy scouts began to disappear into the sand by arrows shot with expert precision while others were taken down as Joshua had done. After the last scout was done away with, Joshua pulled his men back to him and said quietly, "We will move slowly, but not too slow that we don't catch up to them…" He ended with a nod. His men returned the nod. "We will get as close as we can before letting them know we are here. I estimate there to be about six hundred of them." The number didn't seem to alarm his men. Their attention was on the matter at hand: getting their loved ones back. With a wave of his arm, they began to move.

As Joshua's men were taking out the scouts, Acts and his group had moved past Telok's group on the west side headed for their northern position.

Telok was lying on his stomach and watched from the top of a small hill as the enemy scouts were taken care of. He could see Joshua's group moving in to engage the enemy. Joshua and his men crept closer and closer to the Amalekites. He motioned for his men to get ready.

Salmon had watched the same thing and now could also see Joshua moving closer to the Amalekites and he readied his men as well. Their muscles flexed with power and each one had in his heart the fight that it would take to win… and die if they had too. A thought passed through Salmon's mind: 'most of these men were several years older than he and Acts; a few were of the same age or just a year or two older; yet they followed without question.' He let the thought slip away and returned his attention to the matter at hand.

Moses had made it to the top of the Great Hill and could see the entire scene being acted out in front of him. The Lord was giving miraculous sight to Moses, Aaron, and Hur to the point they could see the very facial expressions of their men. They had seen the woman of dark skin lying in the sand. It caused pain to all of their hearts and brought to memory some of the same feelings that Naoon was experiencing of their days in Egypt. They watched as the last scout was removed and now Joshua was only thirty feet or so from the back of raiding party. They searched the crowd of carts and noticed there seemed to be more captive than what was expected. Then, they spotted Klee and Naoon.

Hur could see Klee in the front of the march of the enemy, and Naoon riding in the back of a cart right beside her. Both of them right behind the leader and he made the comment, "Naoon looks alright, but why would he let her ride in a cart and not Klee?"

Moses answered, "Because she will be the first he will take. She rides so that she is not worn out from the walk." The thought moved his anger to the very top of his soul. "Lord, what do I do?"

"You raise your hands to Me Moses and watch Me… fight for you. Raise your hands Moses in praise to the Power of My Right Hand."

Moses took the staff and held it out in front of him parallel to the ground, as a warrior would surrender his weapon, in obedience and honor to the Lord God.

~

Joshua was just about to make contact when one of Shyhestany's men turned to look for their scouts. When he turned, all he could see was the face of Joshua only a few feet from him. He was barely able to get out the start of a shout when the staff of Joshua hit him right in the throat. Knocking him to the ground he made no other sound than his body meeting the dirt. It was just enough of a sound to alert the others who were close and soon the alarm sounded throughout the band of men. Shyhestany had assigned specific men to stay with the captives and others to engage any enemy that might follow; men who enjoyed killing for the sake of killing. The men assigned to fight moved with precision and speed into a battle formation. The men with the captives instructed them to sit on the ground in one big group, as they stationed themselves around them with spears and swords ready to kill when the signal was given by Shyhestany.

Klee was on one side of the group while Naoon and Elim had been moved to the opposite side. Naoon and the baby had been taken out of the cart and put on the ground.

Joshua's men met the enemy raiders with a great shout and the battle began. Joshua moved like a mighty warrior cutting away his enemy. He would kick, and flip men as if they were children. Watching Joshua gave his men great courage as well as tips on how to fight.

Telok was readying his men. As they got into position he held them back until the right time. As soon as he recognized that most of the enemy was engaged in battle against Joshua, he moved in with a loud shout throwing confusion into the men of Shyhestany. The little king looked and could see them approaching and yelled to some of his men to move to the west. As Telok's men engaged in battle they began moving the band of Amalekites back in on themselves. They were getting too close and were in danger of hurting each other with their own weapons.

As the battle waged, Moses' arms were beginning to become very heavy, and the staff felt like it weighed a hundred pounds. As his arms began to drop, the band of raiders began moving the Hebrews away from the captives and Shyhestany.

Joshua noticed the change and questioned in his mind as to why the sudden reversal. Even with Telok and his men engaged with the enemy from the west, Joshua and his men were still being pushed back. As he looked at his men, he could see the struggle they were having and then Joshua remembered and looked to Moses. He could see that the arms of Moses were not being raised to the Lord and that the Lord was not helping them. After several minutes of fighting Joshua turned again to look at Moses. He could see that he had raised his arms and Joshua shouted to his men as new strength and courage arose. The enemy again was being pushed back.

As Telok fought his way toward the captives he caught a glimpse of Klee and then at Naoon, who was on the opposite side of the group. As he looked at the group of captives, he could see that there were many different people groups sitting with those taken from Israel. But as he was accessing the captives, he was attacked by three of the enemy. He pushed his staff up under the chin of the man in front of him and then spun to his left blocking the blade of the second man. He looked with his peripheral vision at the third, he moved his staff behind him at waist level pushing the tip of his staff, with great force, into the man's stomach bending him over. He came back to the second man and blocked his blade again. The man was amazed at his ability to fight and then he noticed that Telok was an Egyptian. Being distracted with that thought was fatal as Telok struck the man in the side of the head, killing him instantly with his staff. The third man was still bent over so Telok addressed the first man once again. Telok could see where he had hit him under his chin. The gash was bleeding profusely. In fact, the man's lower jaw had been crushed by the blow and he was swaying like a tree in the wind. Telok struck the man in the throat crushing his windpipe and the man fell to the ground with no other movement. Telok turned his attention back to the third man by blocking a downward move of his blade. Telok turned to his right and hit the man in his back, just over the man's left kidney. With amazing speed, he spun back to his left and caught the man in the side of his head with his staff, flipping the man all of the way over in the air before crashing to the ground, motionless. Telok looked at the girls and he could see they were safe for the moment. He whistled at Joshua and directed with his eyes toward the girls.

Joshua cut a quick glance at them and then looked to the east and could see Salmon and his men moving in. This caused alarm to the men in battle with Joshua. But even then, with Salmon's men attacking, Joshua could sense the battle's sway, and the advantage was given to the enemy. Joshua pushed his staff directly into the middle of a warrior's face and turned to look at Moses; his arms were down.

Aaron shouted to his brother, "You have to keep your arms up. The Lord fights for us when you keep your arms up!"

"I'm trying," Moses answered. But unknown to Moses there were unseen enemies bringing an attack on him in the spiritual realm. Such an attack had never been attempted on Moses by the demonic world. Satan had commanded four specific demons, high in his ranks, to get to him no matter the cost. They were not loyal to Satan out of any kind of emotion, but they were bound by spiritual law because they had chosen Satan over the Lord God. As they made their way to Moses they questioned in their own minds, 'why had it been so easy to reach him?' But no matter; the task at hand was to bring his arms down and allow him to watch the defeat of his men. They began pushing down on the staff of God, making it seem heavier than it really was. With each passing minute, they laughed as they pushed harder and harder.

Hur looked around and found a rock just tall enough for Moses to sit on. Even though it was very heavy, he and Aaron were somehow able to put it under Moses. He sat on it, and they took their posts: one on one side and one on the other and they each held an arm of Moses up in praise and worship to the Lord.

The demons began to yell and curse them. They spit at them with hate and disgust, but the humans were unaware of their presence and the battle soon swayed again to the advantage of the Hebrews.

It was at this point that a Cherub, seventeen feet tall, appeared behind Moses. He was holding a blazing double-edged sword that was thirteen feet long. His wings outstretched, spanned twenty feet. His golden eyes burned with the Holiness of God. He said with a voice that shook the ground: "I am Dettreon… and I stand in the presence of the Most High God. I guard the very Holiness of the Lord and this man before you… Is Moses; He stands in the gap for these people and has intimate fellowship with the Lord. His fellowship with the Lord has brought him into the very Holiness of God. You will leave this man… Now!"

The demons could not move or speak out of fear. Dettreon looked at them and marveled at what sin had done to the beings that were once angels. They had never met him since their fall from God's presence and he could not recognize them any longer. His gaze was so penetrating they felt as if they would be consumed by it.

Dettreon spoke once more, **"GO!"**

Moses, Aaron, and Hur began looking to the sky for the thunder cloud that had boomed over their heads but did not see one.

The demons stared at this marvelous being for only a second longer and then they fell over each other in reckless abandon trying to get away. Screaming in terror they flew off to the northwest, right over the battle that was taking place in the human realm. As they topped a hill a small distance from the battle the four demons ran straight into Semper, Turion, Axon and Shadow. All were standing with wings outstretched and weapons ready. The four demons knew there was no way out but to fight.

One of the demons looked at the ground for a moment remembering a faint memory before the battle in heaven and the great fall. His memory was so faint but still clear enough to remember being a holy angel being in the presence of the Living God. He remembered and let his hate build inside of him because he had been cast down. It only took him believing Lucifer for one moment to be sentenced to eternal separation. Because there is no salvation for demons, he hated the very ones standing in front of him. He raised his head; and without a word started straight into Semper, who was in the middle of the half-circle of angels. He only got within a spears length before the angel sent him to the pit. In the blink of an eye the other three demons were gone just as quickly and then the angels looked to each other. Semper said, "Now, back to our families."

In an instant, the four were standing over Klee, Naoon and Elim. They were ready to end the life of any human or demon that would try to take theirs… but they would allow the threat to get in human terms; dangerously close before acting.

Dettreon remained behind Moses and loved him with great admiration. He had not considered the moment that he would be given the privilege to stand next to the man… The Lord God of the

Universe called His 'Friend'. His heart wondered at the complexity of humans and just how great the Lord God loved them.

~

Now with the movement of the battle pushed in favor of Joshua, the enemy raiders were backing away. Shyhestany looked at the three directions his men were being engaged. He turned to his men standing over the captives. He gave the order for them to get ready to kill half of them. Axon held his spear ready to kill any human that approached Naoon with the intent of ending her life and Shadow gripped his sword with the same intentions.

Just before Shyhestany was about to give the 'Kill Order,' he heard a shout come from behind him. It was Acts and his warriors attacking from the north. Immediately Shyhestany pulled men back to meet the charging Hebrews. Acts was leading the approach, and his fierce anger could not only be seen in his face, but in his ability to fight as well. Shyhestany took notice of Acts and was impressed that such a young warrior could fight so well having been raised as a slave. He gave orders for one of his bodyguards to engage Acts. And then he turned to see that Salmon was moving closer to his position.

As Acts moved closer and closer to the center of the battle, he met the bodyguard assigned to kill him which is exactly where Satan wanted him. He had dispatched over a hundred demons to bring an end to the human boy's life.

As Acts met the bodyguard, he could see the lust for blood in his eyes. The smile on his face showed Acts that this man was a well-trained soldier and was determined to kill him, even if it meant his own life. All at once the battle slowed in the mind of Acts and in the mind of the soldier facing him. There was no sound except for their breathing. For that moment in time, they were the only two in the battle. They walked in a circle estimating each other's ability and unknown to either man was a battle that was being played out in the spiritual realm above them. The man smiled as he brought his sword up pointing the tip at Acts in an attempt to intimidate the young warrior. Acts looked back at the man and readied his staff; the man charged. His sword pointed at Acts' chest. Acts pulled his staff up just in time to deflect the blow. As the blade passed from his right to his left, he turned to the left, pulling his staff around with great speed and power. It met the man in the middle of his back causing the man to stumble for a step, but he regained his stance and turned to charge Acts once again. He raised his blade and brought it down on Acts at an angle starting at Act's right shoulder and directed downward toward his left hip. The man was intending to cut Acts in two, but Acts brought his staff up with his right hand and guided the blade out from his body. The man used the momentum and turned to his right bringing the blade level at the belly of Acts. Acts jumped back just as the blade cut his shirt showing the very flesh the man was trying to cut. Acts stopped as did the man. He looked down at his shirt and then back to the man. His smile hit Acts like spit on his cheek. Acts looked deep into the man's eyes and then tilted his head slightly to one side and the man took it as if Acts were making fun of him and his rage flared. He raised his blade and pushed his sword out while taking two powerful steps toward the chest of Acts.

"Got close that time didn't I, boy?" the man taunted.

As he did, Acts spun to his left. Time seemed to slow to the point that sweat drops falling from their faces seemed to almost stop in mid-air; their facial expressions relaying every thought and intention. All at once… time seemed to catch up and Acts slammed his staff into the man's upper left arm as both of them heard the bone break.

The man's arm went limp, but it was not the arm holding the blade. He spun to his right and pulled his blade back toward Acts in an attempt to strike him at his right thigh; to bring Acts down to the ground so that the warrior could finish this boy. Acts moved just out of reach as the blade passed him. The man was in great pain and Acts could see that panic now gripped the man's face. As he looked Acts in the eyes he shouted and charged once again with his blade pointed at the chest of Acts. Acts felt as if time began to slow again, and he could see the sweet drops falling from the brow of the man from under his helmet. He could see the panic etched in his face and he knew this would be the last blow he could muster at him. Acts felt in his heart sadness for the man… but he knew what he had to do. His staff met the man in the middle of his forehead just under the edge of his helmet and made an indention in the man's head stopping him cold in his move. The man swayed like a tree and then Acts spun and put the tip of his staff into the side of the man's neck. The force knocked the man off of his feet and he fell, lifeless on the sand. Acts turned and looked at Shyhestany. He felt that this was the target he must reach, but he could tell that more and more men were starting to also target the war lord.

~

In the spiritual realm, at the very moment Acts was engaged in battle, Rend had stepped up with his bronze-colored sword and blocked the blade of the demon. He held the blade with his for a moment never taking his eyes off the demonic warrior. The demon stood a foot taller than him. Rend stood nine and half feet with sandy blonde hair and a dark red head band. The demon looked down at him in amazement. The strength of the Angelic being was tremendous, but no matter, he would end the boy's life anyway. The demon raised his blade again but Rend stepped in front of him and blocked the attempt. That's when the demon put his complete attention on Rend. Rend looked back at the demon with a stare that seemed to have no emotion; no fear; no rage. It puzzled the demon, "Why is he not trembling with fear?" he thought to himself. "No matter, I will put fear into him!" He pulled his sword back to strike at the head of Rend but Rend stepped in close and brought his bronze-colored sword across the demon's thigh, cutting it. Red liquid, almost black, oozed from the wound as the demon screamed in pain. The demon stepped back to gain a better perspective of his foe. The demon began to spin to his left bringing the edge of his blade level with Rends neck. The demon was intending on doing something no other demon had done… take the head of an Angel. As Rend bent down and the blade passed over his head, he could feel the heat of the blade and it served as a reminder that this fight was to the pain. Rend allowed the blade to pass without a block and as the back of the demon was exposed in the turn the Angel put the tip of his blade at the base of the demon's skull. It stopped the demon cold. The demon could feel the point of the sword pressing in on his leather-like skin.

Rend addressed the demonic warrior, "If you choose, you can take your leave in any direction you wish… but you must choose now."

The demonic warrior thought for a moment and reasoned that if he did take his leave, he would have to answer to his lord Satan. That thought was very unpleasant, for he could not even imagine the punishment Satan would dream for him… But if he stayed to fight, he could end up in the pit… which was a thought that was the very beginning of anguish. As he lowered his blade he turned to look

Rend in the eyes. It was at that point that he noticed the dark green eyes of the Angel. They were beautiful. For a split second, the demon recalled being beautiful before the war in heaven; before he chose the wrong lord. Even as the thought flowed through his mind sin brought his thoughts back to the moment. With a snap of reality, the demon began to pull his sword up toward Rends neck. Rend pulled his sword into his chest and spun to his right leaving the sword of the demon behind and then Rend extended his blade and as he did the edge of the blade met the base to the demon's skull for the last time. The blade passed through the demon's neck; as it did the life of the demon began imploding into a cloud of red smoke. In the very last seconds of the demon's life on the surface of the world, he looked into those dark green eyes for the last time and suffered; knowing only he was responsible for his own fate by choosing Satan as lord and not the Great I AM.

Chapter 25

Finishing the Battle

Acts knew that he was fighting to the best of his ability, but there were so many of them coming at him. Everywhere he turned there was a man trying to bring a blade or club down on him. He was beginning to falter in his pace and soon he was getting hit all over his body. He was struck in the back with a club and then his thigh by the handle of a spear. Another man hit him with the butt of his blade, but only because Acts rolled forward catching the man in the middle of his chest sending him to his back. Acts quickly recovered and used the man's own sword to pin him to the ground. All of the actions seem to be a dance that was leading to the climax of his death.

Rend was battling over one hundred demons all of whom were after the life of Acts. His blade moved so fast that it seemed to almost appear as a shield as the demons were being cut down. But Rend, noticed Acts as he began to falter in his strength.

~

Acts was soon spinning trying to keep up the fight, but it was too much. A man was able to hit him in the shoulder with his own club and Acts fell. Being on the ground was the most vulnerable position a warrior could be in on the battlefield. The man raised his blade to release Acts of his head and in that moment: time seemed to stop as Satan and the demons watched. The demonic realm held its breath as they took in the very last moment of the boy's life.

Acts was on his knees, and he could see the blade that was being brought down on him. He did not close his eyes but looked straight into the eyes of the man swinging the blade. As their eyes met a split second in time allowed the warrior to admire the bravery of the young man and then a staff came crashing down on the man's arm. Acts watched the man's arm brake, and the blade fall to the ground just short of his neck. The man screamed in pain and looked to see where the staff had come from. Joshua turned to his left and brought the end of his staff up and caved in the back of the man's skull. The man was hit so hard his body turned a complete cartwheel in the air and then landed on another enemy soldier's shoulders, knocking him to the ground.

~

Rend stopped to see what had happened. He looked at the path he must take to get to Acts, and he began to spin like a tornado, he cut thirteen demons in half in a single move and the last demon standing had his blade poised at the neck of Acts. The demon stopped to look at the color of the eyes of the boy. His eyes seemed at peace with no fear of death. That moment of pause would be fatal. Rend stepped to his right and then pushed off of the earth with his left leg pitching him into the air and he drove the tip of his blade down into the demon's neck and into the middle of its chest. As he pulled his blade out, the demon collapsed in a pile of ashes. Joshua looked at Acts and smiled, "Thought you could use some help." Extending his hand; pulling Acts to his feet. "Can you carry on?"

Acts looked into the eyes of his brother and captain and said, "To the death!" As the words fell from his lips, both of them were engaged in battle again.

Rend looked around and could see the hard part of the fight was over for Acts and he took his place in readiness beside him. No other demon dared to approach Acts. His heart beating with praise for the Lord giving him the victory and he was not going to stand in his own strength, but in the Strength of The Lord.

~

The northeast had opened a door with all of Salmon's men caught up in battle. Salmon looked out from his position which was on the east side of the battle. He could see Naoon. She was in a sitting position with an enemy soldier right over her with his blade at his side. He looked to his right and could see Joshua helping Acts to his feet and men from every direction attacking them. He turned his attention to that direction and as he did a blade 'swooshed' over his head. A raider had come dangerously close to ending his life. Salmon turned to block another swing of his blade splintering his staff. As the shaft broke apart the blade cut into his right upper shoulder creating an opening of three or four inches. He flinched at the pain but maintained his focus. Salmon rolled on his left shoulder and in the process grabbed the sword of a dead Amalekite and stood to meet the man eye to eye. The man was amazed at the agility of the young warrior and now seeing he was armed with a sword only made the 'game' that much more interesting. He played at Salmon, jumping toward him and back again. This dance continued for a couple more jumps. Salmon grew tired of it and said, "Enough!!" He charged the big man. Salmon held his sword high as to give the intention of bringing the blade down on the man's head. The man held his sword up to block, but Salmon moved his strike and hit the man just above his left hip; slicing the man open. As the man looked down at his wound in amazement, Salmon turned to his left and brought the blade level with the man's neck, releasing the man's head from his body. On the other side of the man was Acts; he had been watching the fight only as long as it took for the strike of Salmon to connect with his attacker. Acts looked at Salmon and as their eyes met, they encouraged each other with a single glance.

The battle waged well into the afternoon with Aaron and Hur holding the arms of Moses. The raiding party was being cut down to the point that some of them were running to the northeast. It was the direction with the least number of Israelites.

Shyhestany looked and could see his men running. He looked at his position and surmised that he was surrounded and was in the battle to the end. Three warriors had fought their way dangerously close to him. He then gave the order for all of the captives to be killed. With that command, the three warriors turned their attention to the men standing over the captives.

Shyhestany was a man of tall stature and stocky build. He looked ever-bit the warrior type and he showed no fear in the face of the Hebrews as they battled toward him. He walked over to Klee and took her by the back of her head. Grabbing her hair and pulling back he raised his blade and Klee said something. He stopped. He wanted to hear her last words. She looked up into his face and said, "I want you to meet my husband." It was spoken softly so Shyhestany said, "What!?" She spoke again only a bit louder, "I want you... to meet... my husband."

As what she had said began to register in his mind, he turned to look behind him and met the eyes of Joshua. In a full run, Joshua hit the big man in his shoulder with his own, knocking him completely off of his feet, and away from Klee. Joshua took one look at her and saw the cut on her bottom lip. He seethed with rage! He turned his attention back to Shyhestany; his eyes fixed on his target. Shyhestany got up off of the ground and as he did, he was captivated for a split second by the gaze from this warrior. The two warriors looked at each other, each one sizing the other and looking for weaknesses. Joshua was six feet tall and was of slim build, with well-defined muscles. Shyhestany was nearly seven feet tall and out-weighed Joshua by at least seventy pounds or more. Joshua moved around Shyhestany slowly, never breaking eye contact.

~

Telok had moved in close to Naoon and Elim. The warrior over them had raised his blade as well and was in the process of bringing it down toward Naoon's head as she covered Elim with her arms. Suddenly the man jumped backwards. Telok had grabbed the man by the hair and pulled him so hard his feet left the ground and then he let go of the man allowing him to land squarely on his back. It was the safest way to keep the blade from hitting Naoon. Telok began walking toward the man who had rolled on his back coming to his feet. Even in catching his breath from the fall, the man ran at once at Telok with his blade over his head. As Telok moved to counter the strike, the man stopped short and caught Telok off balance. He hit Telok with the butt of his sword in the shoulder. Telok stumbled just long enough for the warrior to whirl around bringing the blade through the air; the edge aimed at Telok's ribs. As Telok blocked the blade at the cost of his staff; the tip of the blade caught him and had cut him open along his lower right ribs. The cut was about five inches long and the blood was soaking his shirt. Telok now held a piece of his own staff in each hand. He brought his left hand down on the man's blade arm. The man flinched at the blow but continued to turn and bring his blade around again. Telok swung the part of his staff in his right hand up catching the man in the ear and tearing it almost all of the way off. The man yelled and stepped back regaining control of his blade. The man reached up and felt of his ear. The hate in him built as he moved toward Telok aiming for Telok's right thigh. He was going to break him down to his knees before killing him. Telok jumped straight up as the blade passed under his legs. The warrior looked at him in amazement. It was in that moment that Telok brought his left-hand down meeting the man in the center of his forehead with the piece of staff, splitting his head open. As his feet touched the ground, Telok began a powerful turn to his left swinging with such force; when it hit the man in the side of his head it broke his neck and flipped the man completely over and into another enemy warrior. The man that Telok's assailant hit began to push his spear toward Telok. Telok caught the tip of the spear between both of the pieces of his staff and snapped the shaft of the spear in two. As his enemy's eyes opened wide Telok brought his foot straight up under the man's chin knocking him to the ground on his back. Telok watched him, but the man didn't move; dead or alive he was out of the fight. He turned on his heels to Naoon and Elim. As he stood over them; no other enemy came close.

~

In the spiritual realm, Turion had stepped out from behind a cart to face the two demons casting the attack on Telok. He stood eight feet tall and had yellow hair and dark brown eyes. Just like other angels, he was beautiful in form; well defined muscles with a lean build. His shirt sleeves hung just above his elbows, and he was holding a sword that was six feet long; single edge halfway down the shaft and then the sword became double edged with a fine tip. The blade glistened in the sunlight and when catching the sun just right, it reflected the sun directly into the eyes of the enemy. They flinched at the brightness of the light.

He spoke in an even tone that was low in pitch, "I am telling you... leave now." Like Rend, there was no anger, no hint of emotion toward the demons... at least not yet. They looked at him in disgust and hate; neither of them felt any fear... after all there were two of them and only, he stood before them. The demons that Satan had dispatched were all very large and each of these stood, eye to eye with Turion. They looked at Telok and then to Turion. As one turned toward Telok, Turion took a step forward. They stopped. "Is this Angel really about to attack both of us?" One whispered to the other.

Then they tested him again; the one on Turion's left turned toward Telok while the other stayed looking at Turion. As the demon turned Turion spoke once more, "Move one more step... and the pit is where you will wake." This time he spoke with more force and a deep vibration of strong intention. But the demons did not seem to be bothered by his stronger tone. As the demon on the left continued to turn toward Telok, he turned his back to Turion expecting the other demon to protect him as he ended the life of this... Egyptian. While in the turn the demon on the right took his eyes off Turion only a second to watch his partner turn toward Telok and that is all it took; Turion moved with a powerful thrust and pushed the blade through the demon. He pulled the blade from the demon's body and as he did it dissolved into black ash with the demon's eyes being the last thing to disappear. Turion dipped his blade and then raised the point so that it hit the second demon under the chin. The blade passed through the demon's head and came out of the top. The demon began to dissolve like the first, but in the last split second of his life on the surface of the world, he looked at the angel and felt the very Holiness of the Lord God, and as he vanished; sent to the pit just as every demon that is defeated on the world. They would awaken in complete darkness, empty and void of the Lord God's presence. Even in the world, demons felt the presence of God; but the pit was the place The Lord God had removed Himself from, and not any creature on earth had ever experienced that. The demons would now wait, alone and in complete knowledge of what they had done to deserve this punishment. They would recall every single detail of giving their will over to Satan and not to the God who had made them.

Turion looked at Telok; he was safe standing over his wife and daughter, and he watched the battle come to an end with enemy running to the northeast. Turion then looked around to see his brother's smile at him and he knew that this battle was almost done.

~

Joshua and Shyhestany looked at each other for what seemed to be a long time. The battle waging all around them; but for that moment they were the only one's present.

Shyhestany began to swing his sword back and forth in front of him, but Joshua's face did not register any fear. Joshua held his staff in front of him with his left hand, leading and his right hand on the lower end of his staff.

Shyhestany began to move forward and crossed his blade twice toward Joshua, but he knew that Shyhestany was only testing his ability. Joshua stepped back with ease. As Shyhestany moved toward Joshua again, Joshua pushed the tip of his staff into the chest of Shyhestany just below the breastbone slightly knocking the wind from him.

This got the attention of the warrior-leader and now he looked at Joshua with anger. He moved around Joshua to his left, putting Joshua in a perfect position to use the lower end of his staff. He pulled his staff up and hit Shyhestany in the jaw. Shyhestany flinched but didn't lose eye contact. He shook his head and then stepped toward Joshua again. As he did, he suddenly turned on his heels, bringing his blade around to hit Joshua in the ribs, but Joshua blocked the blade, splintering his staff into two pieces just as Telok had. He quickly looked around and saw a spear lying beside one of the bodies of the fallen enemy.

He rolled forward under his enemy's blade and grabbed the spear and rolled up to his feet. Shyhestany laughed at his move.

~

As the fight between Joshua and Shyhestany began, Semper, the Guardian Angel of Joshua now faced a powerful and deadly demon named Scorch. The demon carried an "S" shaped sword the color of scarlet; the edge burned black with the blood of the human sacrifices offered to him. He had served as one of Satan's top leaders and had never failed in any of his missions. He had hair only on the left side of his head and his features seemed smooth. So, when seen from his left side he could almost be considered handsome; but the right side his face was burnt with his skin peeling away from his facial bones. His fangs; always showing from the burnt side and his eye has no eyelid. As he turned to face Semper, the demon's left side showed a smile, and his left eye narrowed, but his right eye only bulged in a constant stare. With hissing from the right side of his mouth he addressed Semper. "Sssso the mighty Michael has ssssent Ssssemper against me. Isn't… it interesting… that we now look upon the ssssame human; again."

Semper had been assigned to another human long ago in the time of Enoch. The human he guarded was a friend of Enoch and before the Lord took Enoch, He used Enoch to teach this human the ways of the Lord. In the time of Enoch instructing this man, he had become a target of an attack from Satan. Scorch was the demon sent to kill the student of Enoch. The demon could not even approach Enoch, so the order was given to kill his friend. In the fight that lasted an entire day, Semper received orders to step back so that the man could be saved through death, and he was then led into paradise where all of the saints before him waited for the wonderful 'Day of the Lord'. Scorch did not ever know what happened to the human and thought all of this time he had defeated Semper and sent the human to the pit. But Semper knew the truth.

~

Shyhestany began to move his blade in front of him with speed and then he ran at Joshua with the tip pointed at his chest, but when he got close, he dove into Joshua's legs knocking Joshua to his back with Shyhestany landing on top of him. Shyhestany wore a glove on one hand that had three small spikes on the knuckle. Hitting Joshua with his fist, he tore an opening in Joshua's face on his left cheek. Shyhestany leaned back on his legs and grabbed his blade with both hands ready to pin Joshua to the ground. Joshua raised his body with his shoulder pitching Shyhestany over his head and causing Shyhestany to hit the ground face-first. Joshua jumped to his feet before his enemy and readied his spear. Shyhestany rolled and got to his feet, and for a big man… he did it with speed. Joshua could feel his cheek bleeding, but he paid no attention to it. Shyhestany moved around Joshua in a big circle. When he began to move toward Klee, Joshua rushed the big man. Shyhestany dropped to one knee. He leaned slightly down with his shoulder catching Joshua just below his waist, Shyhestany stood up pushing Joshua with his arm lifting Joshua into the air. Time almost stopped as Joshua could see dust particles in the air and the facial expression of Shyhestany as he exerted the strength to lift him. Joshua began to look at where he was going to land. He flew through the air several feet before hitting the ground on his back. It knocked the air from him, but he managed to stay focused and get back up. Shyhestany could see that he had hurt Joshua as he moved in to strike again on the leading part of his right side. Joshua prepared, but Shyhestany suddenly turned to his left bringing the tip of his blade across Joshua's thigh cutting his right thigh mid-way between his hip and his knee. Joshua flinched with the strike and as he did, he stepped to his left; turning his body in the direction that Shyhestany had charged him. The move brought him into position to bring the tip of his spear up and hit Shyhestany in the back of his head causing a gash. Shyhestany stumbled. He wobbled a couple of steps and then brought his attention back to Joshua. Joshua considered throwing the spear, but the distance between Shyhestany and Klee was too close. If it were blocked it could mean death for Klee, who was on the ground to his left. Joshua knew Shyhestany would prefer to kill her before succumbing to defeat so that Joshua would suffer the anguish of losing his mate. Shyhestany would leave him with that pain even if he died and Joshua lived. Joshua didn't think he could stop the big man from a full charge. While Joshua had the spear in his hand, he was a threat to Shyhestany; without it, it would be extremely difficult to take the man hand to hand.

Telok watched as he stood over Naoon and Elim. He knew that Joshua would want to handle this himself, but the thought crossed his mind, if Joshua lost, he would have to pick up the fight. And that meant having to leave Naoon and Elim unprotected.

Shyhestany paused a moment and charged toward Klee. Joshua moved slightly away from Klee confusing his foe. Joshua hit the big man with the far end of the spear in his back. Joshua's hit was able to knock him off balance. As he struggled to regain his footing, Joshua turned to his left, pulling his left elbow up under the chin of the big man. This brought Shyhestany straight up and Joshua spun to his right, his eyes meeting his enemy's. Shyhestany and Joshua were in striking distance of each other and as Shyhestany began to bring the tip of his blade up toward Joshua's heart, Joshua began to Spin. As he came around… time slowed. *Every piece of dirt in the air, every drop of sweat falling from their faces froze in the air as the two warriors looked at each other… knowing this would be the final blow.* As time resumed, Joshua finished his spin; Shyhestany moved his blade with power and speed; but it wasn't fast enough. Joshua raised the tip of the spear under the chin of the big man (A move that he had pounded in the head of Telok while in practice back in Egypt.) The blade tip of the spear entered

the bottom of Shyhestany's neck, cutting through his tongue, burying the tip of the spear deep within the man's head. Joshua let go of the spear as the big man swayed.

Shyhestany dropped his sword and put both hands on the shaft of the spear; as he did he began to fall backwards like a mighty tree. Shyhestany hit the ground with the spear shaft pointed up in the air supported by his head. The fight was over, and Joshua immediately turned to Klee.

~

As the spiritual battle continued, Scorch taunted Semper, "Ssssince our last meeting, my lord, Ssssatan, has put me in command of legions of his warriors. I have had many victories, and I have even been worshiped by the humans to the north in Canaan." He paused and tilted his head slightly, "Have you ever been worshiped… Ssssemper?"

Semper spoke in a clear and even tone, "I only worship the One who made me. That is my joy."

"A joy that is falssssse!!" He yelled back. Placing the tip of his sword down on the ground and leaning on the tang Scorch calmed himself, "I'll tell you what real joy issss… It issss the day I killed the human friend of Enoch."

Semper looked back into the eyes of the demon warrior and told him without any expression or guile in his voice, "The human you speak of was never sent to the pit as you have believed. He was taken into paradise where he awaits the wonderful 'Day of the Lord'."

"NO!! I defeated you and you lossst the human. I ssssaw him die and his life was ssssstained with the ssssin of Adam!!" Scorched screamed back in disbelief; but he knew in his own mind that the angel spoke the truth because they cannot lie. In his rage, he raised his sword and began to bring it down at Semper. Semper blocked the blade with his own sword. The demon again and again brought his sword down, first over his right shoulder and then his left. Each time Semper denied him the satisfaction of victory. The rage in the demon was tremendous as was his strength. Each time the blade came down, its block was getting weaker and each time the blade came closer and closer to the face of the angel. On a final time, the demon raised his sword; intending on ending the life of this angel, if such a thing could happen. As the blade cut through the air with the greatest force the demon could conjure, Semper stepped to the right and the tip of the sword went into the ground. It buried the sword two feet in the ground. Semper stepped back and prepared himself again. The demon looked at him in panic; his blade stuck in the ground. He pulled the sword out, throwing dirt through the air. He pulled his "S" shaped sword into his body and began to spin bringing the blade around at waist level. Semper allowed the blade to pass and then raised his double-edged sword, which was eight feet long, and brought it down on the demon warlords left calf. He screamed in anger, not pain, and pushed the tip of his sword toward Semper. Semper took one step back and then pushed the tip of his own sword through the left wing of the demon. Scorch pushed and pulled his sword back and forth, while advancing toward Semper. The blade caught the tip of Semper's wing and punched a hole in it. The pain only registered slightly in the face of the angelic warrior. Scorch felt he was turning the tide in this battle.

"PAIN! You will feel more… *holy one*."

Semper then did a noble thing; he gave the demon the opportunity to walk away. "You may take your leave and never approach this family of Joshua again."

"Do you think that I would turn from ssssuch an opportunity as thissss? I will have my greatesssst victory in defeating you. I will be praisssssed as the greatesssst!" Turning on his good leg, he brought the blade around in a powerful swing. It hit Semper's sword so hard that he almost lost hold on it. The demon raised his blade up toward Semper's hands intending on cutting the blade from him, but he was able to move to the side just as the demon's sword whisked by.

Semper decided to take the fight to Scorch. He raised his sword and began to bring it down, first on the left side of the demon and then on the right. Blow after blow the demon would take a step back and finally the demon grabbed his blade in both hands, holding the sword out in front of him, parallel to the ground to stop the angel's sword and as he did Semper pulled his sword back and thrust it through the demon's chest and out his back. He took a step back pulling his blade from the demon's body. The demon swayed and looked back into the beautiful green eyes of the Holy Angel. A dark thick liquid, which smelled like rotting eggs poured from his chest. He tried to pick his sword up to cast another blow, but Semper pushed the blade down and said in a low voice, "Now you will await the Judgment Day of the Lord in the pit." He stepped back and with one powerful swing, cut the demon in half. The demon; staring with complete fear of where he was being sent dissolved into ash.

Semper took a step back and rested a moment. He looked up to heaven, smiled and praised the Name of God. In his praise, the healing of the Lord washed over him, and his wing was completely restored. His brothers raised their weapons in a show of victory and then Semper looked at Joshua as he stood over his bride. Semper smiled and said in a soft voice, "You are safe… you and your wife."

Chapter 26

Safe Return

Acts and Salmon had met up in the battle and were now fighting back-to-back. They were countering each other's attackers with moves Joshua and Telok had taught them. Soon the boys realized that the men were starting to pull out and run to the northeast. They stood watching, breathing heavily and almost completely out of strength. They turned to look at each other and moved over to where Klee and Naoon were.

Joshua was standing over Klee on one side as Telok stood over Naoon on the opposite side; with all of the people who had been taken as captives between them. Acts took the south side of the captives and Salmon stood to the north. The four of them made a human square of protection over them all. Unknown to them their Angels were standing in positions directly related to theirs. Joshua turned and looked toward Moses standing on the hill that was directly east of their position. Moses looked down and watched as Joshua raised his fist in triumph. Telok turned and as he stood with his captain he raised his fist as well. Then as each warrior of Israel was able to stop, they all held their fists up in success and honor of the Lord.

They were silent at first, but then Salmon could not contain it any longer and he gave the shout of a warrior, and all the men joined him. The shout was so loud that the last of the raiding party running to the northeast thought they were being chased and ran with even more fear in their escape from the Israelites.

Satan looked down on the scene and could not believe his eyes. The boy had managed to live once again. Not only him, but Joshua still breathed as well. He began kicking and slapping his minions all around him. He spat and hissed through his fangs, foul curses toward the Holy One. As hate filled his heart, he turned to look at Acts and Joshua and hissed their names, being repulsed as he said them. "These mere humans will not defeat my plans. For this ragged bunch called, *'The Children of Israel'* will yet praise me just as they do Him. Scorch failed me, but I will set another plan in place. I will have the deaths of this Acts and Joshua, and now the Egyptian will die as well." He thought for a moment and then added Salmon to that list. He laughed and spouted in pride, "I will have their deaths or the death of their wives."

Joshua knelt beside Klee and asked, "Can you stand?" The action opened the cut on his right thigh, but he didn't care.

"With your help," Klee said looking into the eyes of her husband.

He put his strong arms under her arms, lifted her up, and held her as she whispered in his ear, "They killed a woman for trying to help me," as her voice cracked.

Joshua whispered back, "I know," as he squeezed her tight. He held her like he had never held her before.

After several minutes, she pulled back and looked into his eyes and said, "What took you so long?" Joshua knew then that she would be alright.

As they held each other, Telok sat down beside Naoon and put his right arm around her opening the wound on his right side. Naoon took part of the cloth from the bottom of his shirt and tore it. Folding it, she pressed it to his side. Telok put his left hand on the forehead of his baby girl. Looking at Telok, Naoon said, "Well, I guess we have a story to tell our daughter." He smiled at her and said, "It is more than good to see you." Naoon answered back, "And it is more than good to see you, my husband."

Acts and Salmon were standing a little taller now. They were standing as warriors.

Joshua rallied his men and stood looking at them. He looked at Acts and then Salmon and asked, "Are all of your men present?"

They each looked to their units. Each man that had been assigned ten men in his squad held up a hand signaling Acts and Salmon that all ten men in their squad were present and all ten squads were present. Act and Salmon both turned back answering, "Yes sir."

Joshua looked at Telok and he answered, "Yes, my Captain."

Joshua gave the command to all of the men, "See to the wounded first while I and my unit see to the needs of those who were taken captive." There were people from many different nations mixed in the group of captives along with those from Israel. He looked back at his men and then added, "After everyone has been taken care of, go and take back *everything* the enemy has stolen. Gather all their weapons but leave their personal belongings." He caught Salmon by the arm and said, "You will come back here after seeing to your men and Klee will look at your arm."

"Do I have to? I mean... it doesn't look that bad, does it," Salmon countered trying to hide the blood still coming from the cut.

"Yes... you do," Joshua said in the command of a big brother more than that of his commanding officer. And as Salmon turned to see about his men Joshua smiled and thought, "He is becoming a leader."

Every man gave a shout and turned and began to bandage up the wounds of each other. The enemy's loss was 450 men and Joshua estimated around two hundred men had run off. The men of Israel had not lost a single man, but some of the wounds were serious and would take some time to heal. As he touched his cheek, he felt the tenderness beginning and it started to bleed again. He also noticed that the swelling to his eye was beginning to make it hard for him to open. He looked down at his right thigh, it was bleeding as well. Klee turned to Joshua and walked him over where Telok and Naoon were sitting. She looked at Telok and then to Naoon and said, "I think we have some stitching to do."

Naoon answered, "It sure looks like we do."

Klee looked at Joshua and said, "Now I want you to sit down while I check the carts to see if I can find some thread and a needle. I will stitch your cheek up... and then your thigh. After that you will be ready to lead these people back to Moses." As she looked at the people who had been rescued, she commented, "And it looks as though there will be more of us than when we left." He smiled at his wife even though it hurt, and he sat down to wait on her. For a few minutes, Joshua and Telok just listened to Elim cooing. It was calming and was good for their soul and hope for the future. As Telok looked at her, she looked back at him, and she smiled. Naoon looked at her and said, "She knows her daddy." Telok smiled and repeated the words softly, "Daddy."

Naoon looked at Telok and said, "I told her that her daddy was coming... And he did." She turned back to Joshua and said, "I want to thank you... for coming." A tear began to fall from her cheek. She put her hand on Joshua's and said, "I have never been so afraid in all of my life..." Turning to look back into the eyes of Telok she added,

"And that counts for being in Egypt too." Joshua and Telok could see that she was opening up her heart to them. What she had experienced that day was agony for her. "I was in hope that our Lord would not let it end like this. And I knew the type of men Klee and I had married. But even in that knowledge the fear still bit at my heart."

Joshua and Telok allowed her time to gather her thoughts because they knew she needed to share what she was feeling.

"Klee… and the woman who died…" She paused and had to start again, "Klee… she stood for me when I was failing in my strength. Elim needed to nurse and being out from under the pillar of cloud… the sun was so hot. But when I looked out and saw you… I knew then we would be rescued." As she finished talking, she looked down into the eyes of her baby.

The thought had not crossed the minds of the men, "Out from under the pillar of cloud?" Joshua and Telok looked up and closed their eyes to the sun and realized that Naoon was right; the sun was extremely hot even when it had almost set in the western sky. Joshua looked around at his men and could see that the sun was in fact, taking its toll on them also. He got to his feet and as he did, he raised his right hand, getting their attention he told them: "I want all of you to get a drink from the water carts whether you feel like you need it or not. I then want you to remind each other, every few minutes to get a drink." So, the men dropped what they were doing and all of them walked over to the water carts; carts the enemy had taken. They drank deep and were refreshed.

Klee walked over holding some thread and a needle she had found in a cart loaded with colored linens from Egypt. She smiled and prepared herself. She told Joshua, "Now sit down. This will be the first time I've stitched you up! You do know that I learned it growing up with my brother… who seems to get hurt a lot."

This brought a laugh from all of them. Joshua sat down and felt some sweat fall into the wound on his cheek. The action of wiping it with his hand pulled to wound open and it began to bleed. Klee just shook her head and as she knelt beside him and with a wet cloth, she wiped his cheek. Tears formed in her eyes as she did, and she had to pause until she could see clearly. He took her hand and squeezed it.

"You do know… you are safe," Joshua said in a low and comforting tone.

"I know… I just can't get over the Lord allowing me to be your wife. I am amazed at your love and your powerful protection; your leadership and your ferocious friendship to my brother and Salmon…" She looked over at Telok and said, "This goes for you as well, my brother." She looked back into Joshua's eyes and continued, "Your strong relationship with Telok is a wonderful testimony of what the Lord can do in friendships; even if the friendships were born in slavery. You treat him more like a brother… You don't even see the Egyptian in him any longer." Joshua smiled at her even though it hurt his cheek and said, "Thank you… my wife."

In a rare moment, Telok only smiled because tears were forming in his eyes, and he had a lump of emotion in his throat.

Klee wiped the tears out of the way and began to move the needle and thread through his cut. It was swelled up and she had to clean it several times to be able to see where to pull the edges together. Naoon watched and commented, "Even though I stitched up Acts, I think Klee is much better at this than I am." Turning to smile at Telok she said, "But… I will get to practice here in just a few minutes."

Klee put eight stitches in his cheek and eighteen in the cut on his thigh. After she was finished Joshua asked, "So, how do I look?" The area around his cheek had now swollen to the point that it closed the bottom part of his eye, and he was having a hard time seeing anything from it.

Acts and Salmon walked up behind Joshua and Acts said, "We've just about got everything together and the men have all of the wounds bandaged. Some of the wounds were severe enough that those men will have to ride in the carts, but other than that we are ready to move out when you say, my captain."

As Joshua turned around to them, Salmon exclaimed, "Wow! That is some cut." And then bending over for a closer look he added, "Those stitches look great!" Acts looked at Salmon and said, "Yea! I have had a few of them myself. Let me tell you it's not that fun… but the end results look's neat." He looked over at Salmon and said, "It looks like you will get to experience Klee's handiwork too." Salmon grimaced as he touched his right shoulder and replied, "Really?" Klee smiled and said, "Yes. You will need that closed up!" Acts just smiled and took a closer look at Joshua's face and asked with gritted teeth, "How can you see out of your eye?"

"I know!" Joshua replied. "It is beginning to be more difficult."

Klee looked over at Salmon and said, "Your turn!" Salmon looked at her and knew there was no getting out of this. He sat down beside Joshua and Joshua just looked at him with half a smile through one eye. Klee took hold of Salmon's arm and wiped the blood from the area. It started to bleed again. Salmon turned his head toward her and looked over his shoulder like he would in peeking over a rock, "Do you think it will take many?" his voice going higher in pitch as he said it. "Oh... I don't know yet," Klee responded. She opened it a little to see how deep the blade had cut. After inspecting it she began to pull the edges together working the needle and thread. Salmon flinched at first but then settled into the rhythm of the needle. It took twelve stitches to get his cut closed. She commented, "That was pretty deep Salmon. I want to take another look at this tomorrow." He looked at her with a brotherly smile and said, "Yes ma'am."

Turning to Joshua, she said, "When we get back, I want you to lie down and rest. I want to see if we can keep your eye from swelling anymore. We will need to put some salt and oil on it."

"Man...! That's the part that really stings," Salmon commented.

"Well, you may as well get ready because you and Telok will get the same treatment," Klee said with a stern voice. "Oh! Yea! I forgot about that. The salt always stings," Salmon added.

Joshua said, "As soon as Naoon gets through putting stitches in your side we will head back." Naoon took the needle and thread from Klee and told her, "You just have to get past the fact that it's gonna hurt... and stitch to get it done."

It didn't take her long. And as everyone watched, she stopped for a minute; still looking at the wound in Telok's side, and said, "You know...! It's not easy to do this with everyone watching." Acts bounced Elim on his knee and commented, "Oh, don't worry! You're doing a great job." There was a moment of laughter, and she continued adding a total of fifteen stitches to Telok's side.

Joshua exclaimed, "Well, I think we are about ready to head back to camp."

All he had to do when he stood was raise his arm and every man soon stopped and looked at him. Then he turned in the direction they would go and all of them began to move out. Joshua liked giving orders through arm and hand signals; it was good training, and it could very well come in handy in the future.

Moses could see that his men were starting back, and he turned to Aaron and Hur and said, "Let's get back down to the tribe. I w… want to be there when they arrive."

It didn't take long for Moses to reach the tent provided for him. He had eleven runners come to him and he gave them this message to give to the tribal leaders of all eleven remaining tribes:

"From Moses to the tribal leaders; we were attacked and some of our people were taken captive. Joshua took men and did battle with the enemy. Our men have triumphed and are now bringing back what the enemy had stolen. There will be a gathering to celebrate this victory two days from now during the evening meal. We will celebrate the protection of the Lord and His bountiful grace shown in the success He has given us. Tribal elders and leaders with their wives are to come to the tribe of Ephriam. This is where the celebration will take place. It is at mid-point and should not be too long a walk for anyone."

The runners were sent, and Moses sat down to wait with a watchful eye for his men to return. As he waited, he thought about what had happened and the relationship he had with the men he called, "The Four." He spoke to himself, "They are not far away from each other at any given moment." He smiled and added, "Unless, I put them in different positions."

As he sat, he began to ask questions that had come to his mind during the walk down the Great Hill. "What would be the best way of preparing the men for future battles? What would be the age set for the men to do battle? How young should he begin in the life of a child to form them into 'warriors of the Lord'? As he thought these things and expressed them to the Lord, he could sense the Lord's attention even though the Lord stayed quiet. The quiet never bothered Moses because he knew the Lord was always listening.

He then brought his attention back to the moment; he knew it would take them some time to bring everything back. The men would be leading the animals with the carts. Some with injured men in them. There were also men who had been injured and could not walk very fast because of the nature of their injuries. He also knew there would be guests; the captives from other nations. They would need some care before deciding what their next steps would be. He would have to talk with them concerning their lives being pledged to the Lord God and what it would mean on a daily basis if they should plan to travel with the Israelites. They would have to understand that the rest of their lives would be in service to the One True God and following His commands and decrees. It would be a decision that would take careful consideration, but after seeing Him work through the battle; and seeing the pillar of cloud and fire; and eating some of the manna and quail they could not argue that He is truly the One and Only God.

Pondering all of this, Moses quietly allowed his mind to recall a few skirmishes in his younger years while living in the house of Pharaoh. He had also been injured and knew what it took to make it home in pain. He laughed as he told himself, "Those would be some stories that Acts and Salmon would want to hear."

Chapter 27

The Walk Back

As Acts and Salmon walked with the men, Acts looked over at his best friend and said, "I had forgotten how hot the sun is when you are actually directly under it."

"I was so intent on what was happening that I didn't notice it either until the fighting was over and Naoon mentioned it," Salmon replied.

After walking for a while with only the sound of their march, Acts looked up and pointed to the south and said, "Wow! Look at that, Salmon."

As he did, all of them traveling back to the company watched as the pillar of cloud gave way to the pillar of fire. The men had never really stopped to watch the exchange take place. At this vantage point they saw it in a way they could not see in traveling in the line of the company. As they watched, Acts looked around at the people and he could see the wonder and amazement on their faces and in the faces of those rescued with his people; amazement of what the Lord provided them daily. Being out from the company and out from under the cloud had helped them to realize the Lord was truly providing everything they needed… and more.

Acts had listened to some of the conversations between the men as they walked. They were puzzled as they looked back on the battle. Why did the battle have such quick changes; one minute they were beating the enemy and the next they were losing ground? They also noticed how Joshua kept looking up to the hill that Moses was standing on. None of them really had any answers and Acts thought it was interesting.

Klee looked over at her brother and said, "And how did you come through this battle without a cut? I mean… that's un-natural for you."

"I know!! Isn't it? I have some bruises; and I had some really close calls!" as he looked to Joshua, who had saved his life.

"He can come through a battle, but you put him close to a cart and it will take him out." Salmon laughed, and so did everyone else.

As they walked and talked the time passed and so did the miles; up and down small hills in the sand. As they came over the last small hill they could see the company. Small fires were burning, and Acts thought to himself, "Most of them didn't even know what had taken place. It all had happened so fast that trying to get the word to the other tribes for help would have made them too late. He thought if we had hesitated; We might have lost our people. It could have been a story that only a few had lived.

He looked at his family; Klee and Joshua, Naoon and Telok as he held Elim. He also looked at Salmon, who was more like a brother. He thought for just a moment at how the whole thing could have played out. 'He could have lost his sister.' That thought was overwhelming to him and tears began to fall. He couldn't help but praise the Lord in his heart for not letting the enemy win. He knew that the battle was the Lord's, and in his heart, he wanted to express that to Him. He spoke under his breath, "Thank You my Lord... Thank You for being my God and my Deliverer. I do love You so very much." As he looked up, he could see Moses, Aaron, and Hur walking to them. It was so good to see them and when they got within reach there were hugs for everyone... several times over.

The greeting was joyous and tearful for most. Joshua looked into the eyes of Moses and said, "Everything the enemy had stolen is now recovered and brought home. And we have some guests."

Moses stared back into the eyes of the man who had earned the respect of the men who fought for him. "Yes, we do have guests." Moses looked around at the people of the tribe of Naphtali who had walked out with him and said, "Make sure that everything is taken care of concerning our guests." Even as the words were spoken, men and women began seeing to everything they needed.

Soon the story would be told throughout the entire company. Moses would pass the word to the tribal leaders and they in turn would tell the people. Moses would also write it down so that is would be entered into the history of Israel and for Joshua specifically, as instructed by the Lord. Not one word would be altered, and none would be left out. Moses got the attention of the crowd and as he raised his hand he said with his stuttered speech, "You have d... done what the Lord has sent you t...to do." Moses laughed, "But right now... *all of you,*" he said in a louder voice, "need to t...take a bath!"

All of the men shouted, "Yes sir!" as they were dismissed. Moses looked at Klee and pulled her to him with a fatherly hug. Then he held her at arm's length and looked at her lip. "Does the swelling hurt?"

"No… not really," she answered. "Not until I try to smile."

"I wish I could have been there to see Joshua's face when he looked at your lip… That would have been some look." Moses said with a smile.

"Oh… I think the priceless look was on the face of Shyhestany when he turned to meet my husband; face to face. Now that was the look!" she added.

"Joshua!" Moses called out; looking at his eye, swollen and now starting to turn black. and wondering, how he could even see out of that eye? "Why don't you take your wife to the river that flows from the rock and clean up and then get some rest?"

"Yes sir!" Joshua answered with a smile that made him grimace just a bit from the pain in his cheek.

"We will be heading back to Ephriam in the morning." Moses added. He turned to Telok, Naoon and Elim. He just looked at them for a moment. "Well! I guess you have a story to tell your daughter?" The young couple looked at each other and Telok answered, "Yes sir. I suppose we do."

"Your standing with Joshua will be known throughout the company. The Lord has set you in a place of leadership that Joshua will need at his side." He looked at Naoon and added, "You have such a wonderful family. You will be just what Telok needs as he stands with Joshua. The Lord has brought your families together for such a reason." He smiled at them and gave them the same orders he gave to Joshua and Klee. He knew that they needed time to unload the immense pressure they had carried that day. They smiled at Moses as he kissed Elim on the forehead.

Finally, he turned to the only two left standing with him, Acts and Salmon. He looked at both of them, shook his head, and then asked Acts, "And how did you c…come through a battle and not get a c… cut?" The boys laughed and Acts replied, "We were all wondering that same thing on the way back."

Moses looked at each of them, "I want both of you to get cleaned up and eat some manna and quail and then come to my tent." They looked at each other because the opportunity to get to spend time with Moses was something both of them always looked forward to. As he sent them on their way Moses spoke to the Lord, "They left as young men and have come back as young warriors."

"Yes, they have. I have wonderful plans for both of them," the Lord answered his friend.

"You know Lord... I do thank You, for what You did today. I am still a bit fuzzy on the arm thing though. Why did You want me to keep my arms raised?"

"When your arms were raised to Me, you were giving a visual sign of who you depend on. When your arms dropped, it was to show that in your own strength, you cannot win against the enemy."

"I think that Joshua got the lesson, but the rest of the men I'm not sure about," Moses told the Lord.

"This is one of the lessons you will teach to the tribal leaders. This will be told from generation to generation. I want you to write everything down for Joshua. He will need these facts later in life and they will greatly encourage him when he needs it the most."

Moses smiled as he sat down and said, "You never cease to amaze me, Lord," as he grabbed three water skins and went to the water that flowed from the rock just outside his tent; the water that flowed from the beginning of the company to the very last man and animal.

As Acts and Salmon began to get ready to wash in the water Acts reached for his ear and Salmon grabbed for him but he was just out of reach and Acts hit the ground.

A powerful thunderstorm, bigger and more terrifying than anything he'd ever seen was moving toward him. Lightning seemed to show how the cloud was boiling, and thunder shook the ground where Acts stood. A mighty wind hit his face, but it had no sound. The wind swirled all around him, even moving rocks as it carried dirt up into the air. He looked around him and could see people kneeling with their faces to the ground. Not one single person was upright. A sea of people. When he turned back to look at the thunderstorm it parted to reveal a mountain. Acts turned his attention back to the sea of people and rising through them into the air was the snake of mist.

*As it moved toward Acts it started to change into another animal...
Acts then felt the animal wanted him. He couldn't move...*

Salmon held his best friend, but he had no fear for him because
he knew the Lord would not hurt him. What was being revealed to
him would have to wait until the Lord's message was complete.